The Black Silk Hood

A Regency mystery

Jax Edwards

The Black Silk Hood

Cover by J M Giles, Auckland.

ASIN: B0DT3J2FBD
National Library of New Zealand
ISBN: 978-0-473-74050-4
Kindle edition: 978-0-473-74051-1

Dedicated, with heart-felt thanks, to the Mairangi Writers Group for their helpful input. And to long-suffering friends and family who put up with my constant badgering for feedback.

1813. Prologue

It was all coming together nicely. Soon he would be a wealthy man; the years of having nothing, being nothing, would be over. No more servility, hiding his thoughts behind a blank mask. He would have power and respect, a heady feeling. He heard the quiet knock at the bedroom door and went through from the dressing-room to unlock and open it. A footman handed him the tray holding a pot of steaming coffee and buttered toast. Taking it, he placed it on a nearby wall table, then began the morning ritual of drawing back the curtains and letting in the early light.

The hairs on the back of his neck prickled, as if someone watched him. He shrugged the feeling off, picked up the tray again and approached the bed. He had only the slightest warning—a sudden movement, a whiff of something that shouldn't be there, then an explosion and simultaneous flash that sent him staggering back, scalding coffee splattering on the priceless Persian rug.

Chapter One.
1810. Emily.

"Now pay particular attention to the musculature and blood vessels Em. I want the tiniest detail captured, you understand."

My father leaned over my shoulder, his hand lightly resting there. The comforting smell of his pipe overrode the lavender scent of the handkerchief tied around my face to mask a rather unpleasant odour. The subject of our joint concentration, a vivisected rat, lay neatly pinned to a dissection tray on the work table, its inner mysteries exposed for my pencils to capture on paper.

Papa is a well-known amateur botanist, dabbles in anatomy and physiology—all interests that I share—and is also a member of the Royal Society. He calls me his little bluestocking and I have been his 'assistant' since I turned twelve. I am exceedingly proud of that title, though my aunt, Lady Arabella Edale, and my cousins, tell me the *ton* consider it a derogatory name given to women of intellect.

"Really James, the gel will never find a husband if you keep stuffing her head with all that nonsense!" she'd exclaimed, on a previous visit. Papa just smiled and winked at me when she wasn't looking.

Our home, Sweetwater, named after a clear spring that bubbles up in our woodland, is a pleasant country manor with few staff. My father's inheritance from his mother allows us to be comfortably placed but not lavishly so. My own mother died just before my fifth birthday and I remember papa sitting me on his knee, his voice sounding choked.

"Your mama has gone to keep your baby brother company so he won't be lonely in heaven, poppet. As you have me, it seems only fair," he'd added, hugging me close.

Now, I understand, but then, I wondered why they couldn't have *both* stayed with us and saved a lot of tears. Not even clever Mrs Crombie, who had been a midwife before she became our housekeeper—with all her skills—could stop them going. When I smell honeysuckle I remember the feel of my mother's arms around me and hear her warm laughter in my mind.

Mama had been an expert in herbal remedies and she and papa were introduced by a mutual acquaintance when both were attending a Royal Society lecture. I thought it so romantic when my father recounted how they'd met. It was *un coup de foudre*—love at first sight—for both of them, so papa often told me.

"You are very like your mother you know, Em, with your grey eyes and brown hair." Papa squeezed my shoulders fondly. He looked sad and for a moment appeared unable to speak. Then he continued. "I took one look at her and couldn't tear my eyes away. In an instant we both recognised we belonged to each other." His face took on a dreamy quality.

"Remember poppet, don't marry for anything other than love. For all the pain of losing her, *and* your little brother, I have you, and all those wonderful memories." Papa kissed me on the forehead, pulled out his handkerchief and blew his nose loudly.

"One day perhaps I too shall be lucky enough to meet someone who will have interests similar to my own," I sighed.

"Well Em, looking at the insides of rats may not appeal to everyone," papa replied with a straight face, which turned into a chuckle he couldn't contain.

Preferring to keep me close and educating me himself, my father never sent me away to a girls' school, however I have had various tutors. My French teacher, M'sieur Duprés—an elderly, down-at-heels *émigré* from the Terror—tells me I speak it like a native.

"If you did not like working with your papa so much mam'selle, perhaps you could offer your services as a spy to your Viscount Wellington, in the Peninsular," he suggests with a twinkle in his eye. He still has a sense of humour even though his life has been ruined by the political situation in France. I know he is only teasing, and though I should like to travel abroad with papa, the never-ending war makes it very difficult.

Some years ago, M'sieur Duprés had brought a boy with him. The child bowed gravely and I'd smiled back. He was very handsome with blonde curls, violet eyes and about six years old—three years younger than my own age at the time. When he'd spoken, there'd been no hint of an accent in his English.

"May I introduce to you Raoul d'Aynard, the Comte de Beaudeville, m'sieur," my tutor said proudly to papa. "I am his great uncle and his guardian. His grandfather died during our escape from France, and his parents in a coaching accident here in England. My nieces have married Englishmen and moved away from this neighbourhood, and my nephew, his uncle, lives in London." His eyes were sad as he looked down at his great nephew. "Raoul's poor grandmother, my sister, is so frail now she is of little help, so sometimes it's difficult finding someone to care for him when I am teaching," he explained. "I hope you do not object to his presence."

"Of course not, m'sieur. Emily can practice her conversation with him," papa had replied, and so, over the years, Raoul has become a frequent visitor and my young friend.

******

I loathe sewing and embroidery.

"Sewing is an essential skill, Miss Emily, and your father wishes you to learn," said Mrs Crombie, as she dubiously eyed my latest effort.

I can see its practical application; after all, one must be clothed. But embroidery?

"And all ladies know how to embroider. How else do you make your dresses look special? Or cushion covers? And then there's your papa's handkerchiefs. Lady Edale has instructed me to make sure your skills are…adequate," she finished, but I could see the amusement in her eyes. My Aunt Arabella is a very strong-minded woman, so poor Papa's bedroom is decorated with my embroidery efforts. He won't allow them in the rest of the house.

When my nanny retired to live with her niece in the village and my aunt, on one of her rare visits, discovered I had no governess, she was horrified. I know because I overheard papa and her arguing.

"James, she'll grow up a wild creature and will never find a husband! You must employ one immediately!"

"No, my dear Bella, between us, Mrs Crombie and I will make sure that she is reasonably civilised, never fear."

I could hear the firmness in papa's voice and was greatly relieved. My cousins had told me of the tortures their own governess put them through; never allowed to slump while sitting and forced to walk around with a pile of books balanced on the head to correct posture. Bah! Books are for learning! Papa has the most wonderful library which I explore at every opportunity. I'm determined to read every one, no matter how dry and obscure. He instructs me in Latin, which I must have for the scientific work, and also Greek, mathematics, logic, history and geography; all these would horrify Aunt Arabella—if she knew.

I much prefer my dancing lessons. Mrs Crombie plays the pianoforte while papa and I practice the steps. He is teaching me the waltz.

"Lady Stumblefoot, I do declare you are looking divine tonight. May I have this dance?"

Papa bowed over my hand and I fought to suppress my laughter.

"Why Lord Prancelot, I should be delighted," I replied.

Mrs Crombie giggled and missed a note. Papa kept up the foolish chatter all through my lesson and it is a wonder I learned the steps at all, we were both laughing so much.

"Do not tell your aunt I have been teaching you the waltz, Em, but it is all the rage now in London I believe, in spite of her disapproval," he said with a grin.

I have the best father in the world.

Papa belongs to the local hunt and is passionate about his horses. We were riding side by side through the woods, on a visit to our neighbour, I on my beloved Bluebell, the prettiest grey mare you have ever seen, and papa on his magnificent black stallion, Firebrand. He was busily trying to vindicate his hefty expenditure on bloodstock.

"They are my one extravagance, Em, and I know you are equally besotted. After all I don't gamble or spend a fortune on a fine cellar," he declared with a wave of his crop, which caused Firebrand to sidestep and snort.

"You are a model of pecuniary thrift, papa." He peered at me sharply but I could not keep my face solemn and burst into laughter. Papa had the grace to look shame-faced.

I then sternly reminded him. "Have you conveniently forgotten that new microscope you *had* to have and that complete set of Ovid's *Metamorpheses?*"

"Yes, well, hrrmph, I actually bought them for you, poppet," he replied, but he could see by my sceptical look that I didn't believe him for one moment. We have a very comfortable relationship, papa and I. Even before I'd quite turned fifteen, I'd acted as his hostess and attended the picnics, assemblies and dinner parties held by our neighbours; papa says I am very mature for my age. So you see, every day is full and interesting and I do not envy my cousins their fashionable London life at all.

******

This time, when we visited my aunt, she fixed me with her piercing stare. "When you are seventeen you will be coming to stay with us, Emily. I shall see you dressed by the very best modiste and make sure you have at least *one* Season to find a suitable match. I'm positive you can do better than a country squire." And she glared accusingly at my father.

Thank heavens that is still two years away I thought to myself, though I kept as quiet as a mouse. It does no good arguing with my aunt.

My cousins, Sarah and Lucy, think me dull company, and Andrew, the heir, notices me not at all. Sarah, who is coming out this Season, is affecting a lisp of all things and is continually larding her conversation with French phrases. Her accent is awful.

"Lithping ith all the rage Emily," Lucy whispered to me. "Though I do think Tharah thoundth thilly," and she

8

giggled. I covered my mouth to hide a smile and had to agree with her.

Sarah pouted and did her best to look superior. "La, Emily, you are buried in the country tho far from the heart of the *beau monde*. It mutht be thtifling.*"*

"I'm not completely provincial, Sarah. After all I do like fashionable clothes and we have Mrs Peabody, a good dressmaker, in our village who keeps up with the latest from Paris," I replied, a little stiffly, though I had always found it odd that the *ton* aped the fashions of their worst enemy.

"Nothing compareth with Madame Bonet," lisped Sarah. "Thee ith *une tres merveilleuthe modithte*."

I suppressed a shudder.

We were sitting in the morning room and my two cousins returned to reading aloud snippets of society gossip from *The Morning Chronicle*.

"Oooh, I see Lady T has run off to Ireland with one of her footman," exclaimed Sarah in shocked delight. I noticed that for a moment she'd forgotten to lisp.

"Never!" breathed Lucy, hand pressed to her budding bosom. "I overheard mama speaking to Mrs Fenmore in the orangery. She said Lady Tewbury had given her husband two sons and the second looks nothing like her or the earl."

"Oooh Luthy you're not thuppothed to know about thingth like that," Sarah exclaimed in a disapproving voice, then giggled and asked her sister what else she'd heard.

And so it went, all incredibly dull and shallow to my way of thinking, but I'm a guest so I followed papa's advice and said nothing that showed how tedious I found the inane chatter.

Papa and I were in London to attend lectures at the Royal Society and were staying with my aunt and uncle in Mayfair. At present we were in the Edale coach, much more comfortable than ours, travelling back to the house through softly falling snow, my feet kept cosily warm on heated bricks and a fur rug wrapped around me.

"I believe Aunt Arabella thinks of me as a lost cause, papa," I complained dolefully. "She is always finding fault with my behaviour and holds you responsible, I'm sure." I'd observed that life at Sweetwater was far more relaxed,. "I would much rather we stayed at an hotel when we visit the city."

"Just think poppet, it's like killing two birds with one stone. We pay our obligatory visit to your aunt but it happily coincides with our *real* reason for coming to London," he replied with a grin. "Though, of late, I've been a little disappointed in the quality of the Society's speakers. Its heyday seems to have passed Em, and it now lags behind the rest of the world." He sounded quite dejected.

"But papa, *I* think it a great treasure chest full of wondrous discoveries and the lectures are all interesting, though some more than others, I will agree. The one we've just attended on the Amazon jungle's flora and fauna kept me spellbound," I argued hotly. "Think of the amazing plants your friend Mr Lucas brought back and that intriguing blowpipe and darts. *And* the poison made from the bark of a vine. What was it called again. Ah yes, woorara. Surely you can't say we are lagging behind the rest of the world with these fascinating discoveries!"

In the dim light of the coach, I saw papa smiling fondly at me.

"I have invited Mr Lucas to visit when we get home, poppet, so you can exhaust him with your questions."

The confines of the carriage made it difficult, but I gave my father a delighted hug. Now I can't wait to return to Sweetwater, and count the days.

******

10

True to his word, a few weeks later, our visitor arrived in a hired post chaise. Mr Lucas is tall, pocked and very thin with skin the colour of oiled leather. With him came many travelling trunks and at first I thought he had a prodigious wardrobe, but soon discovered my error—they were full of samples! He stayed with us for a month and every day I discovered something new. I filled page after page with detailed drawings of exotic plants and seeds and strange creatures preserved in alcohol; I also took copious notes. Father and I became proficient at using a blowpipe and learned the recipes for making woorara paste of different strengths. Mr Lucas called them one-tree, two-tree or three-tree and then explained when he saw my puzzled expression.

"Apparently the natives judge the strength by the number of trees the monkey can swing to before it drops. It paralyses it you see. The beauty of this poison is that the flesh can be eaten without ill effect. Woorara is only dangerous when it gets into your blood stream."

I nodded in understanding, his description creating a vivid picture in my mind. I loved all these little-known anecdotes and squirrelled them away to take out later and gloat over. On the day of his departure, as a parting gift and at papa's urging, I shyly presented him with a vellum-bound folio containing duplicates of my drawings. In return he left papa the beautifully carved box containing the blow pipe, darts and woorara paste. The house felt sadly empty when Mr Lucas had gone.

Papa believes a lady should be able to defend herself, so has taught me how to use a pistol. Bates, our gardener and sometimes coachman, made me a straw-stuffed dummy on which to practise. Much to my father's amusement, I drew organs and blood vessels on the torso and loudly proclaimed my successful target shooting.

"Aha, have that in the superior vena cava, you dastardly fiend!" I would cry enthusiastically as my shot hit the correct spot. Of course my poor dummy had to be continually patched, re-stuffed and re-drawn with this violent punishment, but it gave me great sport.

My father's older brother is Lord Burncliff and whilst on one of our infrequent visits to Aunt Arabella, she informed us at breakfast that Uncle Rudolf would be calling. My father looked mutinous and Uncle Richard, who was buried behind his papers, poked his head out and hastily informed his wife that he had business elsewhere so would not be at home. I had never met my other uncle but Sarah and Lucy had described him to me, and not in very flattering terms either.

Aunt Arabella looked sternly at papa. "Now James, make an effort for Emily's sake, if not for mine, and be polite. He is your only brother and though he can be tiresome at times, he has many connections for your Emily." And she looked pointedly at me.

I suppose she means the sons of his friends as prospective matches, I thought gloomily. If they were anything like my cousins' description of my Uncle Rudolf… I winced at the idea.

Papa sighed. "Alright Bella, but it will not be easy. He is an idiot!"

"Please James, watch your tongue in front of the gels!" Aunt Arabella frowned and her eyes slewed towards me and my cousins.

Sarah and Lucy were whispering and giggling to each other and not even listening, so just when the conversation promised to get interesting, my aunt disappointingly changed the subject and I never found out why papa thought my uncle an idiot.

We were taking tea when Uncle Rudolf graced us with his presence and I saw what Sarah and Lucy had meant. Where my papa is tall, naturally elegant and, in my eyes, handsome, Uncle Rudolf is short, portly and much older, though he dresses in the height of fashion more suitable for a man half his age. To my mind, this makes him look quite ridiculous. It is hard to believe they are related and I am amazed he could even breathe he is so tightly corseted. I noticed his shirt points were ridiculously high and stiff too, so much so they forced his head back. He wore a snowy white cravat elaborately tied and a waistcoat of the gaudiest colours.

I was introduced to him and as I curtsied, he raised his quizzing glass and one huge eye peered down his nose at me from a few feet away. I heard my father, who was leaning against the fireplace mantel on the other side of the room, give a derisive snort at this affectation. I kept my face lowered and didn't dare look in his direction.

"The gel's rather a dowd ain't she Bella? Can't James afford to dress her properly?" This was said in a voice loud enough for my father to hear.

I must admit my gown was not my favourite, a rather plain, pale blue muslin round gown with little ornamentation, but the air became charged as my father stiffened with outrage. I blushed in mortification and Sarah stifled a nervous giggle.

My aunt intervened to rescue the situation. "Rudolf, do stop being provocative. I want you and James to be civil to each other in my house. Now, are you going to Lady Treddlefield's ball next week? It is supposed to be the most sought after event of the Season and invitations are much in demand."

Aunt Arabella had diverted attention away from me and with relief, I took my seat again. I'm sure he'd been rude just to upset my father, talking to my aunt over my head as if I hardly deserved his attention. For his sister's sake, papa *did* make an effort, though I could see he struggled, and the rest of the visit passed without any more unpleasantness.

However, when my uncle took his leave, I heard papa mutter under his breath, "useless fop."

Oh well, thankfully I need have nothing more to do with him, I thought to myself. I would eventually find out how wrong I was.

Chapter Two
In which an earl and his valet remember the past.

Miles Edward Wolffe, seventh Earl of Firstbridge, looked
sourly at his reflection in the mirror. The London Season
would soon be at an end and he was bored and restless. Not
usually given to introspection, he had lived his life with a
singular desire to utterly please himself. Now, he pondered
on his cursed existence and bitterly admitted to himself that
his past vices and excesses had been the cause of his present
misfortune, though this he carefully concealed from friend
and foe alike.

Wrenching at his neck cloth, with an oath he tore it
loose and threw it to the floor. His valet, Bekkit, standing
behind and to one side, waited for the outstretched hand to
impatiently request a fresh one. At forty-seven, to all intents
and purposes, the earl would still be considered an eligible
catch for the daughters of husband-hunting matrons of the
ton. Well-built, and having avoided the softness of middle
age, his face revealed the truth of his dissipated life. Under a
crop of silver-streaked, artfully arranged dark curls were
heavy brows shadowing cold brown eyes and a hawk-like
nose. Deep lines bracketed a thin-lipped, sneering mouth.

As he again worked on the elaborate knot, his
thoughts turned to the distant cousin who was his heir, and

he ground his teeth. How he loathed the man, would do anything to spoil the fellow's hopes. Naturally this then led to memories of his delicate, ailing wife who had died childless, curse her, the suicide hushed up. He'd never taken a new one. At that moment, he caught his valet's reflection in the mirror, patiently waiting to help him into a perfectly fitting coat of fine blue worsted. The young man was his natural son.

His lordship had been less than twenty—wealthy, arrogant, self-indulgent and already ascended to his title on the precipitate death of his sire in a hunting accident—when the babe had been dumped on the kitchen doorstep at Amberleigh, his country estate, an irate father raging impotently at the man who'd ruined his daughter. Alternately petted and abused, the unwanted child had grown up with the kitchen servants until he was old enough to be put to work in the stables. In time, purely by accident, he came to the attention of his lord.

One day, while walking across the yard to view a recent purchase of prime bloodstock, the earl and his steward, Netherby, came upon a fight amongst a group of young stable hands. The earl recognised his likeness in his son and stood to watch. The boy, now seventeen, was broad-shouldered and handsome in a rough sort of way, with the full sensuous lips and high cheekbones of his mother and the eyes and nose of his father. He'd been set upon by three others; one already lay in the dirt and the other two were coming at him from different directions. The boy lashed out at one of his tormentors, but it appeared to be a feint, for he suddenly spun around and delivered a hard punch to the other.

The earl never knew for sure why he intervened and where his next thought came from. He did not indulge in altruistic impulses, but his valet of many years would soon

16

be retiring and a replacement would have to be trained. Why not this boy?

"Stop!" he roared. Then he turned to his steward. "Have him cleaned up and send him to my study."

The steward knew, without asking, to which one he referred. That was ten years ago.

******

After at last achieving a faultless Waterfall, the earl secured it with a diamond pin then looked at his valet again. An idea had begun to slowly grow in his mind, and as he was carefully eased into his superbly tailored coat he thought, *yes*!

"Lay out my evening clothes for Lady Booth's ball." With these instructions, delivered in the usual abrupt manner, Bekkit watched his master depart and turned to pick up the discarded neck cloths.

Automatically he began his regular chores, his thoughts elsewhere. It relieved his frustration, to slip into a fantasy world while he worked. There, he saw himself not as his lordship's silent valet, but as his acknowledged son, accompanying him to routs and balls, to White's and Boodle's, or discussing horseflesh at Tattersall's and betting on bouts at Jackson's. He would be sort after as an eligible bachelor by the *ton* and there would be an exquisitely beautiful cyprian tucked away in some cosy nest awaiting his pleasure. With a bitter sigh he put away his lordship's shaving gear and emptied the washing water into the slop bucket. He glanced towards the mirror and sneered at his reflection.

"It'll be a cold day in hell before your prospects change," he said aloud to his image.

As he worked on his mindless tasks, he thought back over his life. His first memories were of sleeping by the kitchen fire at Amberleigh, curled up with the cats, a rough blanket thrown over him, and being kicked awake by the pot boys. He remembered the sly pinches and petty tricks played on him and it wasn't until he'd turned six that he learned the reason. Everyone, but he, had been aware that he was the lord's by-blow and a conversation overheard in the scullery finally enlightened him.

"Bekkit, be a bonny-looking lad. Growing more like his lordship every day," said one maid admiringly.

"Oooh another eight years and he be worth a fling behind the stables," giggled another.

He'd gone to the trough where he could see his reflection—black curls, well-spaced, dark long-lashed eyes, the makings of a lordly nose and full generous lips. Up until then he'd rarely seen and never even thought of the master, but after that he looked for and studied, from a distance, the man he now knew to be his father.

As Bekkit gathered up the empty coffee cup and remnants of the ham sandwich the earl had eaten, he thought with a scowl of that long ago cook who'd taken a particular liking to him. He'd been a Frenchman and had escaped to England with his aristocratic master before being employed by his lordship. The cook had beguiled him with jam tarts, and the child eventually understood his motives when, one day, the man discovered him alone in the dry larder helping himself to the honey pot.

Aha my little lordling. You are sweet enough weezout zee honey, *non*? Come, geeve me a kees, *mon amour."*

And with that Bekkit found himself sitting on the Frenchman's lap and having his fingers licked clean of the honey. To a child starved for affection, this attention gave the illusion of love, and thus began his education in the ways of some men with handsome, young boys. It had felt exciting and wicked for a while, but as he grew older he'd discovered that he much preferred girls.

He also remembered that fateful day when his father had finally noticed him. He'd been startled by the shout and stood facing the man with his chest heaving. The earl murmured something to Netherby, then walked off.

"Come boy. Over to the trough to clean up that bloody mess, then his lordship wants to see you in his study. Be quick about it," the steward said impatiently.

As Bekkit washed, he knew fear and a tiny spark of… something. What would happen to him now? Why, after all these years, had he been noticed? Netherby, a young man then, and newly appointed, walked, tightlipped, beside him, but Bekkit felt too nervous to ask if the man knew the reason for this summons.

He soon found out.

The earl sat behind his desk when they'd entered, and stared up, his eyes assessing and cold. In surprise, Bekkit listened as his lordship outlined his future in a bored voice.

"You will be trained as a replacement for my present valet, boy. Tappers will report to me on your progress and you will do *exactly* what he tells you." The earl looked him up and down with distaste and Bekkit became uncomfortably aware of his scruffy, sweaty appearance and smell of the stables, but he let nothing show on his face. "You will be taught to read and write and how to conduct yourself. Now, go find Tappers." He then flicked his hand in dismissal and returned to studying the documents on his desk.

The young man had been given no choice; his lordship had spoken and that would be the end of it.

And so his apprenticeship had begun. He'd sweated over the reading and writing and a smattering of French, but learned quickly and soon spoke like the gentry. As for old Tappers, he'd taught the boy everything he knew, but did it with a sneer, so that Bekkit understood exactly what the old valet thought of him. Just to vex him, he'd excelled at every task set.

Then another sort of training had begun. Instructions began with the best sword master, boxing at Jackson's, and knowledge and accuracy with firearms. He remembered his reverence when handling his lordship's exquisitely decorated and deadly duelling pistols for the first time, the balance and feel sending a rush of saliva to his mouth. At first he'd thrilled at the new challenges. Was his father preparing him to be acknowledged as his son and brought into society? After all princes and dukes did it with their by-blows, even some earls. Why not this one?

As with his valet training he strove for perfection. Occasionally Lord Firstbridge came to watch his progress but never commented. This made Bekkit try even harder.

Suddenly the lessons and the instructors changed; he became an expert fighting with the easily concealed *navaja,* a deadly folding blade that had originated in Spain and been brought back to England by soldiers returning from the Peninsular War. His body also became a weapon as he learned every vicious trick for survival on the streets.

At last he understood. Not only his father's valet, he had also become his guard dog! Bekkit remembered his dream shattering into a million, bitter pieces.

******

Tappers had long since retired and Bekkit now lived his double life as valet and bodyguard. When the mood came upon his lordship, they ventured into London's underbelly, to places sometimes so perverted that even he, used to his master's unhealthy tastes, found it disgusting. He thought of his present life—every day a reminder of those things denied him because of his bastardy—so close to his parent, but never once acknowledged as his son.

After years of longing for his father's approval, Bekkit had come to realise that he actually hated him. Oh, he appeared the perfect valet in every way, make no mistake. He anticipated all demands before they could even be voiced; kept the earl's clothes in immaculate order, polished his boots to a mirror shine, dealt with his tailor and other creditors, organised his social schedule, to name but a few of Bekkit's many duties. *And* he'd saved his lordship's life on more than one occasion. He knew all his master's dark secrets and lived surrounded with wealth and power, knowing that it could never be his.

It changed a man.

Folding the last discarded waistcoat, and returning it to a drawer, Bekkit looked around the dressing room—in good order at last. It would be some hours before his master returned to prepare for the ball. He poured himself a glass of cognac and settled into a comfortable chair to mend a slight tear in a fine lawn shirt. He'd noticed his father's speculative gaze in the mirror and wondered what it meant. His lordship planned something, he felt sure.

Chapter Three.
1811. Simon.

I stepped from the stage coach with a sigh of relief, and my bladder fit to bursting. Every bone in my body ached after a long, weary day spent squashed up against my fellow passengers, the inn stop for a meal, a distant memory. At the front of my mind rested the thought that thankfully we had arrived safely; I'd heard that highwaymen were particularly active on this route, not that I had much worth stealing I philosophically reminded myself. Being well-connected seems of little consequence if one is also impoverished.

It had been a jarring ride, the roads in an atrocious condition after a very wet winter. On one side I was crammed against a musty smelling cleric who constantly mumbled as he dozed with his head on my shoulder and, I suspect, was the source of the silent but ripe farts that lingered in the air. On my other side sat an amply proportioned and attractive widow. This I knew because she kept referring to her *late* husband, *Sir* Paton, simpering and fluttering her eyelashes whenever she turned her pretty, painted face in my direction and patting my knee suggestively, much to my embarrassment. Opposite sat a rather plain, tired-looking woman of indeterminate age and dressed all in brown, even to her gloves and bonnet. She appeared to be in charge of the two boisterous children who spent most of the trip arguing or whining. I guessed her to be their governess and noticed her disapproving look when she caught the widow being overly familiar with my knee. Just down from Cambridge with the ink barely dried on my brand new degree, I wished to get to the address my mother had given me, before darkness set in.

I spied a privy on one side of the yard and beat my fellow travellers there to relieve myself. Deuce take it! The awful stink made my eyes water. The coachman's assistant had by now stowed his shotgun and proceeded to throw luggage from the back storage compartment. I watched carefully, and caught my valise before it touched the ground. The air hung heavy with the strong odour of horse urine and manure, flattened underfoot and ground permanently into the cobblestones.

After politely farewelling the other passengers, who hardly noticed, they were so busy rescuing their own baggage, I walked through the arch of the stable yard into the noise of a narrow and very busy London street. Standing still for a moment, I looked around. I'd been fifteen when we'd moved to Stamford following father's death and realised I'd forgotten the particular smell of this great city—coal and wood smoke from thousands of chimneys, combined with a foul odour from the open sewer of the Thames, made for a pungent mix.

Suddenly a delicious aroma, mingling tantalisingly with the less savoury ones, assailed me. A street seller had set up his cart by the yard gate, no doubt hoping to tempt the hungry passengers as they passed through.

"'Ot pies, beef, eel or mutton! Penny a piece." he shouted. Catching my eye, he grinned and waved one in front of me. "'Ow 'bout it guvner?"

I couldn't resist. Hunger gnawed at my empty belly. Poking through my meagre supply of coins I handed over the penny and removing my gloves and stuffing them into my coat pocket, I proceeded to enjoy what tasted like the best pie I'd ever eaten, or so it seemed, though no doubt it contained mostly gristle and gravy.

Horses and coaches trotted past in the dimming, hazy light at the end of a cool spring day, and people hurried by, no doubt eager to be home before nightfall. I had just licked the last tasty flakes of pastry from my fingers and was wiping them with a handkerchief, when I saw a hackney approach and hopefully hailed it. Luckily it had no passengers and the jarvey pulled up beside me. Shouting out the address—which I'd hastily checked on the piece of paper my mother had thrust into my hand before my departure—I threw up the valise. With a tired groan, I climbed once more into a shabby and odorous interior.

My destination would be the home of an old friend of my late father's. Two weeks before, my mother had sat me down and explained what she had done and why.

"Simon, my darling boy, I haven't wanted to worry you but we are stretched very thinly. You have finished university, so it will be a little easier, but I must think of the girls' futures now. I doubt you will remember him, but your father had a dear friend, a Mr Ferris, who is a magistrate in London. You will probably disapprove of my having done this without consulting you first, but I have written to him to see if he has a position for a keen and intelligent young man as his assistant."

She'd eyed me anxiously, waiting for my reaction. Unsure if I felt altogether happy with mother's decision, I did understand. It would be one less mouth for her to feed and truthfully, I had no idea of what I should now become. I only knew it to be imperative that I seek employment.

"Well, I suppose it can do no harm, mama. I know I have to find a position, and if he has no need of my services, perhaps he may know of someone who does."

And to our surprise, mother had received a most satisfactory and positive letter in reply.

Dear Mrs Mannering,

I am delighted to hear from you. I knew you had moved to Stamford after my good friend's passing but had mislaid your address. And yes, there is every possibility of finding employment for young Simon. If you would let me know the date of his arrival we shall have a room readied for him, while we decide if we are mutually compatible. I am very pleased we have made contact again and look forward to meeting your son. If he is anything like his father, we shall get along admirably.

Kind regards,
Arthur Ferris

So here I am, being carried through the crowded London streets, to meet with a man I could not quite remember—though no doubt he'd been a frequent visitor to our home while I was away at Eton—in the hope that I would impress him with my eagerness to learn. I had done some papers on civil law at university, but common law I would have to study on the job, as it were. I did not even have to worry about the expense of accommodation while he assessed me. Needless to say, I felt extremely nervous.

People, carts, carriages and those on horseback blocked the streets and made for very slow progress, but the hackney finally pulled up in front of a substantial townhouse, one in a row of similarly appointed properties. On the other side of the road I could just make out a fenced-in park, shadowy trees looming in the gathering dark. I paid the jarvey, who tossed me my valise, and taking a deep breath, walked up the steps to the front door. Within seconds of my rattling the knocker, a smartly dressed manservant opened it and light flooded out. I gave him my card and he showed me to a small reception room adjoining the entrance hall while he went to advise his master of my arrival. I hoped the trepidation I felt did not show on my face. Shortly, the butler returned with a maid and while I handed her my great-coat, hat, gloves and bag, he instructed her to prepare a bedroom for me. I then followed him to the parlour to meet the man who would later become my friend and mentor.

Mr Ferris, a widower, is tall and distinguished looking with a cheerful and kindly countenance, in spite of the pressures of his position. He shook my hand then introduced me to his oldest daughter who acted as his hostess. Miss Ferris, a pleasant-faced, fashionably dressed young woman who I judged to be in her mid-twenties—a few years older than I and with a strong resemblance to her father—came forward to greet me.

"It is very nice to meet you at last Mr Mannering. Papa has been regaling me with stories of his youthful adventures with your father." She grinned impishly as she curtsied in greeting and I bowed politely.

Mr Ferris bade me be seated. "How is your dear mother?" he enquired with a smile. "I lost touch with her when she moved from town after your father's sad demise."

"Very well, thank you sir." I included Miss Ferris in my next remark. "Mother asked me to forward her regards and I much appreciate being given this opportunity to meet with you. I did question the propriety of her actions, but hope that I may justify her faith in me by acquitting myself to the very best of my ability."

I made this, in hindsight, rather pompous little speech, which I'd practised in the hackney, with as much earnestness in my voice as I could muster. If the coach driver had heard me he must have thought me mad, talking to myself.. My host and hostess nodded and smiled so it seemed to be well received. A maid then entered with a tea tray and biscuits, and inconsequential conversation followed until the door closed behind her.

"I'm sure you must be very thirsty after your long trip," Miss Ferris said as she poured and handed me a cup; I hoped I didn't betray my nervousness with its rattle.

We talked of my family and his for a short while, then Mr Ferris glanced at his fob watch.

"We shall not discuss business tonight, my boy. We'll leave that until tomorrow. Dinner will be in one hour so you have time to get changed."

I had forgotten that in London they dined much later than at home and felt very glad I'd bought the pie!

With that, the meeting ended and the housekeeper, a Mrs Foot, took me upstairs to my room. She showing me the bell rope, if I needed anything, and discreetly pointed out the water closet.

"A maid will come to escort you to the dining room, Mr Mannering," she said with a smile as she left the room.

Drawing in a long breath and letting it out slowly, I studied my surroundings. The room had reasonable proportions with a clothespress, long mirror, a chest of drawers, a desk with a chair, another more comfortable one for relaxing, a bed and a brightly-coloured rug on the floor. My clothes had already been unpacked and stored away, lamplight glowed, the curtains were drawn across the window and a cheerful fire burned in the grate. Warm water for washing, a towel and my toiletries were on a small side table. Paper, pens and ink lay ready on the desk. Everything looked set for my comfort and convenience.

Well, I have successfully navigated the first part of my adventure, I thought to myself. I washed and shaved then changed from my travel-stained clothes and waited for the maid to show me the way to the dining room. I liked the magistrate and his daughter, who'd received me so warmly, and hoped I had made a good impression. I need not have worried. Much later, after we'd become friends, Rachel Ferris confided in me.

"Papa asked me to take particular note of you, Simon. He values my opinion and would welcome no one under his roof who did not meet with my approval," she'd said with a twinkle in her eye.

"And pray what won you?" I'd grinned rather cockily, knowing this to be a leading question.

She'd looked at me appraisingly, head tilted and with one finger on her chin.

"Hmmm. Outwardly I saw a tall, well-built and rather earnest young man, neatly dressed, if not in the height of fashion, with dark curly hair, weary, blue eyes, and a shy smile. But underneath that I also saw warmth, honesty and depth of character."

I'd had the grace to redden as she'd burst into laughter. "Well you did ask," she'd said between giggles.

At dinner that first night Mr Ferris introduced the other family members. This is a household where the children, once they are old enough to comport themselves well, are included at the dinner table and not banished to the nursery. Miss Felicity I guessed to be the same age as my youngest sister, and Master Blake, his father proudly informed me, would be going up to Oxford in the new term. The young man and I had a lively and amusing discussion about the rivalry between Cambridge and Oxford and I found myself relaxing and enjoying the banter. Once Miss Ferris and Miss Felicity had left us to our port, my host beamed at me.

"Tomorrow, I am looking forward to discussing your duties as an assistant to an extremely busy magistrate, young man. I'm sure you and I will do very well together."

Chapter Four.
1811. Emily.

Some months after our visit from Mr Lucas, Papa and I were having breakfast together—I shall never forget it; ham, poached eggs with toast and butter and his favourite tiny, lemon cakes. Spring had definitely arrived, the sun shone and thrushes sang joyfully outside our open window, altogether promising to be a lovely day. I had already been for a walk and gathered some interesting plants and insects I wished to examine under father's microscope.

"I found a pretty ladybird papa. I've never seen a yellow one with black spots before." We were discussing my find, when papa suddenly paled and gripped his chest.

"The pain, Em! The pain!" I stood abruptly and knocked over my chair as I rushed around the table to his side.

"Mrs Crombie! Help!" I screamed for our housekeeper and heard hurrying footsteps as I grasped papa's shoulders. He slumped forward over the table making strange gurgling sounds.

I shall never forget that terrible day. Mrs Crombie sent the groom on one of the hacks to gallop as fast as he could to the local doctor who lived in the village. Bates and papa's valet, Coates, were called to help carry my father to the sofa. I sat on the floor holding his hand, willing him to get better. He lay pale and silent and never spoke again. The doctor arrived, listened to papa's chest and took his pulse, then with a solemn face patted my head.

"I am sorry my dear but your father has left us."

"Left us?" I asked stupidly, unable to comprehend. He lifted me to my feet and led me towards a chair. I sagged into it feeling weak and disoriented. The doctor opened his bag and drew out a vial of reddish-brown liquid then called for a glass of water and added a few drops.

"Here, take this my child. It will ease your pain."

Vaguely aware that he offered me laudanum, I numbly sipped. It tasted incredibly bitter and I shuddered, but within minutes I felt detached and sleepy. I remember Mrs Crombie walking me to my bedroom and helping me undress. Then nothing.

I woke the next morning with a heavy head and a sick feeling in my stomach. The house remained eerily silent, with none of its usual noises. Even the birds seemed quiet. One of the maids, Nettie Perkins, sat in a chair near my bed and for a moment I wondered why, then noticed a black ribbon on her cap and memory returned, flooding me with grief. My darling papa had left me and I cried my sorrow into the pillow.

"Would you like a cup of tea, Miss Emily?" Nettie asked timidly. Through my own tears I could see she had been weeping too—her eyes and nose were pink. My father had been a kind and
considerate master.

"Th-thank you Nettie." I sat up and tried to control myself. The maid quietly withdrew and in no time Mrs Crombie entered carrying a tray with tea, buttered toast, and dark clothing draped over one arm. She dropped the garment on the bed, set the tray on my bedside table, and poured me a cup, before pulling a chair closer and sitting down with a weary sigh.

"I know you will be devastated at your father's passing my dear, as we all are. I have sent messages to Lord Burncliff, Lady Edale and Mr Felter, your father's solicitor, so I'm sure they will be here shortly. Your father is in the parlour if you wish to sit with him. Would you like me to send Nettie to help you dress when you've eaten?"

I have never felt the need of a personal maid, as my stays and dresses are conveniently designed to do up in the front and I'm quite capable of plaiting my own hair and pinning it up, but suddenly I couldn't bear the thought of being alone, so I nodded.

Mrs Crombie patted my arm comfortingly. "This will do for you to wear until the dressmaker is sent for, my dear," she said, patting the garment she'd brought with her. "I shall have several of your older dresses dyed as well."

While I'd slept she'd found a black gown buried in a trunk in the attic and had spent half the night altering it to fit me. Between sobs I thanked her. She looked exhausted and on the verge of tears herself as she rose to go.

Nettie returned; I washed and she helped me dress, both of us too full of sorrow to speak. With heavy steps I slowly walked downstairs and entered the parlour. Mrs Crombie had draped it with black crape and Coates, his face a picture of grief in the dim light, sat silently by the trestle table upon which my father lay. I later learned that he had refused all help in preparing his master's body and insisted that it would be one last service he could do for him. He saw me, nodded, and quietly left the room. I dropped into the vacated chair and talked to papa all day.

Mrs Crombie tried to draw me away. "You must eat, my dear. I have a tray here for you; you can take it to your room. Your papa would not want you to make yourself ill."

"No, Mrs Crombie," I whispered. "I can't leave him. They will take him away and I have so much to tell him before they do." She patted my shoulder, and left me to my sorrow.

Finally, numb with grief, my voice failed me and the housekeeper insisted I have a hot drink laced with a sleeping draft, before ordering me to bed. Late that evening, while I slept, our house of mourning and silence came rudely awake. Papa's family and his attorney had arrived. Apparently Mr Felter's and Aunt Arabella's coaches arrived together followed by Uncle Rudolf 's splendid equipage half an hour later. As dinner time had long past, individual supper trays were sent to their rooms and Mrs Crombie explained to our guests that I would greet them in the morning. Thankfully, I remained unaware of this invasion, deep in poppy dreams. Slowly the house settled into silence again.

At breakfast the following day I braced myself to meet my family and did my best not to burst into tears.

"How are you, my poor gel?" Aunt Arabella asked with a sympathetic face. She is nice enough but not a motherly sort for which I am grateful as I knew an affectionate hug would have shattered my composure. "Edale sends his apologies by the way; laid up with gout— he's impossible to live with at the moment," she added, slathering marmalade on her toast.

My Uncle Richard is the most mild mannered of people so this was hard to imagine. I made some vague reply; if I'd told her how I *really* felt, she would be shocked at my impropriety. In Aunt Arabella's eyes a young lady should always conduct herself with modesty and decorum; to display deep emotion was for the lower classes who, according to her, knew no better.

Uncle Rudolph's greeting was brusque. "Sorry to hear about your father, Emily. Never knew there were any heart problems in the family. Dashed unlucky."

I looked at him and the thought crossed my mind at how unkind fate had been to take my wonderful father and leave my uncle. At that moment I'm afraid I was not feeling very charitable towards papa's brother.

Mr Felter smiled kindly at me as he helped himself to bacon and eggs. I miserably stirred food around my plate as my aunt and uncle reminisced about papa. Their memories were nothing like mine. We finally moved to the study and I sat in the corner listening to them arguing.

"I'm sorry Lady Edale but your brother's instructions were very clear. He did *not* want an elaborate funeral. I have already sent orders to the village carpenter to prepare his coffin and the rector, Mr Poole, will be here shortly to discuss the service with you." Mr Felter adjusted his gold *pince nez* firmly on his nose and stared over them at my aunt. She made a sound that I can only describe as a snort.

"Really Mr Felter, it is just not good enough that my dear brother should have so little consideration for propriety. After all, as the son and brother of an earl he should have a funeral furnisher to see to the arrangements. It will *not* do sir!" Her face appeared quite flushed, but I hardly cared. I wanted them all to go and leave me to mourn.

Then Uncle Rudolf, who had been ogling Nettie with his quizzing glass, as she brought in a tea tray, suddenly spoke into the charged silence. "Bella, do stop fussing. If a simple funeral is what James wanted, then let him have it."

These words startled me out of my grief. Why would Uncle Rudolf be so obliging? I immediately felt suspicious.

After this, Mr Felter went through the details of papa's will. My father had bequeathed to my aunt some fine china and paintings she had admired, and various gifts and pensions to the staff, but as our home was not entailed, everything, including the inheritance from his mother, came to me, with all sorts of protections to stop it being sold or spent by whoever became my guardian. Mr Felter, who had been appointed as executor, glanced at me, but most of his words were directed at my uncle. I had a strong feeling he did not like him. Papa's solicitor, and also his friend, belonged to a poorer twig of a very ancient and powerful, ducal family tree and had no fear of a mere earl.

"You and your husband, Lady Edale, have been named as Miss Southey's guardians," he concluded with a smile at me. I surreptitiously watched my uncle's face. He looked extremely annoyed at Mr Felter's announcement.

My aunt, obviously pleased at her inheritance, spoke happily. "Well this certainly gives Emily a most satisfactory dowry. I am sure she will get many offers of marriage."

My heart was breaking and she was thinking of marriage?

"Yes, quite, Bella. But the gel is not yet sixteen, so I suggest, in the meantime, she live with me until she turns seventeen. She will be a suitable companion for my Sophie."

Uncle Rudolf had been widowed a few years before, and as soon as it was deemed decent, had found himself a new bride, barely eighteen. I remembered her paying a call on my Aunt Arabella when papa and I had been visiting; a pretty but rather empty-headed female I'd thought at the time. Sarah had informed me she was the only child of a country squire, blessed with a very substantial dowry and much ambition. And now my uncle suggested that I should keep her company! I froze in horror, but my aunt nodded.

"Yes, an excellent idea Rudolf. She will learn a little town bronze with your Sophie to guide her, before she comes to me."

I had not been addressed directly, my fate being decided with no thought of consulting me for my wishes. I cried inside for my dear papa but felt powerless to change things, so I sat, mute and miserable, and my uncle looked well satisfied.

Mr Felter left for the city that afternoon and would return for the funeral. Aunt Arabella arranged for our village

34

dressmaker to call and Mrs Peabody arrived, bobbing her head and curtsying several times, overawed by my aunt.

"I wish for my niece to be measured for three day gowns, two of black and the other grey, a black pelisse and also two black dinner dresses. They are to be completed with all speed," she demanded imperiously.

Poor Mrs Peabody. She was thoroughly intimidated by Aunt Arabella, fumbling with the fashion plates as she showed my aunt the designs, and nervously taking my measurements under her haughty stare. I knew the dressmaker and her girls would work day and night to complete the order, such is the force of my aunt's personality. Mrs Crombie had given an old bonnet of mine new life with dark ribbons and Aunt Arabella presented me with black gloves and a reticule embroidered with jet beads. My clothing would now be as sombre as my heart.

The funeral service passed in a blur. At first my aunt had insisted I could not attend, assuming that I would not be able to contain my grief, but I promised I would not cry so she reluctantly agreed. I sat and stood with everyone else and answered politely when people spoke to me, feeling like a puppet with my father's brother and sister pulling the strings. Mourners were invited back to Sweetwater for a funeral repast and I survived it all in a state of detachment. Mrs Crombie was an angel, thankfully seeing to all the details.

I felt greatly relieved when Uncle Rudolf left for home the next day. Several times I had caught him looking my way and it made me uneasy. Was he wondering how he could get control of my money now that Aunt Arabella had become my guardian? He must know that papa, who disliked him so, had never intended for me to be left in his power, yet, in spite of that, I would be forced to live under his roof until I turned seventeen.

Aunt Arabella stayed on to release most of the staff and discuss with the housekeeper which rooms should be closed. Only Mrs Crombie and Bates would remain as caretakers. I presumed casual staff from the village would be employed when cleaners were needed.

"Emily you simply must have a personal maid," my aunt stated one morning at the breakfast table. I had managed perfectly well without one up until now, but I didn't have the heart to argue.

"I shall be speaking to that Perkins girl. She has no training but I haven't time to waste searching for better," she informed me. "However, you may sit in on the interview as it will be instructive."

Nettie looking petrified, perched on the edge of the chair in papa's study, as my formidable aunt fired questions at her.

"Yes, milady, I can read and write and do my sums. Ma taught me, she being a vicar's daughter before she married pa," she shyly admitted. That was all it took. Nettie became my personal maid immediately and I could see her great delight at the promotion.

Other than Bluebell and Firebrand, the carriage, papa's curricle and all the horses were to be sold off. I had to fight for papa's favourite and bravely argued with my aunt.

"He is far too high spirited for a gel, Emily. You need a sensible, quiet gelding or mare—much safer to ride than that unpredictable stallion."

"No, Aunt Arabella. Papa loved him and Bluebell will soon be too small for me. I have already ridden him and know we will suit," I pleaded, hoping I would be forgiven for my little white lie. My father had never allowed me on the stallion's back, but he would have—eventually. For once my aunt listened and allowed me my small victory.

The days passed in a blur. M'sieur Duprés and Raoul called to offer their condolences and goodbyes and I thought about those I would be leaving behind.

"I shall miss you Emily. May I write?" Raoul, now twelve, asked wistfully.

I was one of his few friends and knew he understood how I felt, being an orphan himself. Though Raoul owned an empty French title, having been born in England, he sat awkwardly between two worlds. He, no doubt, had felt the scorn to which many *émigrés* were subject, as they struggled to survive, most of them having arrived on English soil with little more than the clothes on their backs. The suspicion of spies hidden in their ranks did not help either.

"Yes, do please write, Raoul. I shall miss you too, and who else will I have to correct my French, *mon ami?*" He blushed with embarrassment when I hugged him fiercely. His clothes were shabby but clean and he felt so thin. "Perhaps one day I shall be able to return," I added hopefully, though I knew it would probably be years before I would see Sweetwater again.

******

Dust sheets covered the furnishings and the house seemed to be going into hibernation, which I suppose it is, as most of the rooms will be closed. It no longer feels like my beloved home. Nettie helped me pack my belongings and I had permission to take a few mementoes of my father - his fob watch and pipe, and miniature portraits of my parents - but when I asked for the microscope, Aunt Arabella exclaimed in horror.

"What nonsense, gel! You will have no need for that in your new life! I trust you will learn to behave like a lady and I expect to see great changes in your attitude after your sojourn in your uncle's house. At least your father had you taught *some* useful accomplishments. These will stand you in good stead."

37

I presumed she referred to my needlework, French and music lessons, dancing and art classes; certainly not logic and mathematics or my scientific work. I wondered what Uncle Rudolph's library would be like and mourned the one I had to leave behind.

My aunt left me then to give further orders to Mrs Crombie. I knew I had two choices; either bend to her will and become a person totally at odds with what papa had taught me, or follow his advice— stay quiet, observe, and remain true to myself. It wasn't really a hard decision and when I caught Nettie pulling a face at Aunt Arabella's retreating back, we both stifled a giggle. Perhaps having her with me in this new life would make it not quite so bad after all.

That night, when everyone slept, she and I struggled down the servants stairs to papa's workroom carrying an empty travelling trunk between us. There, we carefully packed the microscope, my treasured dissecting tools and other small, scientific instruments which were gifts from my father. The beautifully carved, yard-long wooden box holding the blow pipe, darts and woorara paste, went in next, then my own collection of notes and drawings, and various valued reference books, which included my mother's herbal medicine compendium. In spite of my aunt, I hoped to set up in the stillroom at Mornington, my uncle's estate, on the pretext that I could prepare salves and potions to keep the family healthy.

When we had squeezed as much as we safely could into the trunk, we struggled back to my room and Nettie packed clothes around and over my treasures so as to hide our guilty secret.

Chapter Five.
Still 1811. In which Nettie begins her new life and writes home.

Dear ma and pa,
Dreadful things have been happening here. Mr Southey dropped dead of a heart attack and everything is in upheaval. Miss Emily's family descended on us like the tread of doom.

Nettie thought that very dramatic. She continued writing, her tongue between her teeth as she concentrated on her spelling.

You will never guess. Her family had a meeting to hear the will and decide what to do with Miss Emily and I am to be her lady's maid! I feel very sorry for the poor girl left an orphan at fifteen. Mr Southey's family are not like him at all. Her uncle, Lord Burncliff has a roving eye. I felt him ogling me when I brought in the tea; so fat and old too! And as for Lady Edale, she's rather cold and high in the instep.

She'd read *that* expression in a novel borrowed from the circulating library in the village and it suited Miss Emily's aunt to a tee she decided. Nettie knew her mother would be delighted. Not about Mr Southey's death of course.

Her ma didn't know him like she did, so couldn't be expected to be overly sad. But ma, being a lady herself, before marrying Nettie's father, would be proud of her. Her parents now ran an inn, with extensive stabling, on the main route north. It had an excellent reputation with the *ton,* mainly because her mother knew how to set a good table and the sheets on the beds were always clean and well aired.

Thinking of home, brought Nettie's brothers to mind, two older and two younger ones, with her in the middle— how she missed them. They could all read and write and do their sums—their ma saw to that. But *her* life would now be with her dear Miss Emily, and she looked forward to it with a thrill of anticipation. After some thought, she decided to cross out the bit about Lord Burncliff. Nettie didn't want her mother to worry.

The latest gossip is that Mrs Crombie and Bates will be staying on but everyone else has to go, except for me of course. I feel so sorry for Mabel, the other maid. You remember, I told you about her. She got herself in the family way with the baker's son, him as took the king's shilling and never came back. Mrs Crombie persuaded the master to employ her and she's been so grateful, she works twice as hard as anyone else. Whatever will Mabel do now? I wonder if Lady Edale will write references, but she doesn't really know any of us. Perhaps she'll talk to Mrs Crombie.

As she wrote this she huffed a sigh of relief. Nettie was very grateful she didn't have to look for another job, knowing how the more comely of the maids were treated in some of the other gentry families, and though she worked hard here, it had always been a well-run house; no having to avoid lusty masters, their guests, or wayward sons. Mr Southey was not a man to prey on his staff and had been both courteous and kind, making an effort to acquaint himself with all of his employees, no matter how lowly. As a consequence, he had been given their admiration and loyalty.

She'd heard he had a lady friend in the village—a discreet and obliging well-to-do widow—an arrangement that suited both their needs, no doubt. There was never any question that he would replace Emily's mother, the love of his life, so Mrs Crombie had said, and Nettie thought this so romantic.

She reflected back over her time at Sweetwater. The housekeeper was her godmother; that's how she'd got her job in the Southey household four years before. Ma believed it would be good for her to get experience away from the inn. She'd just turned thirteen when she'd been taken on as an upstairs maid; well, to be truthful, she really filled in wherever the need. Miss Emily had been eleven at the time and such a clever little thing too. There was only her and the master to look after, the mistress having died some years previously. They were always a bit short-staffed at Sweetwater, owing to Mr Southey spending so much on his horses. In spite of this, it remained a happy house. She shook herself out of her daydream and continued writing.

Mr Southey has been ever so generous in his will; all the staff got something and I got a nice little sum to put by for my dowry. Miss Emily will be staying with Lord Burncliff until she's been 'polished up' enough to have a Season in London, which means I'll be moving to an earl's house, and then to London! I'm going up in the world! What do you think about that ma! I hope you and pa and the boys are well.

Your loving daughter,
Nettie

There were a few ink blotches where she'd overloaded the quill, but Nettie took pride in her penmanship and spelling and looked forward to keeping her ma up to date with all the exciting news.

******

After Lady Edale had delivered her decision about Mr Southey's microscope, her mistress had looked positively miserable. Later, when Nettie helped Miss Emily undress for bed she'd noticed the still downcast face. As she brushed and plaited, she'd eyed her mistress's lovely hair and looked forward to trying out some new hair styles—though, from the sad face reflected in the mirror, perhaps now would not be a good time to make suggestions. Her thoughts were interrupted when Miss Emily suddenly wailed.

"Oh Nettie, how am I going to survive!"

Her maid paused in her brushing. Should she suggest it? She smiled tentatively.

"Well, Miss Emily, there is that spare trunk I haven't filled yet."

Nettie held her breath as her mistress stared back and comprehension slowly dawned. A grin of delight lit her face and the new lady's maid felt very pleased with herself.

"Nettie you are so clever!"

She didn't think herself so clever when, later that night, she struggled up the servant's stairs, puffing at the lower end of an extremely heavy trunk with Miss Emily, holding a candle and equally exhausted, dragging on the other.

Chapter Six.
Simon.

Dearest mother,

I hope I find you well, and the girls also. Tell them, when I am in funds, I shall send for you all for a visit. You would not believe the number of poor, sorry creatures clogging the roads. They say it is because of all the wounded soldiers returned from the Peninsular and no work to be had. For all that, London is a wondrous place, but I had forgotten how exceedingly smelly it is and also prey to choking fogs. I am settling comfortably into my new home and Mr Ferris is all that is amiable. It is an elegant address and I have a charming bedroom overlooking the rear garden.

I absent-mindedly nibbled on the end of the quill and gazed unseeing out the window. Had I used too many glowing adjectives? Perhaps I should not have mentioned the beggars—she may worry—but paper cost a great deal and I couldn't afford to start again, so I continued writing.

I am kept very busy. In the week I have been here I have met two dukes and a bishop plus attended Mr Ferris while he passed judgement on numerous thieves and pickpockets.

43

I didn't mention that there were also strumpets and mollies brought before the magistrate by the Bow Street Runners, not wanting to offend my mother's finer sensibilities.

He set me a task to solve a crime that had puzzled the Runners, and I seem to have a gift for logical thinking for, from the evidence, I deduced the perpetrator!

I wondered if perhaps I'd bragged too much but then decided that mother would be proud of me. I fully understood the sacrifices she'd made to educate me and wished to show her I had been putting it to good use. University life has given me a thorough grasp of the vulgar tongue, however I didn't mention that my knowledge of the underworld has broadened considerably and my vocabulary has been greatly extended with thieves' cant. It crossed my mind that I now moved amongst people from the highest in society to the lowest, giving me an interesting perspective.

Mr Ferris has kindly seconded me to White's. Fortunately my connections are considered to be elevated enough for this great honour. I shall have to buy a new wardrobe as I am sadly not the fashion, but do not fear mother that I shall exceed my allowance.

Again I wondered if I had said too much. I sighed and continued.

Miss Ferris is a most charming young woman and the whole family have made me warmly welcome. I miss you all, mother dear, and hope I may see you in the not too distant future.
Your affectionate son,
Simon.

I realised I had written 'charming' twice but decided not to alter it. With relief at a task completed, I sanded and folded the one page letter, wrote mother's name and address and fixed it with a wafer. I left it on the hall table to be franked and taken with the household mail, having been advised by Mr Ferris that I could include my letters as a benefit of employment. Now my duty was done, I joined Miss Ferris and her younger brother and sister in the sunny garden.

They were playing pall mall, a game with which I am not familiar. It appeared to be a matter of driving a ball through small hoops set in the ground with a sort of mallet. They explained the rules and with a great deal of hilarity and fierce competition I entered into the fun.

Chapter Seven.
Emily.

Nettie and I travelled with Aunt Arabella and her maid, as she intended seeing me settled before she returned to London for the remaining months of the Season. The luggage would follow in a hired coach, with grooms sent from Mornington to ride Bluebell and Firebrand, in easy stages, to my new home. I strained to see the last sight of Sweetwater, eyes glazed with tears as a turn in the drive finally hid it from view.

It proved a long, but not uncomfortable, journey to the Burncliff family estate as we passed through picturesque countryside. Quaint villages tucked into the creases of the land gave way to gently rolling patchworks of fields interspersed with wooded lots. Aunt Arabella dozed most of the way which suited me as I had no desire to make conversation, and Nettie and my aunt's maid were as quiet as mice. We stopped several times to change horses and at one busy inn, secured a private parlour and stayed for a quick luncheon.

I had never been invited to Uncle Rudolf's—understandable with the antipathy between the brothers—so I gazed out the window with some interest, for we were now passing through ornate gates supported by impressive posts, atop which sat stone eagles, wings spread as if ready for flight. A wide, tree-lined avenue curved ahead, then we rounded a bend and, to my delight, a stunning vista opened before us of a stately manor bathed in late afternoon sunshine. Mornington Hall is truly beautiful. Close to the house were shrubs and flower beds filled with spring colour, and a perfectly manicured park surrounded a small, but pretty, lake. *This is where my papa had grown up. Perhaps I shan't mind living here,* I thought to myself. I had no memory of my grandparents.

I could see it impressed Nettie; her eyes widened with awe. The coach stopped at the imposing entrance, the steps were lowered and with Aunt Arabella preceding me, we approached the front door which was opened by a liveried footman, an elderly butler waiting to receive us. The housekeeper took the two maids to her private sitting room and I knew Nettie would be very nervous in her newly elevated position. Aunt Arabella and I were announced, then ushered into the drawing room. Aunt Sophie, together with my uncle awaited us there.

Lady Burncliff reclined on a chaise longue looking very pretty and rather round, not the sylph-like creature I remembered. The thought crossed my mind that she must be increasing. *That will be why she is not in town for the Season and needs a companion,* I thought. *Someone to run errands and plump up her cushions.* I felt my heart sinking and knew this to be correct when she spoke.

"Pray do be seated. I do apologise for not rising." She looked down and contentedly rested a hand on her stomach.

Uncle Rudolf, who had been standing by her side, leaned forward. "My dear, you already know Arabella and you may remember my niece, …er Emily. As I told you, she will be staying with us for the next year or so until she comes out. You will have so much to teach her, my love."

Sophie—I simply could not think of her as 'aunt'— smiled sweetly at Aunt Arabella, after glancing speculatively in my direction.

Aunt Arabella bustled forward and settled herself on a chair. "Yes Sophie, you must take every care of yourself. And thank you for graciously accepting the training of Emily. I know she will have a lot to learn from you. Her manners have been sadly neglected and your refinement is just what is needed." She glanced sternly in my direction. I had seated myself as far away as I could and tried to look eager, though I fumed inside. Sophie gave me a considered stare and I dropped my eyes in case she could see my thoughts. Listening to Aunt Arabella, I imagined myself as a dog being taught new tricks. For a moment I forgot my anger, and suppressed a giggle.

"You must call me Sophie, child. I declare calling me aunt is too ludicrous. I am hardly more than a year or two your senior," she tittered and rolled her eyes roguishly at Uncle Rudolph who gazed adoringly back. She at least agreed with me on *that* point.

The next hour stretched endlessly. At last Aunt Arabella rose and excused herself to dress for dinner; she would be staying overnight before taking the long journey back to town. I followed her meekly and wondered how Sophie felt having her 'unpolished' niece foisted upon her. What argument had my uncle used to convince her? A maid appeared to escort me to what would be my only private space for some time. It was a pleasant room, spacious, and with a lovely view of the park. When I entered Nettie turned from putting away my belongings in the clothes press.

"It's ever so nice here, Miss Emily, and I have my own little room next door so I'll be right handy when you need me," she exclaimed. "I've laid out your new dress for dinner. You're going to look a picture!" Nettie is such a sunny person and even though she's been my maid for only a short time, she somehow always manages to lift my spirits when I'm low.

She arranged my hair with a black velvet ribbon to match my stylish mourning dress and I daringly wore a silver locket set with a small amethyst that had belonged to my mother. In spite of missing papa dreadfully, I walked to the drawing room feeling all the crack—a favourite expression of Sarah's—until I saw Sophie, a vision in black silk. The design of her exquisite gown cleverly concealed her condition. Pearls were looped around her neck and threaded through her golden hair. The candlelight caressed her lovely complexion and I felt entirely set back and rather plain and unfashionable.

However, my uncle greeted me kindly enough and introduced me to the other dinner guests. Firstly, there was a dark, silent gentleman, Lord Firstbridge, who stared at me rather rudely. His estate bordered my uncle's, I was told. Then a Sir Timothy Badger, who I believed to be the local magistrate and coroner, and his wife—acquaintances of long standing. My uncle's steward, a Mr Small—an intense young man with a pronounced stutter, who had obviously been added to make up the numbers—was last. Lord Firstbridge escorted Sophie into dinner, Sir Timothy offered his arm to Aunt Arabella and Lady Badger accompanied my uncle.

A blushing Mr Small and I brought up the rear. When I realised he felt even more nervous than I, I forgot my own shyness and made an effort to put him at his ease. In a very short while his stutter almost disappeared and we were chatting amiably. I may not be a diamond of the first water like Sophie, I thought to myself—another expression of Sarah's—but at least I can hold up my end of an intelligent conversation, for I had observed that Sophie's was limited to flirting and banal remarks.

The evening passed pleasantly. Sir Timothy made sure to include me in the general conversation and even Lord Firstbridge spoke to me across the table, though papa considered it impolite. In spite of what Aunt Arabella thinks, my father had taught me *some* manners. However we were a small party and most informal, so on giving it some thought, I allowed it to be acceptable. I listened to Aunt Arabella telling Sophie about Sarah's coming out.

"She has already been presented at court and danced at Almack's," she announced proudly. "The invitations to balls and routs have flooded in and she has a flock of admirers. I expect good news before the Season is over, though James' death has rather upset things." She spoke as if my father had planned it deliberately to inconvenience her. I wondered if Sarah hoped for love or was a title more important. Surely it is possible to have both—if one is lucky.

Aunt Arabella rattled on. "No doubt you still remember the excitement of your Season, Sophie, after all it is not that long since clever Rudolf snapped you up."

Sophie simpered, I have no other word for it, and lowered her eyelashes coyly. "Oh, I could not resist him, he courted me so persuasively, and showered me with gifts and the most beautiful poems."

I looked at Uncle Rudolf—who was beaming at his wife's praise—with barely concealed amazement.

Eventually, Sophie rose and we ladies retired to the drawing room. I found Lady Badger a kind and nice-natured person and warmed to her immediately.

"I do hope you will be happy here Miss Southey. It is hard to lose a loved parent *and* be moved from familiar surroundings," she murmured softly to me while Sophie talked to Aunt Arabella. "If ever you feel the need, please know you will be most welcome to call on me. Leafybrook is within walking distance and my oldest girls would be delighted to meet you." She turned as the door opened. "Ah, here are the gentlemen. I do find this separation of males and females after dinner rather tedious. Their conversation is far more interesting." She grinned at me impishly and I could not help but smile back.

Lord Firstbridge approached and took a seat beside me. Sophie's eyes followed him across the room and I wondered at her petulant expression.

"You are looking very elegant this evening Miss Southey. May I offer my condolences on your recent loss."

"Thank you, milord. I miss my dear papa dreadfully." I tried very hard not to sniffle.

"You are fortunate Lord and Lady Burncliff are able to give you a home."

I felt like a hypocrite when I agreed with him.

"Do you ride Miss Southey? There are some marvellous trails at Amberleigh and I have mounts trained to sidesaddle if you need one. You are more than welcome."

Happily he had chosen a subject close to my heart and we spent the next little while discussing bloodstock. He'd definitely risen in my opinion and I quite forgave his rudeness.

Altogether, I'm sure that I conducted myself in a way that papa would have approved. Thinking of him discomposed me for a short while but I doubt anyone noticed. I had survived my first dinner party with strangers and felt very grown up. My new life had begun and papa would expect me to be brave, but I faced it with little hope and much trepidation.

Next morning I farewelled Aunt Arabella, she being most anxious to return to London. It had been over a fortnight since papa's death and cousin Sarah would be needing her.

"Goodbye Emily. Now make sure you heed Sophie's instruction. I expect to see a great improvement when next we meet."

She gave me a hurried kiss on the cheek and in a flurry of farewells to her brother and sister-in-law and impatient instructions to her maid, boarded her coach, which soon disappeared from view down the drive. Apart from

51

Nettie, I was now alone among people who really didn't know or even care about me.

A few days later, when I tentatively broached the subject of my setting up in the stillroom with my herbal remedies, Sophie looked at me with horror.

"In this house we have servants for that sort of thing, Emily. *You* may be used to dealing with herbs and suchlike but here that is *not* a lady's occupation. How can you suggest such a thing? Besides, you will be far too busy attending me."

And so it proved.

Sophie had me fetching handkerchiefs, shawls, smelling salts and books, discussing fashion and reading aloud the gothic novels of Mrs Radcliffe and other romantic authors until I felt like screaming. It is all so…mundane. Though I must admit that I did fall under the spell of *Sense and Sensibility*, a newly published work by an unknown author who simply calls herself 'a lady'.

The highlight for me is our weekly visit to the circulating library in the nearby market town. Nettie and I are left in peace to browse the shelves and choose volumes that appeal to us, while Sophie gossips with her friends in the tea shop next door.

******

I have discovered Uncle Rudolf's library! When I peeped through the door I could see towering shelves marching away into the gloom, the occasional ray of sunshine stealing past sombre window drapery to make dust motes glitter and light up gilt-lettered spines. The room has an air of abandonment, as if the person who'd lovingly assembled it had long gone. I walked its length, reading titles, and thought of papa's, which is more towards the sciences, though it does have the Greek and Roman classics.

At Mornington however, it is not only the classics, but the works of Walter Scott, Jonathan Swift, Daniel Defoe, Alexander Pope, Richard Sheridan and many others. I delighted in this discovery and promised myself that when I could escape from my 'improving' lessons with Sophie, I would hide in this room. I had soon learned that neither my aunt nor my uncle were great readers, so seldom visited here, she much preferring her morning room and he his comfortable, less imposing and easily heated study.

Here, I also found a portrait of a young gentleman in the clothing of last century—powered wig, long waistcoat under an elaborately embroidered coat—and the background was of this very room! It hung over one of the two fireplaces that bookended the library. Immediately I knew who it was, the likeness to my dear papa being so strong. The grandfather I did not remember must have loved books as much as I did, I guessed. Over the other fireplace hung the portrait of a plump and pretty young woman, dressed in the height of fashion for the day, with a baby in her arms and her hand on the shoulder of an equally plump boy of about ten— no doubt my Uncle Rudolf. Beside him stood a little girl— Aunt Arabella. Tears welled up as I looked at my darling papa and I stood there for a long time…remembering.

Through the summer we dined with other prominent families in the neighbourhood and they in turn dined with us. On sunny, still days we went on picnics, but they were such elaborate affairs, we might as well have eaten indoors. Sophie decided it was acceptable for me to accompany her on these sedate outings though I would quite happily have stayed at home. I don't particularly like my uncle's wife and she doesn't like me I'm sure, so ours is a strained relationship. In the privacy of my room, I still succumb to bouts of weeping and Nettie rocks me in her arms to comfort me.

Sophie never walks, is afraid of horses, and prefers to travel everywhere on wheels, however I often rise early and Nettie and I escape into the countryside, glad to be out of the stifling and uncomfortable atmosphere. Arm in arm, we explore nearby woods and walk the fields and lanes. Whenever I can, I flee my duties to ride Bluebell, with a groom accompanying me. One day I found Firebrand growing fat and idle, so now I exercise him as well and I must say he is a much more exciting ride than my darling little mare. So I can sit astride, Nettie has reluctantly helped me create a new habit with a divided skirt, as I have outgrown my old one. Firebrand has not been broken to the side saddle you see. Though I suppose this will have to be attended to if I am to ride him in company.

"Really Miss Emily, it is most unladylike for you to ride like a man," Nettie scolds me with a frown. But I don't care.

"You sound just like Sophie," I tease. "Papa never minded and we *are* in the country so hardly anyone sees me except the grooms." I knew if my aunt *did* hear of it, I would be forbidden to ride astride, but I was sure no one would report me. I don't think the staff are very fond of her ladyship and her pettish ways. With Firebrand I feel closer to my father and it is as if he is still with me.

******

It is the last of the summer days now and Sophie's baby is due in autumn. I have become very fond of Sir Timothy and his wife and count them friends, and Lord Firstbridge has also called quite frequently. Uncle Rudolph had disappeared with his steward on this particular day when his lordship visited. We received him in the morning room, which is furnished to Sophie's taste with pastel shades, the Chinese patterned wallpaper being very pretty but, in my opinion, spoiled by chairs and tables with an over abundance of gilt decoration. I was sitting by the window and had been reading aloud to Sophie— who never reads herself if she can avoid it—when he was announced. Reclining on the chaise longue, with a flirtatious smile she bade him join us. I have to admit my aunt made a delightful picture with the sunlight glittering on her curls, and dressed in the latest fashion now she is out of mourning. One hardly notices she is nearing her lying-in, she still looks so ravishing.

Lord Firstbridge leaned over her outstretched hand before flicking the tails of his coat and sitting at her feet.

"Do you not find the country dreary milord?" she sighed. "I know you are not interested in hunting and shooting and must long to be back in town with all its many pleasures. No doubt you will be returning at the end of this hot weather, or do you intend joining Prinny in Brighton?"

"Alas, the pleasure of the prince's company is not to my taste, Lady Burncliff. Now he is regent, I find him rather a bore." His smile was more a sneer and Sophie tittered.

"How naughty of you to say so, milord. Burnie finds him quite entertaining. There is talk of the Marine Pavilion being redesigned—again." She looked enquiringly at her guest.

"Yes, I believe Prinny is considering it, and completely obsessed with the oriental style." He pulled out a jewelled snuffbox and delicately took a pinch, making it obvious he no longer wished to discuss the Regent.

I sat quietly listening to this vacuous talk, having nothing to contribute as it was so outside my own experience.

"Of course there is the coming Season to look forward to milord. Surely *that* will not bore you—all that fresh, young beauty to admire." She glanced at him archly from under her lashes.

"My dear, none could be more lovely than you," purred the earl with a knowing smirk. "I prefer my beauty a little more...polished." Sophie blushed prettily and prattled on.

"La, milord you flatter me. Now, tell me, what is the latest *on-dit,* as you have been to town more recently than I. It is incredibly dull rusticating here at Mornington and I intend returning as soon as I am able. I have so missed it these past months." She now sounded sulky and dispirited.

His lordship proceeded to amuse her with sly and titillating gossip, some of which quite made me blush. I sat listening to their suggestive chatter and doubted despairingly that I should ever learn the twists and turns of these word games. Flirting seems to be all the thing. And pinching. Nettie tells me the prettier of the serving maids keep well out of Uncle Rudolf's reach. Perhaps this is the way the *ton* always behave. It is a puzzle to me. I was drearily reflecting on my inadequacies when a voice spoke sharply.

"Emily! Pay attention! Lord Firstbridge is addressing you!"

"I apologise milord. Pray forgive me." I knew I couldn't blush as charmingly as Sophie.

"Only that you must be looking forward to your own coming out and the pleasures of the Season, Miss Southey," he repeated politely.

"Oh yes, very much so." I tried to inject enthusiasm into my voice. Lord Firstbridge smiled at me and it made him look not quite so saturnine.

"I shall be attending the opening of parliament so will be returning to town at the end of October and I am looking forward to listening to the lectures of Mr Brodie, at the Royal Society. He is speaking on the influence of the brain on the action of the heart and on the generation of animal heat. An elegant speaker."

My eyes opened wide and I gasped with pleasure. "Ah, I should so love to hear it milord! I have attended many amazing lectures in the past with my dear papa."

"Then when you come to town for your coming out, may I have the privilege of escorting you there?"

That still remained a year away I thought, with resignation for even if Sophie were to return to London after the baby was born, I doubted she would want *me* with her, but I thanked him profusely. I could see her pouting at the turn of the conversation, and not long after Lord Firstbridge took his leave.

"You should not be so forward Emily. It is unbecoming in a girl barely out of the schoolroom," she snapped at me when we were alone. "Now go and fetch my smelling salts. I am feeling a little faint."

She could not spoil my pleasure however, until the gloomy thought occurred to me that his lordship had said it, only to be polite.

******

Uncle Rudolph has gone, without Sophie, to join the Prince Regent in Brighton; she is much put out but too uncomfortable to travel. Country life does not agree with either of them; he misses the London clubs and his cronies and she, the balls and theatre, flirting and endless gossip. It is as well that my uncle has a competent steward in Mr Small. But even Sophie does not like town when the city swelters in the heat of August, even smellier than usual. Then the *ton* desert it, fleeing to the seaside or back to their estates to prepare for grouse and pheasant shooting in the autumn and fox hunting in the winter.

However, with parliament due to re-open in November, as Lord Firstbridge had reminded me, those families of our acquaintance who do not enjoy outdoor pursuits will return to their town houses or rent one for the coming Season. Not Sophie though—as she is due soon she must remain at Mornington. This makes her quite irritable and I am the butt of her ill humour. Everything I do or say is criticised.

"That hairstyle is most unbecoming Emily. Far too old for you."

Nettie had devised it and I thought it rather flattering. I said nothing, but wondered if it would have been better to have disagreed with her. Were the continual little digs designed to prompt a reaction from me so she could then complain to my uncle how difficult she found me? I decided that would be too complicated for Sophie. She is just spiteful and shallow and taking out her own discomfort on a younger person who has no one to defend her. So, as much as I can, I ignore the petty jibes and conjugate Latin verbs or the rules of the Pythagorean theorem in my head, which works beautifully.

I hear an eminent man-midwife is travelling from town for Sophie's confinement. I wonder if it is fear that makes her so waspish. I do not like her but I wish her no ill will and pray for a safe delivery. Perhaps I should make an effort to be more conciliatory and not judge her so. I don't know what I would do without Nettie. Poor girl, she patiently listens to my complaints as she helps me dress.

"But just think Miss Emily, when you have your Season and once you are wed, you'll be mistress of your own home," she reminds me gently as she arranges my hair in another becoming style. Nettie has borrowed a book from the library called *The Duties of a Lady's Maid* and has studied it assiduously.

"Unfortunately I shall have to find a husband first," I reply despondently.

To that, Nettie has no answer.

In the privacy of my room I often think of my dear papa and how much I miss him. I shall turn sixteen in October so it will still be another year before I can escape to my other aunt for my coming out. A year ago I had dreaded it. I have to admit, my hopes have certainly changed. However, one must never make plans when one is an orphan and subject to the whims of others.

Had I but known, my future was already being decided for me.

Chapter Eight.
In which Nettie writes home again.

Dear ma and pa,

Mornington is beautiful! I love my dear little room next to Miss Emily's. It is perfect! When we first arrived, the dragon of a housekeeper took me to the servants' hall to be introduced to the staff and then we went to her private sitting room to take tea. I felt really scared, but remembered all the things you'd taught me and behaved in a most ladylike manner. I watched Lady Edale's maid for guidance. I've read The Duties of a Lady's Maid *from cover to cover—twice—so I'm sure I didn't do anything to embarrass myself.*

Nettie loved writing about taking tea and making polite conversation. It sounded so refined.

There is an army of servants here, so different from Miss Emily's old home. The footmen are all tall and handsome in their smart livery. One even winked at me! Poor Miss Emily is struggling to fit in. She's like a wild bird with wings clipped and forced to live in a cage; a beautiful cage but still a prison.

That had been taken, almost word for word, from a novel Nettie had borrowed from the circulating library in Blakesley, the nearest market town. Her mistress had generously bought her an annual subscription as she knew how much her maid loved to read. Nettie thought it described Miss Emily's situation perfectly. She dipped her quill into the ink and continued writing.

Until I came to this grand house I never really understood how special it is to be a lady's maid, ma. I'm regularly invited to take tea with the housekeeper and don't mix with the lower servants at all, though sometimes I do miss their cheeky chatter. If it wasn't for the fact that my mistress is so unhappy, I would be quite content. In my opinion, Lady Burncliff is mean-spirited, for all her beauty, and seems to take pleasure in making Miss Emily's life a misery with her nagging and unkind comments, pretending that she is trying to 'improve' her dear niece. The cow! And like mistress, like lady's maid. That Jersey is an ogre! Lords it over me, she does, because she is Lady Burncliff's maid and therefore much superior. I do my best to cheer Miss Emily with amusing stories from below stairs, but I can see how far her spirit has sunk. She's even looking forward to staying in London with her aunt! That's how bad things have become.

Nettie had filled a page. She thought of turning the sheet sideways to continue, but as she knew her ma found it difficult to read when overwritten, she squeezed in a fond farewell and her signature at the bottom, and with a satisfied sigh, sanded, folded and addressed it, ready to take to the village for posting.

Chapter Nine.
Simon.

I am thoroughly enjoying my new life. Six months have passed since I became Mr Ferris's assistant and I am firmly established in this cheerful household. The Inns of Court, the Bow Street Runners and the seamier side of London life are now also very familiar to me. Mr Ferris has encouraged my detection abilities and I'm gaining a reputation—not to mention the satisfying monetary rewards—as a solver of crimes. My clients in the *ton* are comfortable discussing their personal problems with me; they consider me 'one of them', my noble background having been carefully scrutinised, and of course, it is my employer, a much respected gentleman, who has vouched for me. I've learned, however, that not all magistrates are so upstanding and honest. Some are as corrupt as those they condemn and I am very thankful for my mentor's high principles.

This improvement in my finances now enables me to dress appropriately for a follower of fashion. Today, I'd met up with Michael Slater—a friend from my Cambridge days —at White's and asked for his advice regarding my wardrobe.

"Look Mannering, there's Beau Brummell," Slater whispered, reverently, indicating an immaculately dressed gentleman, who had just walked into the club, surrounded by a laughing group. "Now there's what you should aim for," he said with awe. "They say his valet cleans his boots with champagne!"

I discreetly eyed the great man and had to agree he made a picture of subtle elegance. Slater then took me to his favourite tailor in Savile Row and eventually I settled on several waistcoats of muted colours, my favourite being a soft grey silk stripe which would go well with my new charcoal grey wool tail coat. I couldn't resist a quizzing glass, though there is nothing wrong with my sight, and several tasteful fobs to decorate the ribbon of my watch. I left with pockets weighing a lot less. However, when I saw myself in the bedroom mirror, fully dressed, I believe I looked as well as any man and felt bang up to the mark, though I'd stopped short of the ridiculously high shirt points and extravagant neck cloths of a dandy, and abhor the lurid waistcoat colours they favour. Rachel passed me in the hall as I left to dine with friends.

"My, Simon, you cut a very fine figure!" That woman loves to make me blush!

******

Mr Ferris called me in to his study one morning recently and gestured for me to be seated.

"Simon, would you like to invite your mother and your two sisters to spend a week in town? I'm sure you have missed them and they would be most welcome. Rachel is anxious to meet them as well. I shall absent myself from my magisterial duties and it will be a pleasant break."

The thought of seeing my family again, filled me with pleasure. "That's most generous of you, sir. I'll write immediately!"

Mother accepted with alacrity, so I am now at the yard impatiently expecting the mail coach's arrival at any

63

moment. My employer's carriage is waiting out in the street to convey my family through London.

The horses finally trotted through the gate, lathered and exhausted. A groom opened the coach door and the steps were let down. Looking tired and rumpled my mother alighted first, followed by the older of my two sisters. Rebekah, who has the same hair and eye colouring as mine, looked around with excitement, then seeing me, her face lit up.

"Oh Simon, you look devilish handsome!" she exclaimed and received a frown from mother.

"Pray don't be so vulgar, miss!" But as my mother lifted her face to me to receive a kiss on the cheek, she whispered in my ear. "You do indeed, my love."

Next, Prudence, the baby of the family, at eleven, tumbled out into my arms. With a laugh I set her on her feet.

"My legs have quite gone to sleep, Simon, and I'm beyond disappointed we didn't see *any* highwaymen." Prudence is an avid reader and, unbeknownst to mother, she informed me later, had devoured Charles Johnson's *History of Highwaymen, Murderers, Etc.*

I gather one of mother's economies has been to do without a personal maid, so little Tillie who I remember as cleaning the bedrooms and changing the sheets, climbed out last and, eyes wide with awe, looked timidly around.

The bustle of collecting valises took but a few minutes and then we loaded everything into Mr Ferris's carriage. Finally, as the gas lights were being lit, much to Prudence's amazement, we set off across London. One would not believe my family had spent the whole day travelling in some discomfort to see my little sister's bouncing delight when I pointed out places of interest as we passed.

"Ooh Simon, we have nothing like that at home. How do they get the gas to the light? And is that the Tower of

London where Henry VIII had Ann Boleyn beheaded?" Prudence, who was a very little girl when we'd left London, has a lively curiosity with a rather ghoulish bent.

I noticed Rebekah eyeing me appraisingly. "That coat fits you like a glove Simon, and the cloth looks exceedingly fine." She leaned forward to finger the fabric.

I affected a casual air. "Oh it's a Weston. He's the best tailor in London, you know."

Rebekah smirked. "And I suppose your boots are by Hoby?"

Before I could stop myself I asked, "how did you know?" Then felt foolish when she started to laugh.

"Oh Simon, just because we live in Stamford doesn't mean I'm unaware of London fashion. The young men of my acquaintance all talk endlessly of Weston and Hoby as if they were gods."

I grinned a little shamefacedly. I love Rebekah but she is a trifle too knowing at times. My sisters chattered on happily but mother sat with her eyes closed, and I knew she longed for the end of this weary journey.

Mr Ferris and Rachel, stood waiting at the front door to greet us and without further ado the ladies were whisked off to their rooms to refresh themselves and change before dinner. We met again in the drawing room and it amused me to see Blake, home from Oxford for the break, blush and gaze with wonder at my oldest sister. Even though it is only six months, I have to admit that Rebekah has grown and changed since I last saw her and is now quite the beauty. She looked particularly ravishing in a very modish gown of pale peach with trimmings of cream lace. I have become much more conscious of fashion now I move in London's polite circles.

It was a jolly and relaxed evening full of merriment and laughter. Felicity Ferris had found a fellow soul in my younger sister and I guessed the two of them were destined to be the best of friends. I observed Rachel's awareness of how much her father's face lit up when he talked to my mother and I saw her smile to herself. I'm very fond of Rachel—as a brother—and understand there is a widowed barrister who has been courting her for the last year but as she could not bear to leave her father to manage on his own, she has resisted his ardent advances. However, if circumstances were to change….I turned to talk to Mr Ferris, but the thought lingered in the back of my mind.

And so a week of wondrous pleasures began. Mr Ferris took us all to Astley's Amphitheatre to watch amazing equestrian acts, jugglers, acrobats, rope-dancers, clowns and strongmen.

Prudence clutched my arm with eyes shining. "Oh Simon, I would dearly love to be able to ride like those amazing girls. Do you think I could ask them to teach me?" she murmured softly, but mother overheard.

"Don't be silly Prudence. It is not a ladylike occupation." She saw my little sister's disappointment and added. "However, I do believe Simon's old horse is still eating his head off at the stables. I kept him for Rebekah but she seems to have no desire to ride, so when we get home I shall arrange for lessons for you."

Prudence threw her arms around mother and squealed with delight. As I could now afford stabling in London, I had been to Tattersall's and bought myself a showy gelding called Charlemagne, so did not mind in the least.

The ladies enjoyed visiting the shops and warehouses to buy fabrics and trimmings and exclaim over the latest fashions from Paris. We saw a balloon ascent at the Vauxhall Gardens and attended the theatre, where Mr Ferris had rented a box. Mother looked lovely in a new gown of dark blue silk and the young bucks in the pit ogled my ravishing sister, much to Blake's displeasure, he showing all the signs of being desperately in love. I enjoyed seeing my family having such a happy time.

Life has not been easy for mother since my father's death—we all still miss him very much—but this week has taken the strain out of her eyes and given them back their sparkle. As with Rachel, I am aware that my employer is not unaffected by my mother's charms, and so allowed myself to quietly hope for a happy outcome.

Finally the time arrived for the guests to leave. The ladies hugged and kissed and there were promises of letter writing. Mr Ferris and his family stood with me to bid them farewell. He had kindly offered the use of his comfortable coach for their return journey and as it trotted smartly down the road, he remained watching until it disappeared from view.

My employer leaned forward to quietly murmur in my ear. "Your mother is a damned fine woman Simon. Do you have any objection to my keeping in touch with her?" A flush suffused his cheeks and I knew his swearing to be an indication of his heightened emotions.

"Of course not sir! I'm more than happy." I grinned to myself at my employer's discomfort.

And so life returned to normal, though the senior members of the household noticed how eagerly the master awaited the mail each day, and when certain lightly scented letters arrived, addressed in a feminine hand, he would retire to his study with a satisfied smile.

Chapter Ten.
In which an agreement is reached.

Lord Burncliff cleared his throat uncomfortably. "Ah, sorry Firstbridge, a man should meet his gambling debts. A matter of honour. However I've had a bit of a financial setback. Ship I invested in hasn't returned from the West Indies. Sunk no doubt," he surmised gloomily. "Fact is, I can't meet those vowels you're holding; find myself cleaned out at the moment, don't y'know."

The two men were relaxing in Lord Firstbridge's study, lounging comfortably in wing chairs before a cheerful fire and sipping glasses of fine cognac, compliments of a smuggling contact. His host knew Burncliff gambled hard—cards, horses, dice—and always seemed to be on the edge of ruin. Firstbridge on the other hand, husbanded his wealth. He gambled, yes, but assessed the odds, withdrew when expedient, and enjoyed the power to be gained from having others in his debt, his nature being rather cold and calculating. He marvelled at his guest. That silly chit of a wife came with a very respectable dowry. Had the fool disposed of it already?

"No problem, my dear Burncliff. But perhaps we can help each other. I have decided to marry again and I'm looking for a biddable young bride. If you can suggest someone and recommend me, well, perhaps we can tear up those vowels, hmmm?" He held his glass in both hands, looking over its rim at his guest, and wondering if the fellow would be smart enough to understand his meaning.

Lord Burncliff looked startled, then speculative, and slowly smiled.

Chapter Eleven.
Emily.

Autumn has arrived; the days are mellow and the nights cool. Uncle Rudolf has returned for the birth of his hoped-for son. His first wife had only produced daughters and they've long since been married off. I don't recall ever meeting any of them and they never call at Mornington now their father has re-married. To think I might pass one of my cousins in the street and not even know her. That is what happens when family's fall out, I sadly acknowledged.

He brought with him the man-midwife, and what an unctuous fellow he is. Sophie is quite taken with him though, so that is all that matters. I expect to have a new cousin any day now and I am hoping that his or her arrival will occupy my dear aunt so much I shall be left in peace. I read to her, rub her back and rearrange her pillows, fetch a shawl or a handkerchief or play softly on the pianoforte to soothe her nerves, but I'm weary of the constant correction.

"Really Emily, don't slouch so. A lady always sits with her back straight." Or "Emily, I have noticed you are far too familiar with your maid, she is Perkins *not* Nettie. You will encourage her to take liberties and one must always be conscious of keeping the servants in their place."

No doubt Sophie has found me a great trial. It does not help that I dislike card games which is one of her passions. And I shall continue to call my maid Nettie, in spite of my aunt's strictures, I think mutinously.

I am so glad that Sir Timothy and Lady Badger will not be going to town.

"The oldest girls are still a little young for London's social life," she told me one day when they paid a visit. "Perhaps next year. I do not want to rush them to the alter. I should miss them too much. And besides, Sir Timothy is so busy with his magisterial and coronial duties, he really cannot afford the time." She looked across the drawing room with affection at her husband who sat talking to my uncle.

"I prefer the quieter pace of country life anyway, and if I require intelligent and interesting conversation, I have you close at hand," she added softly so that no one else can hear, and looked at me with a smile.

I am warmed by the compliment. With the Badgers as neighbours, I feel I'm not entirely alone. And of course I also have my dear Nettie who keeps me from despair.

******

Distant wailing woke me this morning. Nettie bustled in with my morning cup of hot chocolate.

"Well, Miss Emily, your aunt is brought to bed, as no doubt you've heard, so the house is at sixes and sevens. That man-midwife has everybody running and Lord Burncliff is to go riding with Lord Firstbridge. I fear the master is quite put out by the racket."

I can always count on Nettie keeping me informed. All day the pain-filled cries continued. My uncle sent a note to say he would remain with his neighbour and for news of the delivery to be sent there. I felt sorry for Sophie but I enjoyed not being at her beck and call. I took Bluebell for some much-needed exercise though a chill wind blew, and feeling very refreshed, I then galloped Firebrand along the

71

trails through the woods. He is being trained to the side saddle but I still prefer to ride him astride whenever I can. Papa always said that a side-saddle was a death trap on a spirited horse. I came back to the hall to find the house still in an uproar. Having changed from my riding habit, and eaten a quick luncheon, I took myself off to the library to spent a happy afternoon.

Late in the day my uncle finally had an heir.

"He's a bonny lad if the sound of his lungs is anything to go by," Nettie informed me as she helped me dress for dinner. "A wet nurse has been hired and that Jersey says your aunt is resting and not to be disturbed." This was said with a sniff. I knew Nettie's opinion of Sophie's lady's maid.

At dinner that night Uncle Rudolf positively beamed. He'd invited Lord Firstbridge so I played hostess in my aunt's absence. I noticed our guest's usually rather cynical face looked bleak and I remembered his childless state. He made an effort to be cheerful.

"Congratulations Burncliff. You are a lucky fellow. Here's to your heir." And he raised his wine glass in a toast.

My uncle laughed. "You should get married again, Firstbridge. After all you don't want to leave it too late you know."

I noticed he looked at me as he said it and wondered why. The conversation then moved to the matching pair of carriage horses Lord Firstbridge had recently purchased so I withdrew using the excuse of a slight headache and left the two of them to their port.

The following morning an invitation came to visit the new mother and view the baby. I scratched at the bedroom door and when Jersey admitted me I walked into a blast of hot air. All the windows were closed and a fire roared in the grate. Sophie lay buried in piles of covers and looked very pale in spite of the heat—not her usual lovely self—which did not surprise me, after her recent ordeal. She signalled me closer and I noticed the nurse standing nearby with a shawl-wrapped bundle in her arms.

"Come and meet your new cousin, Emily." Sophie spoke in a tired, soft voice. The nurse offered him to me and I carefully held him in my arms. He weighed almost nothing. I looked down at the tiny face and thought him a dear fellow; his rosebud mouth moved in a sucking motion and one little hand waved in the air. Unfortunately he'd been so tightly wrapped I couldn't see anymore of him.

"He's a darling, Sophie. You are very clever." And I meant it.

My aunt smiled and then closed her eyes. Jersey, who had been watching her intently, took the baby from me and hustled me to the door.

"That's enough for now, Miss Emily. Milady is very weak and the man-midwife will be here shortly to bleed her *again*." She said this with such distain, I gathered he'd not made himself popular with the household staff. Outside the door, I realised I'd forgotten to ask the baby's name.

A few days later my uncle sent a footman to call me to his study. This was most unusual as, other than mealtimes, he usually ignored me. He stood in front of his desk, and started speaking as soon as I walked through the door.

"Now Emily, I've had an offer for your hand from Lord Firstbridge. He is quite taken with you my dear."

I stood stock-still and stared in shock at this surprise announcement as his lordship had never shown the slightest sign that he had a *tendre* for me. Well he *had* given me permission to ride one of his horses, and promised to take me to a lecture at the Royal Society. Did that count? Uncle Rudolf then passed me a letter addressed in Aunt Arabella's familiar hand.

My dear Emily,
Your uncle has informed me that Lord Firstbridge wishes to offer for you. While he is somewhat older than you, it is an extremely good match as he has vast holdings all over England and is related to at least three dukes, therefore, after discussing it with my dear Edale, we are happy to give our consent. I trust you will comport yourself with all propriety and we look forward to placing the betrothal notice in the Times.

Yours affectionately,
Aunt Arabella

In the back of my mind—the part not paralysed with surprise—I thought it highly unlikely that Uncle Richard, had voiced any opinion whatsoever, he being a man of large proportions but few words, and thoroughly hen-pecked to my mind. I wondered if her happy compliance had been because she would no longer need go to the trouble of bringing me out. I believe this life I am leading has made me rather cynical.

With his eyebrows raised expectantly, Uncle Rudolph obviously waited for some reaction from me.

"I-I am honoured," I stammered, my thoughts in a whirl, "but this is rather sudden," I finished lamely.

"Oh, he will be calling this afternoon, my dear," he replied airily. "There is no doubt it would be a brilliant match for you. We shall be close by so you can still visit Sophie."

Presumably, my uncle thought that would be an added incentive to accept the offer. I excused myself and fled to the library. I didn't want to speak to Nettie until I'd fully absorbed this startling development. Curling up with my feet tucked under me in my favourite chair—the fire had not been lit to take the chill from the room as no one else ever came here—I considered my situation.

My sixteenth birthday would occur at the end of October. Not accepting this proposal, would mean spending another whole year in a household that had only brought me unhappiness, and then what if I didn't find a husband in my first Season? Would it mean a return to Uncle Rudolf and—perish the thought—Sophie? It was all very depressing.

I gloomily came to the conclusion that of my few options, the best one would be to wed Lord Firstbridge. After all, Aunt Arabella had told me that marriages in the *ton* were seldom for love. Wealth and position were all that counted. If affection came afterwards, well it would be pleasant but not really necessary. I put aside my childish and romantic dreams and accepted this new future into which I found myself being reluctantly propelled.

When I told Nettie, she squealed with delight. "Oh Miss Emily, you will be free of Lady Burncliff! And mistress in your own home! I shan't be sorry to see the back of that Jersey either."

At least someone appeared to be happy with this offer, I consoled myself, and hid my own misgivings. Soon, it would be six months since my dear papa had left me and I wondered if he looked down and saw what a muddle my life had become. I had forgotten his advice to marry for love and only remembered, when it was far too late.

Lord Firstbridge, when I'd shyly joined him in the drawing room, took my hand in his and bestowed a dry kiss on it.

"Dear Miss Southey, I admire and respect you and would be honoured if you would accept my hand in marriage."

His eyes met mine and he smiled. For a moment I saw something there that unsettled me and sent a shiver of unease down my spine, but in a flash it passed and I told

75

myself I must have imagined it. It seemed not the most impassioned declaration, and on later reflection, more like a contract being settled, which I suppose it is. However, whatever the future might hold, I had chosen my path.

"Thank you Lord Firstbridge. I am delighted to accept." My reply sounded stilted but in keeping with the formality of his offer. I blushed as he then lightly kissed me on the cheek.

"Please call me Miles, it is my given name, and I shall call you Emily."

He slipped a magnificent diamond and ruby ring on my finger and just like that, I was betrothed.

Chapter Twelve.
Emily.

We were married in the village church on a bitterly cold autumn morning, and also the day I turned sixteen. Aunt Arabella and Uncle Richard—no doubt he had been bullied into accompanying her—arrived from London the night before with exciting news. Aunt Arabella couldn't wait to tell me.

"Sarah has accepted an offer from a very suitable young man, Emily. Most likeable and of impeccable lineage," she said with satisfaction. "They are to be wed in early spring. He is the son and heir of a general in Wellington's army, you know, and the wedding is to be before the new offensive."

My aunt carried a letter for me from Sarah. We had never been close but when I read it I could see her obvious delight shining through the writing and though I felt happy for her, I could not help but compare it to my own rather emotionless betrothal.

Nettie dressed me for the wedding in my new gown of violet-coloured velvet with rows of embroidered flowers around the hem. Over this I wore a darker, fur-lined redingote as the wind blew like flying ice. I would carry a matching fur muff instead of flowers, though my future husband had sent a dainty bunch of autumn violets from his conservatory, to be pinned to it. Earlier that morning, Nettie had been quite emotional when she'd presented me with a pair of lovingly-made embroidered slippers for my birthday. I thanked her and kissed her warmly.

"Oh how your dear papa would have loved to see you looking so beautiful," she said sadly. I felt very close to tears myself. "And I wish Mrs Crombie could have been here too, Miss Emily," she added, looking even more forlorn.

Actually, I did too. Growing up in a motherless household, Mrs Crombie had been a constant presence in my life, and eventually my mentor, gently explaining about the changes that came to a young girl's body. Though I am familiar, in theory, with the reproductive process because of my studies, I am completely ignorant of what passes between a man and a woman in the bed chamber. And Sophie, who could have helped me, would be the last person I would want to talk to. I have never heard it discussed in polite society and Mrs Radcliffe and the like did not go into details in their books, beyond heaving bosoms and passionate kisses. Other authors barely mentioned it at all.

Nettie usually tries to sound very confident and grown-up—though she's only two years older than I—but she still snuffled dolefully as she arranged my pretty new bonnet over my curls.

"I've already packed most things Miss Emily and while you are being wed, I shall be transferring to your new home to prepare for your arrival." She sighed, obviously a little sad to be leaving her cosy room adjoining mine.

I knew Nettie had quite enjoyed her stay at Mornington. Being a lady's maid gave her a high status in the servants' hall, only superseded by the housekeeper and Jersey, but seeing my unhappiness and ill-use had dimmed her pleasure somewhat.

Sophie would not be attending; her lying-in had now lasted six weeks and she still remained too weak to walk far, owing in part I believed to the many blood-lettings she had endured at the insistence of the man-midwife. Uncle Rudolf gave me away and as my hand passed from his to my new husband's, I felt the oddest sensation of being bought and sold. I occasionally have the queerest notions.

It was decided the wedding breakfast would be held at Amberleigh as Sophie is so unwell. I had been there as a visitor before of course, but now I viewed it with different eyes as the carriage swept up the driveway to the entrance. This would be my home from now on and a little voice inside me murmured, *hope for better, it could hardly be worse.*

It is an enormous place, wings added on over the centuries and in differing styles, but somehow it still has a satisfying cohesion. The grounds are even more impressive than Mornington's with formal gardens surrounding the manor itself, and a ha-ha separating them from a glorious park of grassy swards stretching into the distance with groves of magnificent English oak, beech and chestnut. Deer roam freely. I knew from previous visits that a lake—larger and even more beautiful than my uncle's—filled the view on the south side.

The household staff were waiting at the entrance and the butler, Peebles, went slowly down the line making introductions, the females curtsying and the men bowing. I had already met Mrs Peebles, Amberleigh's housekeeper, and no doubt the butler's wife, so I felt relieved to see a familiar female face. I suppose they thought me a very young mistress, incapable of running such a household, but as I had been papa's hostess for some time before his death, I am not entirely without experience. Mrs Crombie had trained me well.

When we came to my husband's valet, I felt a jolt of recognition. This would be my lord's natural son. It had been one of Nettie's bits of gossip gleaned from my uncle's coachman. He is a handsome young man and I could see the family likeness. He stared boldly at me with dark, calculating eyes—exactly like his father's—before dropping them and bowing. We passed on and I put him out of my mind.

Mrs Peebles took me upstairs and along hallways to my new bedroom, and Nettie, who had already unpacked and tried to make everything look as homely and familiar as possible, welcomed me. We stood in a prettily decorated room, with a huge silk-curtained bed and walls papered in a pattern of exotic birds and flowers.

"It's much bigger than Mornington, Miss Emily. Oops I mean milady," she corrected herself with a grin. "There's a dressing room through that door, and my room's beyond that so I'm still right handy." She drew me to another door on the other wall and opened it.

"And here's a dear little private sitting room with a lovely view overlooking the lake. I believe that door over there leads to his lordship's room," she finished.

I carefully tried not to think about that other bedroom and its occupant. No doubt there would be a dressing room and valet's room on the other side as well. Altogether, it made an impressive suite.

Nettie removed my redingote and hat, tidied my hair and wrapped me in a warm, beautifully patterned shawl in violet, silver and black. Though the room felt cosy with a cheerful fire, the long hallways were not. The wedding breakfast would be served in the formal dining room and when I opened my bedroom door, a footman waited to guide me there. Just as well as I would surely have got lost without him.

A sumptuous meal had been prepared—a whole roasted salmon, ham, cold meats, pies, eggs cooked in various ways, muffins, seed cake, honey cake, savoury and sweet buns, fresh fruit, hot chocolate, tea, coffee, fruit juices and of course champagne for the wedding toasts. To top it all, a beautifully decorated wedding cake took pride of place in the middle of the table. Unfortunately I had little appetite and sat quietly as Aunt Arabella and Uncle Rudolf dominated the conversation. The vicar and his wife were there and Uncle Richard talked amiably to Sir Timothy and Lady Badger, but it was only a small party.

"And where do you plan on going for your honeymoon, my dear?' asked a smiling Lady Badger.

"Lord Firstbridge promised to take me to London to attend lectures at the Royal Society, but we are leaving the trip until the new year, when hopefully the weather will have improved," I answered shyly.

I did not mind the delay; it meant I would have time to familiarise myself with my new home and get to know my husband better, as he remained almost a complete stranger to me. And the thought of removing to London to face the expected round of balls, musical evenings, morning calls and all the other social obligations of my new position as a countess, filled me with trepidation.

My husband sat beside me, now, talking pleasantly to the vicar and occasionally turning to me with a comment. I wondered if he could feel my eyes observing him. I had no idea of his age—he had never mentioned it and I thought it impolite to ask—however I could see that it would be close to that of my uncle; perhaps even older than my father had been when he died. He must have been quite impressive as a young man, but now, when his face stilled, it seemed as if his experiences had stamped it with discontent and cynicism. During the wedding service I had learned his family name— Wolffe. I had not, until then, known even that small fact about the man to whom I was now wed.

For the life of me I could not see why I had been chosen when he could have had any one of a number of beautiful young women as his bride. For whatever reason, he had, and now I must make myself as agreeable as possible so that he wouldn't regret his decision, for I knew that marriage could be made intolerable if one incurred a husband's anger. Nettie had told me a horror story of one of the local landowners, who on the surface appeared perfectly amiable, but behind closed doors beat his wife mercilessly. She'd given him only daughters. I understood then why I had never seen her without long sleeves, and often veiled.

The wedding guests finally prepared to leave. We clustered in the entry hall as hats and coats were donned. Lady Badger gave me a hug, looked at me searchingly and spoke in a soft voice. "Will you be alright my dear? I felt it was Sophie's place to talk to you as you've no mother to advise you, so didn't like to interfere, but…"

At that moment Aunt Arabella approached to make her farewells and Lady Badger moved aside, her sentence unfinished. My aunt pecked me on the cheek and whispered in my ear.

"Now Emily do be obliging, and comply with whatever you are asked." With this small and rather vague bit of marital advice I supposed I would have to be satisfied.

Uncle Richard went to follow my aunt but before he did he surprised me. He took both my hands in his; he is a big, stout man and they were swallowed in his giant paws. He glanced at his lordship who was talking to Sir Timothy, then looked intently at me.

"I know I haven't been much of an uncle to you my dear, but remember, if you ever need help, come to me." This he spoke in a soft rumble so that no one else could overhear.

Several years later, I discovered he'd heard some disquieting rumours about Lord Firstbridge, but as usual had been overruled by my forceful aunt.

Then Aunt Arabella, who'd moved towards the front door, called impatiently. "Come Edale, we have a long journey ahead and I fear there is a storm brewing."

With that, he kissed me on the cheek and released my hands. "Yes, my dear," he replied, and with a final concerned look into my eyes, followed his wife to the waiting coach. I realised I had misjudged my Uncle Richard and felt comforted. But I wondered why he had thought I might need help? First Lady Badger and then my uncle had spoken as if concerned for me. Straightening my spine, I squashed any misgivings and keeping a friendly smile on my face, I bade the vicar and his wife goodbye.

My new husband turned to me as the last guest left and the door closed. "I thought you might like to take a tour of the house and hear a bit of its history, Emily."

I gratefully seized on this offer as a sudden feeling of panic had gripped me. He presented his arm and we made our stately way up stairways, through galleries hung with ancient family portraits, and barely-used rooms filled with wonderful treasure. In a neutral voice he informed me of the house's long and venerable history. At last we came to the library, and it took my breath away. Unlike Mornington's, this one felt alive, a room loved and lived in. We paced its length and I could tell by the way he spoke, that my husband felt at home amongst the books. Perhaps here we could find a meeting place of souls and make this odd marriage work.

In the small family dining room we ate a late and light luncheon; in spite of my nerves I now found myself exceedingly hungry, having eaten little at the wedding breakfast. His lordship made an effort to put me at my ease.

"I hope you have found much to admire at Amberleigh, Emily. The library is one of the most extensive in all England," he said with justifiable pride. For a moment I forgot my shyness.

"Yes my lord, I am looking forward to perusing it," I answered with all honesty.

"I understand you have a strong interest in the sciences. There is a large section devoted entirely to scientific and medical writing—Newton, Lavoisier, Davy, de Condorcet, Morgagni, Fielding, the Hunter brothers, to name but a few. There are even some treatises translated from the Arabic tongue." His eyes, which I had noticed were normally cold and guarded, lit with enthusiasm. It was obvious that he had a strong interest in medicine. At the time it did not occur to me to wonder why, after all, papa and I had also studied medical texts. We discussed books for a time then he changed the subject.

"Do you sail, my dear? No? There is a small yacht on the lake. When the weather improves the steward can give you lessons if you wish." I noticed he had not offered himself. Then he continued. "Speaking of the steward has reminded me I have some urgent business to attend to this afternoon, so shall leave you to your own devices and see you again this evening."

With a small smile he excused himself and left the room. I must admit it filled me with relief to be alone at last; other than talking about books or horses, keeping up polite conversation with this self-contained man had been a strain. Is it because he has an aura of something dark and disturbing? I knew I must be letting my imagination run away again, and put it down to nerves. Shrugging off my disquiet, I decided to explore the wonderful library, lose myself between pages and forget what loomed ahead that night. I did, however, acknowledge to myself that though my understanding of these things is limited, as with the weather, it appeared to be a rather bleak wedding day.

Chapter Thirteen.
In which Bekkit remembers.

When he had been introduced to the new Lady Firstbridge by old Peebles, Bekkit noted how young she looked—hardly out of the schoolroom in fact. Pretty eyes, but quite shy-looking. Not to his taste at all. He liked them a lot bolder. No doubt she would be a little mouse to his father's cat. Or more likely a wolf he amended, thinking of the Firstbridge family name. Their coat of arms featured two snarling wolves rampant, however, the motto, *statera iusta in omnibus*—balance in all things—hardly applied to his lordship. Excess in all things would be much more apt, he acknowledged cynically. If Bekkit had been a caring man, he would have pitied her—but that emotion had long since been stifled, and all that was left was dark emptiness.

He vaguely remembered his lordship's first wife; back then he'd been a lowly stable boy. Now *she* had true beauty—cornflower blue eyes, sun-gold curls and plenty of sparkle. She'd loved to drive her curricle around the estate and had been a first-rate whip. Sometimes, when she chose to ride, she would request a groom to accompany her; her eyes would fall on him and his heart would pound. Even though still a child, he'd fallen half in love with her. Mounted on a pony and trailing behind, he would daydream about being the lord and wearing fine clothes…and kissing her. He huffed a snort of derision. What a young fool he'd been, aching for something he could never have.

Many years had past since then. He'd watched her slowly wilt, like a flower without water; sickness, then miscarriages and stillbirths following one after another until she became a sad little shadow of her former self. One day they'd found her face down in the lake. The story was spread that she'd been out sailing and fallen overboard and drowned. But all knew the truth. Bekkit didn't really know his father then, a figure so far above him, he seemed almost another species.

His thoughts returned to the new Lady Firstbridge. You could never tell with the quiet ones but perhaps she'd be made of sterner stuff than her predecessor. Married to his father, she'd have to be. Bekkit knew himself to be no angel, but as his lordship's bodyguard, his eyes had been opened to real depravity. The notorious Hellfire Club of last century had long been disbanded but the legends of its excesses lived on and were certainly emulated by the more dissolute of the present day *ton*—his father amongst them. He made sure his lordship never knew of the thoughts hidden behind his carefully blank face—had no idea how much Bekkit both despised and envied him. Orders were followed, however degrading, and sometimes Bekkit even enjoyed them.

Chapter Fourteen.
Simon.

I decided to walk home. Mr Ferris had taken the coach but I felt a need for exercise after spending the day in court assisting my employer with the never-ending work that being a London magistrate entails. And all for the reward of seeing a job well-done, for there is no remuneration attached to this thankless labour of defending English law. It is a system open to corruption and Mr Ferris and I had spent many evenings pondering the problem. *My* salary came out of my employer's own pocket.

The autumn wind sliced through me, tall buildings on either side of the street acting as a funnel. Even so, the smoke from thousands of fires choked the air. Now I regretted my decision to go on foot but there wasn't a hackney in sight so I continued, ploughing my way along the crowded footpath, beaver hat pulled down over my ears, gloved hands tucked deep into my great-coat pockets to give extra warmth, and watchful for the young rascals who could skilfully relieve me of my valuables if given half a chance. I had used quite a few of them in my detection work so knew how clever and cunning they could be, had even befriended some and learned of their brutal, short lives.

Most had spent their early years suckling gin, instead of mother's milk, to quieten their hungry cries. If I ever found myself in a position to help the children escape that terrible poverty, I vowed I would. Even so, I employed as many as I could afford and had been cheekily informed by one of my favourites—a street-wise, endearing rascal named Spiff, of around seven, it being hard to tell his true age, his growth having been so stunted—that they considered themselves my troops and had adopted the name of Mannering's Militia.

My thoughts turned from Spiff to Mr Ferris. This brought a smile to my face. He had been a little absent-minded of late and I wondered at the cause, though I had my suspicions. Not that it interfered with his work; he remained as sharp and efficient as ever, but there were moments when his eyes glazed over, his mouth curved up and he went... somewhere else.

The detection work has now become so profitable that I could set up on my own if I wished, but my loyalty to Mr Ferris, who is in a large part responsible for my good fortune, will not allow me to desert him. The magisterial load is enormous and if I can alleviate it in any way, I am determined to keep doing so. I know how much my employer appreciates my aid, and our mutual admiration works to the benefit of us both.

With relief, I finally arrived home, quickly mounted the steps to the front door and before I could raise the knocker our cheerful butler, who had heard my footsteps, opened it.

"Ho Rendall, it's a brisk day out there. You wouldn't consider swapping jobs would you?" I joked as I removed my hat and gloves, shrugged out of my great-coat and handed them to him.

"No, Mr Mannering, I haven't got the brain for all that court fandangle. I'm much better at butlering," he replied straight-faced, but with a twinkle in his eye. I knew he had a soft spot for me.

"The master is in the study and would like a word before dinner," he added.

Intrigued, I walked down the hall, knocked, and upon hearing "come," opened the study door. Mr Ferris stood in front of the fire, hands behind his back.

"Sit down, lad. Hrrmph. I've something of a personal nature to discuss with you but before I talk about that, I want to tell you, we have been invited to stay for a few days with my friend, Sir Timothy Badger, in Northamptonshire, near Blakesley. He is the local magistrate and coroner. We have been friends for years and we like to meet occasionally to discuss mutual legal problems."

"I should be delighted to accompany you, sir." The idea of a trip into the country pleased me enormously. I much preferred it with its slower pace and fresher air, though I had to admit that London had improved my life financially.

"We've also been invited to stay with another friend of mine, a Mr Berryman, in Stamford, after our sojourn with Sir Timothy."

I watched my employer's face redden slightly. Stamford is my home town where my mother and sisters still lived. It suddenly dawned on me the significance of this. Mr Ferris fiddled with the fob hanging from his watch chain.

"You no doubt have guessed by now that I have strong feelings for you mother and am hopeful of your approval to my asking for your mother's hand in marriage." This came out in a rush and his face reddened even more.

"You have it wholeheartedly, sir, and I am delighted to be connected to a family which has made me so welcome." I jumped up and shook Mr Ferris's hand enthusiastically and my employer beamed from ear to ear.

"I have every reason to believe your dear mother will look on my suit with favour, my boy." And he rang for Rendall to fetch the best brandy for a toast and to ask the young people to attend him so he could inform them that there would be very good news shortly. Of course the whole household knew that something momentous was afoot, so it came as no surprise. They kissed their father and hugged him.

I watched Felicity dance around with delight. "Prudence will share my bedroom won't she papa? Oh please say yes!" She squealed and clapped her hands, and I could see that Blake regretted he would be up at Oxford in the new year so would be unable to gaze daily at his goddess.

As for Rachel, she remarked quietly to me, and with some satisfaction, that her place as hostess would soon be supplanted, so I knew her ardent admirer would shortly find his dearest wish granted.

"I've passed my load to a fellow magistrate. He can stand the strain for a few weeks." My employer grinned boyishly at me.

So bags were packed, farewells made and in no time at all we set off, the carriage rumbling its way along the turnpike road to Northamptonshire. A change of horses had been arranged at the inn where we would stop for luncheon and I admired the picturesque countryside and quaint villages through which we drove. Our destination is one of the prettiest shires in all England I had been told, and when we at last arrived, I had to agree.

Chapter Fifteen.
Emily.

I came to my wedding night in nervous ignorance. However, nothing could have prepared me for what followed. When it ended and I could think again, I wondered if I should cry or be angry.

My maid helped me prepare for bed. Dinner had been a nerve-wracking affair as I made stilted conversation and pretended I was not petrified. In spite of that, when it came to an end, I wished I was back at the beginning again. Nettie seemed as anxious as I, fussing over me like a mother hen. I wore a beautiful night rail, all filmy lace and ribbons, with such a pretty matching cap to tie over my curls. Nettie doused all but a few of the candles, gave me a quick hug, wished me goodnight, and left me sitting amongst the pillows, waiting, my heart fluttering.

I heard footsteps crossing the adjoining room, the door opened and my husband walked in. He wore a richly-patterned dark green banyan over his night attire and he carried something black in his hands. He approached the bed, the candlelight dancing on the planes of his face, and then he spoke.

"My dear, to protect your finer sensibilities I should like you to wear this." He held out what looked like a black hood.

I stared at it like a fly in a web, faced by its spinner. Aunt Arabella had told me to obey, so I swallowed and nodded. I was beyond speech. He pulled the black silk over my beautiful nightcap and tightened it around my neck. Thankfully, I found I could still breathe.

"Lie down my dear." His voice sounded emotionless —cold, even.

So I complied. After a pause I felt the covers pulled back and my husband climbing onto the bed. I can hardly bear to talk of what happened next; it was so awful I tremble when I think of it. I felt hands push my night rail up and my legs were pulled apart. With an effort I kept my arms rigidly at my sides as fingers probed, then something hard forced its way into me. I froze in terror and pain and almost suffocated as I gasped for breath. The pounding continued for what felt like an eternity, then he collapsed on top of me with a grunt. Finally, I felt his weight lift and heard the rustle of clothing. I lay as still as I could, afraid it would happen again. My night rail was pulled down and at last my husband removed the hood. He stood by the bedside staring down at me, a strange expression on his face, one I could not identify in the flickering candlelight. I gazed numbly back and flinched as he gave me a kiss on the cheek.

"Good night my dear. I shall see you at breakfast." And with that he walked from the room.

Now, you will understand why I didn't know whether to cry my heart out or be angry. After the shock had passed, I felt utter disappointment. I'd always thought novels gave a rather romantic picture of marriage and the truth would fall somewhere between that and Aunt Arabella's obscure advice. What I had just experienced passed way beyond my understanding. I knew procreation to be necessary for the next generation. I'd watched mating displays of birds, seen the bull serving cows and, against father's orders, crept into the breeding shed and peeked, when Firebrand had been put to a mare. It embarrassed me terribly at the time but I had vaguely assumed that as we were superior beings to animals, procreation for humans would be somehow more…refined. After all, at times I can still faintly remember my mother and father in each other's arms and feel their gentle love all around me. I curled up in a ball, trembling with shock, and it was many hours before I finally slept.

When Nettie brought me my hot chocolate the next morning, she took one look at my face and drew me into her arms. I clung to her but could not bear to tell her of the night's horror. When I had gained some composure, she helped me to dress, and feeling sore and embarrassed, it took all my courage to go downstairs and face my husband at breakfast. He came to me as if nothing had happened, pecked me on the cheek—he'd never once kissed me on the lips—then sat down to eat and read his morning papers. I filled my plate from the sideboard and took my seat at the other end of the table. We ate in silence.

He finally looked up from his reading, "I'm going riding with your uncle this morning and will probably stay for luncheon. I thought you would want to have a meeting with the housekeeper, so that should fill your day admirably and I shall see you at dinner. Oh, and I took the liberty of inviting your aunt, if she is well enough after the birth, and your uncle and Sir Timothy and Lady Badger to dine in a sennight, so that will give you time to discuss the menu with Mrs Peebles, my dear." He rose, nodded towards me, and left the room.

The crying and the anger were still warring with each other. Was this loveless, emotionless existence to be my future? It appeared so. Well, I thought stubbornly, I shall carve out a life for myself and not let my sham of a marriage destroy me. I shall learn how to run this great house efficiently, set up a place in the stillroom for my healing remedies in spite of Sophie's condemnation, and create a workroom for my scientific interests. I doubted milord would be the least bit interested as long as I acted decorously as his hostess, and interfered as little as possible in his life.

Sir Timothy sent me a note advising that he would have house guests, so I wrote back and included them in the invitation for seven days hence. My nights continued as had the first—hooded, brief and brutal—but gradually I became inured to this treatment and bore it stoically. My days were filled with all the things I loved to do, such a far cry from my life at Mornington, and I tried to forget what lay ahead after dark. At least it did not last long—for that I was grateful.

I enjoyed planning the menu for our dinner—white soup, followed by fish with wine and mushroom sauce, stewed mutton with hothouse asparagus, roasted, walnut-stuffed venison, pot herb pie, sweet pickles and for desert, syllabubs, preserved fruits and lemon cheesecakes. The choosing of the wines I left to Peebles. He is an expert and familiar with his lordship's preferences.

The evening of my first dinner party as a married woman finally arrived. As mourning for my dear papa had ended just before my wedding, I donned a beautiful new dress with a short train, a soft blue, but with a daringly low-cut bodice and pleating on the sleeves and hem.

"Do you not think it is rather too low in the neckline Nettie?" I looked uncertainly at myself in the mirror and tried to pull it up a little.

"No, Miss Emily, you have a lovely figure and it shows it off to perfection," she stated firmly. I must admit it made me feel very elegant and I determined to resolutely face our first guests and not let anyone suspect the travesty of my marriage, for I had come to believe that even those who only wed for wealth and connection would surely not have to endure one as cold and demeaning as mine.

I wore a sapphire and diamond necklace with eardrops to match, that complemented my dress. When he'd shown them to me, my husband had said they were family heirlooms and I wondered how many long-dead women before me had worn them—including his first wife. Then I put aside these morbid thoughts, for the colour highlighted my grey eyes fringed with their dark lashes—my best feature—and I felt quite lifted up. And, of course, Nettie's lavish praise gave me confidence.

His lordship, looking darkly saturnine in his black evening clothes, met me at the bedroom door and offered me his arm. I wondered if he would speak as we descended the stairs to receive our guests. I felt no desire to make conversation. But he surprised me.

"You are looking very well tonight, my dear," he said in his bored voice.

"Thank you milord." I could think of nothing else to say, as we crossed the hall and the footman opened the door into the drawing room. What a cold, formal couple we are.

Other than the library, this is my favourite room in the whole house. The walls are panelled with dull gold-coloured mouldings and painted with beautiful pictures of idyllic country scenes. Chandeliers hang from the high ceiling, flooding the room with soft candlelight and the scent of beeswax is mixed with the perfume of flowers. A series of tall, arched french doors with pale green, silk curtains open onto a terrace and give a fine view of the lake during daylight hours. The white marble fireplaces at each end of the room have exquisite carvings of nymphs, flowers and animals, and I'd had the giant porcelain vases filled with roses and lilies from the estate hothouses. The furnishings are in perfect scale for this lovely room and the sumptuous rugs on the floor bring everything together. I have often wondered if this had been the style of milord's first wife, and admired her good taste.

Naturally Nettie had made it her business to find out about this shadowy figure. She'd been buttoning me into my dress in front of the full-length mirror one evening, when I was told what she'd learned.

"According to Mrs Peebles, his first wife was a beauty when she married the earl, but faded to a sad little thing near the end, with sickness and many stillbirths. And there were rumours of *suicide*." Nettie's reflection uttered this last with a shudder.

My face remained blank as I looked back. If my husband had treated her as he did me, it came as no surprise, but I kept this thought to myself. I am made of sterner stuff however and will *not* be diminished. Papa said to always stay true to oneself and so I shall.

My uncle and Sophie were shown into the drawing room. With the man-midwife's departure, she has gradually returned to good health and appeared more beautiful than ever in her stunning dinner dress of a soft sea-green silk that matched her eyes and clung seductively to her figure as she drifted elegantly across the room.

"Emily my dear, how enchanting you look. You quite put me in the shade," she exclaimed, which she knows is nonsense. I noticed her eyes slide to my husband standing beside me and sighed inwardly. Yes, Sophie is definitely back on form.

Uncle Rudolph looked cheerful and self-satisfied and I wondered if he was having a winning streak for I know, through Nettie of course, that he is an inveterate gambler.

Sir Timothy and Lady Badger fondly greeted me; I am so thankful to have them as friends. He introduced their visitors—Mr Ferris, a London magistrate, and his assistant, Mr Mannering. He is a charming and handsome young man with a warm smile and I liked him immediately. Sir Timothy took my arm to escort me to dinner and he and Mr Mannering sat at either side.

Through the evening Mr Ferris boasted of his assistant's detection skills so we prevailed upon him to regale us with some of his successes. He blushed at the praise but then had us all laughing at his tales. My husband boldly flirted with Sophie and several times I saw her triumphantly gaze in my direction. If only she knew! I wondered if Sophie had ever had to wear a silk bag over her pretty face. It is strange—watching them, I felt absolutely nothing. No jealousy, no envy. I know I am only sixteen but my experiences over the past months have made me feel so much older in my head. We ladies retired to the drawing room while the men enjoyed their port.

"A delicious meal, Lady Firstbridge. Your cook has surpassed herself. And thank you so much for including our guests in your invitation." Lady Badger's compliment made me blush and it still sounded odd to my ears to be addressed by my new title.

"Your visitors more than made up for their inclusion with delightful conversation." I insisted, especially thinking of the pleasant Mr Mannering.

"Mr Ferris joins us at least once a year supposedly to discuss legal matters with Sir Timothy but in actual fact I rather think it's more the pheasant shooting that draws them together." She smiled knowingly. Then Sophie joined the conversation with talk of her son, Charles, who is now almost two months old.

"May your niece and I call to see your beautiful boy, Lady Burncliff? He will be getting to the interesting age soon," asked Lady Badger who I knew to be an expert on babies, having produced a new one every few years.

Sophie's eyes lit up. "Yes, do come tomorrow. Charles is quite adorable. He has my colouring and mama says he is the image of me at the same age."

I'm sure she is thankful he doesn't look like Uncle Rudolf I thought, then mentally chastised myself for being uncharitable. I never imagined Sophie would be the least bit maternal but perhaps I have misjudged her. Motherhood must definitely alter one's perspective, though she will always be a goose-head to my way of thinking.

The gentleman joined us and we were soon discussing things that concern country folk.

"It's been unseasonably cold for this time of the year. I fear we are in for a snowy winter, making the roads to London almost impassable," complained my husband.

Sophie chimed in with a little laugh. "Oh milord, surely you would brave a little snow to get back to the balls and the theatre. I know I shall make Burnie attempt the journey." And she fluttered her eyelashes at her husband. He smiled dotingly back. My uncle doesn't seem to mind his wife's pet name for him. I can't imagine calling my husband 'Bridgie'.

"And the pheasant shooting season looks set to be a disaster too, between poachers and an overabundance of foxes," Sir Timothy gloomily sighed.

Lady Badger smiled. "Don't be such a pessimist, my dear. I'm sure you've put every poacher in the shire behind bars by now, so perhaps it won't be too bad."

"Yes there has been a prodigious number of the rascals. All these soldiers coming home from the war no doubt, and no work for them," replied her husband.

Mr Ferris nodded in agreement. "Yes, highway robberies have increased as well and there are many more beggars in the city. I wonder the government doesn't do something about it," he sighed with a troubled expression.

"The Enclosure Acts have a lot to answer for and I suppose if you are starving and cannot find work, then poaching and thievery are your only recourse," murmured Mr Mannering in a quiet voice that only I heard. He sat near me and I felt his eyes frequently drift in my direction. It gave me a pleasant feeling and soothed my battered ego.

The depressing turn of the conversation prompted me to suggest cards so the tables were set up and soon all thoughts of bad roads, bad weather and bad men were forgotten in the excitement of potentially winning hands and fierce competition. I'm afraid I am an uninspiring partner for in spite of having an excellent memory, I have no love for cards and played only to make up the numbers. However, it generated much mirth and the evening finished on a happy note. When our guests had gone, my husband complimented me on the success of my first dinner party and we then retired—to the same nightly ritual. When my courses came I had some peace but as soon as that ended, he returned.

Two days before Christmas I started to feel very tired and nauseous in the mornings. We had been invited to Mornington for the festive dinner before my uncle and Sophie returned to London and I wondered how I would cope, feeling as I did.

"I am so unwell, Nettie. I must have eaten something off to make me feel this sick and I am exhausted all the time," I complained to my maid, who smiled with delight.

"Oooh milady, I think you are *enceinte!*"

Nettie has taken to filling her conversation with French words she has memorised from the lady's maid instruction book. Her pronunciation is even worse than Sarah's but I don't tell her that as I would not hurt her feelings for the world. In fact I have been contemplating giving her some French lessons myself, she is so eager to learn. I looked at her in surprise, and then comprehension. I am so ignorant about the process of human reproduction that I had never realised my condition until that moment. In spite of the nausea, a warm glow filled me, tinged a little bit with unease. I'm going to have a baby!

My husband stayed out on estate business all day and did not return for dinner either. Later, I paced up and down the drawing room in a fever of anticipation. It felt most unusual but for once I couldn't wait to see him and give him the news. By the time he came to my bedroom later that night, I was almost bursting with it.

"My lord, I believe I'm increasing." I blurted out as he walked towards me, and then blushed with embarrassment. He immediately tucked the black silk hood, which I had come to look upon with fear and loathing, into the pocket of his banyan and instead sat on the bed. For once his face appeared animated, not politely blank, and when he spoke he actually gave me one of his rare smiles.

"Well my dear, I am very pleased with you. You must take good care of yourself. No more riding until the baby is born and let us pray for a son." I received a congratulatory peck on the cheek and he returned to his own room. I watched him walk away with a profound sense of relief.

He did not come to my bedroom the next evening or any thereafter. My nightly misery had come to an end and for that, I felt deeply grateful.

Chapter Sixteen.
In which Nettie worries.

Nettie had been so worried for her little lamb. Something bad had happened, she knew it. Her Miss Emily hadn't confided in her and she didn't like to press but ever since the wedding night, she'd had a haunted look. Nettie couldn't say she liked his lordship. He seemed a cold fish and never showed her mistress any sort of affection, well, not when she saw them together anyway. She knew she should be calling her 'milady' now and she did try, but to her she would always be her little Miss Emily and it occasionally slipped out, not that the mistress seemed to mind.

Even though they were separated in age by only two years, she felt so much older than her ladyship. There was no doubt that Miss Emily had a clever brain, though. She'd seen her reading a book written in an odd language and been told it was Greek! Nettie had enough trouble with the ordinary French and English alphabet, let alone an entirely different one! Now that her mistress was increasing, the haunted look had disappeared and she seemed a lot happier. This put Nettie's mind at rest.

Then there was Bekkit; she didn't like him either. Oh, he had a handsome face for sure, she would give him that, and he cut quite a dash in his lordship's cast-offs, but his eyes were everywhere, always watching. Nettie had seen him looking at Miss Emily when he thought himself unobserved and it made her feel…uncomfortable. Thankfully, he stayed mostly in his lordship's rooms, and even in the servant's dining hall, he kept himself apart. She knew the prettier maids feared him and avoided him as much as possible. Any time he'd caught Nettie's eye she'd glared fiercely back, which seemed to amuse him, and that annoyed her intensely.

******

His lordship and his odious valet had returned to London and the house felt so much cheerier without them. She'd noticed the improvement in her mistress straight away; a new lightness to her step, and now that the nausea had passed, she seemed almost like her old self again. Yesterday they'd gone to Blakesley to purchase yards of fine lawn for the baby's long clothes. Nettie laughed to herself; she felt so full of excitement you would think it was her who was having the baby. At the moment, she and her mistress were sitting in a little back parlour which had been transformed into a book room; the cheerful fire made it feel so cosy, just the two of them sewing together and gossiping. Nettie prayed this new-found happiness would last.

Chapter Seventeen.
Simon.

I can hardly believe the changes in my life. We spent a pleasant few days with Sir Timothy and his comfortable family and then set out for Stamford. Mr Ferris had dozed off on the long coach ride so I was left alone with my thoughts, which kept circling back to that dinner party with Lord and Lady Firstbridge. The first thing I'd noticed had been the great age disparity between them, she barely more than a child and he looking close to fifty! When Lady Firstbridge had offered her hand in greeting I'd been lost in a pair of the most beautiful grey eyes I'd ever seen.

Thinking back, I believe they were more silver than grey with black rings around the irises and framed with long sooty lashes. Though she smiled sweetly, I felt they held a hidden sadness in their depths, or am I just being fanciful? I grin to myself at my poetical imaginings. Lady Burncliff's much touted beauty, I hardly even noticed, thought her very shallow, and watched with disdain as Lord Firstbridge flirted with her shamelessly. I found myself making a real effort to charm my hostess and hear her laugh. What a mis-matched pair they are.

Lady Badger dearly loves a gossip I'd noticed, so when I'd casually enquired about them on our way back to Leafybrook, she was only too eager to confide in me.

"Poor dear; she's an orphan you know and I rather think her family bullied her into marrying Firstbridge; why he chose her, I can't imagine. He could have had his pick of any of the Season's beauties. She's a sweet girl, so young and innocent, and has a small fortune of her own but that would not concern *him*, he is extremely wealthy. And it certainly does not look like a love match, he is so cold and formal with her I've noticed."

"Hush my love." Sir Timothy had gently scolded his wife. "You must not spread tales. If it should get back to his lordship's ears, and he discovered the source, it would be most embarrassing."

"Oh fiddle, Timothy, you know it's the truth!"

But I'd deftly changed the subject and the problems of Lady Firstbridge and her husband were set aside.

Eventually, the jolting of the carriage woke Mr Ferris and I regretfully stopped thinking of those lovely grey eyes as we discussed our plans for Stamford.

"We shall have dinner with your family first Simon, before I spend the two nights with my friend."

I could feel his eagerness to see my mother again and in the dim light of the coach, noted the grin on his face.

Mother, looking flushed and pretty, greeted us at the door, with my sisters hovering behind her. She gave a shy smile to Mr Ferris and a hug to me. I hastened up the stairs to my old room carrying my valise and not waiting for the maid. The girls followed me, giggling and laughing, well aware of the happenings in the parlour.

"Shush, you scatterbrains. This is a very important occasion. You will soon have a step-papa who will put you to work as scullery maids," I teased.

"Oh Simon, you talk such fudge!" scorned Prudence, bouncing on the bed. "This is ever so exciting! Living in London we'll be able to see wondrous things every day! *And*

I am now an accomplished horsewoman! Peter, the groom, says I have a good seat."

I smiled fondly at my baby sister. "Then I shall have to take you riding on Rotten Row where the fashionable fribbles display themselves," I promised, as I unpacked my valise to spare mother's overworked staff. I'd gathered that my old mount was to be sold and a new one purchased in London for her.

"We shall give mother half an hour alone with Mr Ferris and then go down to congratulate them," smiled Rebekah who, I could see, felt no less excitement than my little sister. She blushed prettily when I teased her about seeing Blake again.

Finally we trooped downstairs, chattering noisily, so as not to surprise our parent in the arms of her intended. Mother's tears mingled with smiles of joy and much kissing, hugging and congratulations followed.

"We shall be returning with my children, and a special licence in a fortnight, Simon. I know they will not let me come without them. After the wedding, we'll all travel back to London to celebrate Christmas there." With his arm around mother's shoulders, Mr Ferris gazed fondly down at her. We ate a late dinner then he reluctantly bade us farewell and went to sleep at his friend's.

The two days passed quickly. Mr Berryman, also a magistrate, proved a genial host and sympathetic towards his distracted house guest, who would drift into a daze with a blissful smile in the middle of a serious legal discussion. I joined them for these meetings and immediately informed Mr Berryman of the cause.

"Please excuse my employer's moments of distraction, sir. I suspect their cause can be blamed on a lady's lovely smile; far more interesting than the squire's missing silver."

Mr Berryman chuckled. "Yes, a lovely smile, does tend to overshadow everything else," he agreed.

Mr Ferris took our poor humour at his expense, with a happy grin.

We returned to London on the last day of November. Then followed much activity as Rachel harried the maids into cleaning the house from top to bottom, a magnificent tree arrived and delicate Christmas tree decorations were carefully unpacked. All soon appeared ready to welcome the new bride who, in far away Stamford, would be busy covering furniture with dust covers, packing, and writing references for staff looking for new positions.

Only the housekeeper would remain as caretaker. The decision whether to let the house or sell would be left until the new year. Rebekah and Prudence would be saying tearful farewells to their friends and quite a few young men would no doubt be devastated to hear that my lovely oldest sister was soon to leave the neighbourhood.

A fortnight later, the whole Ferris family and I were back in Stamford. Fortunately the weather had been reasonable and the journey suffered no delays. We would be staying in an hotel for the one night we were there. The next morning dawned cold and sunny. Mother, looking beautiful in a red wool redingote with a matching cherry-decorated bonnet, became Mrs Ferris in a quaint medieval church. A few friends, including Mr and Mrs Berryman, attended and afterwards we returned to their house for the joyful wedding breakfast, Mrs Berryman having kindly offered to host it as our house was now packed up. I looked at my mother's radiant face and our combined families and thought how her desperate letter all those month's ago had brought so much happiness into our lives.

The guests were finally farewelled and the Berryman's presented with a beautiful vase and a case of fine French wine in gratitude for hosting the feast. At last we were on our way, we children squeezed into the hired coach, already laden with our luggage, which would follow our parents' one to London.

"It's only fair that we give the newlyweds some privacy, Simon. We are all young enough to put up with a little inconvenience after all," Rachel said with a smile. I agreed but wondered if she would still feel that way by the time we reached the city. I felt sure she had never travelled in anything other than her father's comfortable carriage.

In spite of the crowding, an abundance of good humour made the hours pass quite quickly. In fact I noticed Blake seemed perfectly happy squashed next to my oldest sister. We stopped for the horse changes at a good inn and enjoyed supper with our parents who looked flushed and a little disheveled, much to Rachel's and my amusement. It would be well after dark before we arrived in town but a full moon gave us plenty of light and the good weather would not hold forever so we needed to take advantage of it. The fact that there were two carriages would also made it unlikely we would be waylaid by highwaymen.

Mrs Foot had waited up for us with hot drinks and warmed rooms when we finally came to the end of our weary, cold journey, and not long after we were all tucked up in our beds. I thought of my mother and her new husband and went to sleep with a smile on my face.

I am now back at my desk in my employers chambers thinking over the events of the past few weeks and filled with a sense of satisfaction. Yes, my sisters' futures are now secure and I can focus on my own plans. Life has definitely changed for the better.

Chapter Eighteen.
Emily.

I must say that being *enceinte,* as Nettie says, has been interesting from the biological point of view. I am making notes on my changing body and wish I had an inverted eye that could peep inside and see the alterations there. The Christmas feast at Mornington brought no pleasure as the smell of all those elaborate dishes quite turned my stomach. Lady Badger was also a guest so when I confided my nausea to her while the men drank their after dinner port, she pressed my hand.

"How very pleased I am for you Emily." She and I are now on first name terms, we have become such good friends. "The nausea is perfectly normal, my dear, and will soon pass. Do you find you are fancying the oddest things to eat or drink? With my last one I craved sparkling ale and would drink it by the pint until Sir Timothy swore I would burst!" She chuckled at the memory.

"Oh, mine is peppermint candies; I am continually sending Nettie to the kitchen. And normally I don't like peppermint," I replied. Hearing that the morning nausea would soon be over filled me with relief.

As my husband is frequently away and I know I will not be disturbed, I spend hours reading in the library, huddled before a cozy fire, or else mixing tinctures and salves in the stillroom. Once my nausea ended I felt...

wonderful. I think this is partly due to no longer having to endure my lord's nightly attentions, but also the sense of wellbeing that had so long deserted me, has returned. And Nettie is relieved to see me so happy. I have been helping her with her French and she is an eager learner, becoming more proficient by the day. My young friend, Raoul, writes to me frequently and I set Nettie the task of translating his letters.

If the weather is still and the ground not too icy, we tramp the countryside together, well-wrapped up against the cold, our breath hanging in ephemeral clouds in front of us. I must admit Nettie is more my friend and companion than my maid.

One thing I have decided—I will *not* have a man-midwife. Finding my courage, I spoke to my husband one morning at breakfast when he had returned on one of his infrequent visits.

"My lord," I simply cannot bring myself to call him Miles and he has not commented on the fact, "I wish to bring Mrs Crombie here for my lying in. She was an excellent midwife before she became papa's housekeeper and is a firm believer in the teachings of Dr Alexander Gordon. Papa and I read and discussed his book, *The Practice of Physick* so I know I shall be in safe hands." I had rehearsed this little speech and held my breath waiting for a reply.

He looked up from his newspaper with a slightly irritated expression. "Do as you see fit my dear," he said and returned to his reading.

Pleased with my small victory, I hid a smile of success. It crossed my mind to wonder why he called me 'my dear' when he showed so little warmth towards me. However I did not dwell on it for long; I try to think of my husband as little as possible.

******

109

Spring is here and a year has passed since my life was turned upside down with my father's death. The baby is due in late summer and I am sad papa is not here to see his grandchild but I like to imagine him watching over us both. I do miss my riding but have obeyed my husband as he is so obliging over Mrs Crombie. Bluebell and Firebrand have to rely on grooms to stop them getting fat from lack of exercise but I visit them daily with small treats. It sounds odd to say it, thinking about my loveless marriage, but I am content. I put my hand on my stomach and talk to the baby; I feel we already know each other. My other scientific interests have been put aside and I am wholly absorbed in this miracle of nature.

The flutter of the baby's first kick is magical. My husband always refers to it as 'he' when he talks to me at all but I don't mind in the least if it is a girl. Then I remember the earldom needs an heir and I pale and my heart seizes in panic at the thought of the black hood returning. Perhaps, I think hopefully, he will not be so concerned with my sensibilities in the future.

Occasionally Sophie comes visiting. She has just returned from London and I always hope she will bring Charles, who is growing apace, but she never does. "A child's place is in the nursery," she grandly tells me, when I ask.

"I am attending so many balls and routs I've had to acquire a whole new wardrobe. Burnie complains at the cost, but one can not appear in the same old gowns. Madame Cloissone has all the latest colours from Paris and my new dresses are exquisite."

I imagine there must be a great number of French modistes in the city.

I don't believe Sophie actually sees much of her son. Her first pleasure at motherhood seems to have faded and he hardly enters her conversation. When I return the calls, I always ask to see him. After all, these visits give me an idea of what my future holds. Charles is adorable and I wonder how Sophie can bear to part from him, for I know he doesn't travel to London with her.

Because I am increasing, his lordship has never again referred to my attending lectures at the Royal Society, but I am not too disappointed owing to my new-found contentment and preferring the country life anyway. He spends weeks away, to attend to business or parliament he says, however I suspect it is to enjoy the company of his friends and the busy social life of the *ton*. In scandalous whispers, Nettie has repeated to me servant hall gossip about the doings of their betters.

"I've heard, milady, that old Lord Pike has a mistress tucked away in the city and him almost seventy! I wonder how Lady Pike tolerates it with everybody knowing. She must be so embarrassed! Mind you, being thirty years younger than him and having a lover herself, I don't suppose she really cares what he gets up to."

"Shhh, Nettie," I scold, but I smile inwardly. I'm certain there is at least a thirty-year age difference between my husband and myself. Has he a ladybird discreetly hidden away in some pretty little house in town? Strangely, the idea does not bother me. No doubt *she* does not need to wear a black silk hood! I am becoming worldly-wise now I'm a married woman.

Chapter Nineteen.
Emily.

"Lord Firstbridge has released all the servants for the night, except Bekkit, Miss Emily," Nettie tells me one evening. "Even the Peebles have been sent off to visit relatives."

We sit, sewing companionably in my book room before retiring, the early evening light with the addition of lamps, still bright enough to work by. I had requested a dinner tray be prepared for the two of us before the staff departed. My husband and his valet have also left and now the house feels uncommonly quiet. They had arrived back at Amberleigh two days earlier—I cannot pretend any pleasure at his lordship's return—and the relaxed atmosphere of the household has quickly changed to one of wariness.

"Yes, his lordship informed me at breakfast this morning that he had invited a few friends for a card evening and they will all be dining at the inn, where the gentlemen are staying, before coming back here, so my services as hostess will not be required," I replied gratefully, feeling decidedly unsociable in my present condition. I had not met any of the guests and was relieved to have no part in entertaining them. But why he had dismissed all the staff I could not fathom.

Nettie put down her sewing and sipped at her glass of lemonade. "Apparently, these card evenings have been a regular occurrence in the past, milady." She hesitated before continuing. "I've heard rumours that it's not just cards they play at either." Her usually expressive face was carefully blank and I wondered what she was trying to tell me.

"I suppose he misses his clubs and the excitement of the city and only returns to Amberleigh when he absolutely has to, so it is understandable that he requires some livelier entertainment when he is here." I don't know why I was making excuses to my maid on his behalf; I have such a distaste for him and to be perfectly honest, he rather frightens me. However, Nettie, who in spite of our different stations in life has become a friend, would not let the matter rest.

"After these 'card parties', the maids say they have trouble removing stains from the carpet and furniture. *And* the room always smells...horrible, not just cigar smoke and alcohol." Nettie spoke with the emphasis on 'card parties'.

Did she mean they were taking...opium? A shiver slid down my spine. Perhaps it was the unnatural quiet of the house, but I felt a strong sense of unease.

"Nettie dear, would you please take the tray back to the kitchen. I'm going upstairs now. I don't want to be caught down here when the guests arrive." We packed up our sewing, Nettie disappeared through the baize door to the servants' quarters and I walked slowly up the dimly lit stairs, the occasional creak of a tread accompanying me. The silence pressed down like a great weight and I welcomed the comforting familiarity of my bedroom. I had already started undressing when Nettie returned to help me get ready for bed.

"I have a new French novel arrived from Hatchard's today, Nettie. It will be good practice for you to read it to me." My words were muffled as she helped pull the shift over my head.

"Merci beaucoup, comtesse," she answered, with a pleased grin, and shook out my night rail.

113

These days I tire easily, so it felt wonderful to lie down at last with my eyes closed and listen to Nettie's hesitant French, as she sat reading aloud beside me in the soft lamplight.

******

I awoke to darkness, except for a sliver of moonlight striping the floor. My bed curtains had been tied back because of the stifling heat and those at the window, ballooned gently. A soft breeze, with the faint scent of roses, whispered across my face. I was alone—Nettie must have long retired—and wondered what had disturbed me. I left my bed, crossed to the window, and parted the curtains. The lake looked indescribably beautiful, a glowing pewter sheet in a landscape of dark and light contrasts. The air was displaced as something large flew past my window, with a noisy flapping of wings, to land on the black silhouette of a nearby tree. The branch rocked violently with the added weight of a great barn owl, then slowly stilled. I watched as its head swivelled towards me and we contemplated each other. It took flight again, no doubt on the hunt, but I stayed, staring into the night—all remained calm.

With a sigh I closed the curtains and returned to my bed, but I could not sleep and lay on my back…listening. Suddenly a burst of male laughter shattered the silence, followed by the human-like scream of a vixen. The scream came again and was choked off. Had it been the cry of a fox —or a child? Then my now-alert brain remembered we were in the middle of summer and foxes mated in January or February. A child then, but what was a child doing at Amberleigh in the middle of the night? A deeper shadow moved and my heart stuttered.

"Are you awake Miss Emily? It's only me." Nettie spoke softly as she slipped through the dressing room door and crossed the band of moonlight. I stretched out my arm and felt her trembling grasp.

"You heard it too?" I whispered. "Here, climb into bed with me."

Nettie, ever resourceful, first jammed chairs under the doorknobs, then slipped under the light covers. We lay, side by side, trying to breathe quietly so as not to miss a sound, well-aware that we were two defenceless women alone in a house with a cold and disinterested husband, his valet, and any number of men I had never met. But all was peaceful again. Eventually, when nothing further served to frighten us, tiredness overcame our fears, and we slept.

The moon had set when I was woken once again by noises in the hallway. My maid slept on but I heard the murmur of voices, footsteps passing by and my husband's bedroom door opening and closing.

******

At seven thirty, Nettie hastily washed and dressed and went to fetch my morning chocolate.

"The servants are slowly straggling in, milady. I looked into his lordship's study—it's a right mess and smells awful." She wrinkled her nose with distaste as she handed me a tray with a plate of bread and butter and steam rising from a hot drink.

I sat in bed enjoying the delicious flavour of the chocolate, thinking about the mysterious happenings of the previous night. Nettie had by now disappeared again to organise hot water for me to wash, as the house slowly came back to life. Had I mistaken that cry? Could it have been a woman's? I frowned at the thought, for I knew what sort she would be, and made a sound of disgust. Surely my husband would not sink so low? Nettie did not allude to the card party again but I wondered if she knew more than she was telling me; however, I decided I didn't really want to know and put it out of my mind.

My husband did not join me for breakfast. When I enquired, one of the footmen told me he had gone to meet with his friends at the inn. A morbid curiosity drove me to peek into his lordship's study but the maids had already been at work and all I could detect was a faint odour of kerosene overlaid with beeswax. His lordship spent the day away so it was not until the evening that I saw him again. As usual, he appeared immaculately dressed when we met in the drawing room.

"Did you have a pleasant evening with your friends my lord?" I asked as he escorted me into dinner.

I hoped my voice didn't sound shaky; I seldom address him directly. He did not reply immediately, but seated me, then took his place at the head of the table. His dark eyes flickered to the footmen who sprang forward to serve us. I thought I saw a glint of something like amusement as his face turned back to mine—it was hard to tell with the distance between us.

"Yes, a very satisfying time, my dear. I hope we didn't disturb your sleep with our noise." And he stared at me intently.

"No, I slept well," I lied, and dropped my eyes to my plate. I am such a coward!

Chapter Twenty.
In which Bekkit is...Bekkit.

The valet rowed the small dinghy out into the middle of the lake. The moon had almost set but he didn't need much light for what he was about to do. Shipping the oars, he lifted a long, sack-wrapped bundle and carefully lowered it into the water. He watched as it sank quickly, the stones giving it weight. The lake was deep here and would forever hide its secrets. He sat for a moment gazing at the ripples fracturing the reflected starlight and breathed in the cool night air to clear his head. Then, with a shrug, he rowed back to the jetty.

No one saw him.

Chapter Twenty-one.
Emily.

Some weeks have passed since the night of the card party and I have convinced myself that I'd made something out of nothing. My husband returned to London with his friends and life has settled back into a quiet routine. The weather is pleasantly warm and I am so big I'm reduced to waddling. Nettie and I go on collecting walks, my interest in botany having returned. Of course it is Nettie who does the gathering as I am physically unable—I simply point, and she produces her little trowel and adds to her basket whatever has caught my attention. There are always herbs needing to be dried for my medicinal recipes, and even though there is an excellent kitchen garden at the hall, some plants I require only grow in the wild.

We frequently meet Sir Timothy and his family on these expeditions and are persuaded to return to Leafybrook for luncheon. They are such a contented family and it is so pleasant being with them, I never refuse, and afterwards they always send us home in their carriage. The contrast between their household of happy noise and laughter and my own is glaringly obvious to Nettie and me. Then I remember that soon I will have a tiny love in my life and immediately it cheers me.

******

Mrs Crombie has arrived; Nettie and I hug her with delight. We sit in my cosy book room as she recounts stories from home.

"You will be pleased to hear Mabel has found love with the village blacksmith. He's a widower with four children, so an extra one won't matter, and as for Coates, your papa left him a very nice sum so he's run off to America with one of the doctor's daughters. I doubt she'll be chased too hard by her papa, he having five others still to be married off," she said with a wry smile.

I listened avidly and remembered my priggish attitude towards Sarah and Lucy's gossip—how judgemental and superior my younger self had been. I have grown up a lot in a very short time.

"Now lie down on the sofa, my dear, so I can examine you. Just to make sure everything is where it should be."

I am poked and prodded.

"Yes, all is well, milady, and it wont be long now." She gave me a reassuring smile as I struggled back into a sitting position.

"I'll not be needing the services of a wet nurse Mrs Crombie. I intend feeding this baby myself," I tell her firmly. She smiled and patted my hand.

"Of course, my dear. I've always thought it better for the babe to be nurtured by its own mother. He or she is from your body and part of you after all." She's a very wise woman, Sweetwater's housekeeper.

******

I can't wait for it to be over. My husband has come home to be at Amberleigh for the birth. I wish he would stay away; I am much happier when I don't have to see him daily.

However, as the whole point of marrying me had been to get an heir, no doubt his presence is to be expected.

I am so glad Mrs Crombie attended me, and my dear Nettie, who afterwards complained teasingly that she thought her hand would be detached from her arm, so tightly did I hold it. I shall not go into the details, for any woman who has birthed a child will understand. I had been warned about my waters breaking and feared what lay ahead, but Mrs Crombie calmed me and after hours of living in a sea of pain —which seemed endless—when she told me to push, I found the last of my strength and *pushed.* All the agony and suffering seemed worth it in that first moment when I held my beautiful son—and he *was* beautiful. Not wrinkled and red as with little Charles, but perfect. I lay exhausted as Nettie bathed and swaddled him.

"I helped when ma birthed my two younger brothers, so I know all about little boys, milady. He's got all his fingers and toes, *and* the other important bits," she said with a grin as she placed him in my arms.

His dark eyes seemed to look intently back at me and I felt such boundless love, I thought I would surely burst from it. Gazing, enchanted, at his little face as he suckled noisily, I barely noticed as Mrs Crombie gently pressed my stomach which she explained was to remove the afterbirth. The bloody signs of my ordeal were quickly cleaned away, then Mrs Crombie asked to take my son from me and I felt bereft.

"Just for a moment, my love, so his father may see his heir, then I shall return him to you for he'll be hungry after his battle to be born."

My husband walked in and took his son from Mrs Crombie's arms. Such an odd look passed across his face, one of satisfaction but certainly not love, and I wondered at it.

"He is a handsome child, Emily. You have done well."

While he was in a good mood I asked the question that had been concerning me. "May we call him James, my lord, after my father?"

He hesitated, then smiled at me. "Of course my dear. As you wish. I seem to recall a James amongst my own antecedents, also." He passed our son back to Mrs Crombie, came to the bedside and gave my cheek a dry kiss, then without another word, left the room.

Not an overly enthusiastic reaction, I thought, but I had become accustomed to my husband's disinterested manner towards me. However, it surprised me that it also extended towards our beautiful baby. No matter; I did not let it dampen my feelings of delight at our little miracle and thought no more of it.

Lavishly rewarded for the precious gift she has given me, Mrs Crombie, has returned to her proper job as the housekeeper at my old home, leaving Nettie, me and baby James in our own little world of happiness.

Chapter Twenty-two.
Simon.

Stretching out my legs to toast in front of the fire, I sat back contentedly. I have now moved into very respectable, well appointed rooms. My landlady, Mrs Brendon, a genteel woman of straightened circumstances, had turned her home into a boarding house for gentlemen. Not far from my stepfather's chambers, it serves admirably for a young fellow of reasonable substance. My detection work has been growing by the day but I still manage to fit it around my position as Mr Ferris's assistant.

I am not the only one who moved out of the Ferris household when the new members moved in. Rachel Ferris that was, is now married to her long-time suitor and is happily setting up her own household. In fact I have heard a whisper from my sisters that she might already be increasing. Autumn is drawing to a close and my warm and comfortable rooms already feel…homey.

I thought about the upcoming visit to Leafybrook. This time my mother, the new Mrs Ferris, would be accompanying us. They have hired a governess for the girls so she will be in charge of the household while the parents are away. It has been almost a year since the last trip to Northamptonshire and though a healthy correspondence passes between Mr Ferris and Sir Timothy, I know they find nothing quite as satisfying as being in each other's actual company, arguing companionably over glasses of port and with a little pheasant shooting on the side. This turned my thoughts to a pair of lovely grey eyes and I smiled to myself. Surely I would see her again, and wondered if she had found happiness in her spring and autumn marriage. Well, time to pack my valise as we intended making an early start.

******

The carriage pulled up at my address sharp at seven in the morning. I had asked to be informed of its arrival, as my rooms are at the back of the building. Instead of sending a maid, Mrs Brendon scratched at the door herself and called. "Mr Mannering, your carriage has arrived."

I opened it almost before she had finished speaking, a grin on my face. "Thank you ma'am. Much obliged. Take care and I shall see you again in a few days."

Valise in hand. I bounded down the stairs, through the open front door and into the carriage. Mrs Brendon had followed and watched me go with a wistful smile and a wave. She has been hinting at bringing her daughter home from her expensive ladies' finishing school and introducing her to her newest lodger. I've been informed by the others that she is very pretty, but somehow when I think of girls, I remember Lady Firstbridge.

Mr Ferris greeted me with a cheerful smile and my mother, a fond hug. The carriage lurched into motion and soon the tightly packed city houses and shops were left far behind. We travelled through the shires at a leisurely pace, the horses not being pushed too hard. At the half-way, we stopped for the change. Mr Ferris had booked ahead for a private parlour and we enjoyed a leisurely meal at the busy inn, so it was very near supper time when we finally arrived at Leafybrook Park. We all found it a relief to alight after many hours confined and were ushered into the drawing room by Rankin, their butler. Sir Timothy and Lady Badger, William, the heir, and the two oldest Badger girls, Suzanne and Jane, rose to greet us.

"I say Arthur, so nice to see you and young Simon again. Now, you must introduce us to your lovely wife." The introductions were made and Sir Timothy continued. "Dinner will be served shortly but you will have time to freshen up. We held it back, though the younger children have dined already so will have to wait until tomorrow to greet you."

Lady Badger, herself, took us to our rooms. and put my mother at ease immediately. I enjoy the Badgers' company and hoped that mother would like them too.

Following the late dinner, our hostess insisted we immediately join the ladies in the drawing room rather than leaving us to our port, but everyone soon retired as the long coach ride had been exhausting. A pheasant shoot had been arranged for the next morning, so after breakfast, while we men were out with our guns, Lady Badger introduced mother to her large brood and no doubt they enjoyed a cosy chat about the latest *on-dit* from London. It heartened me to see how pleased the two ladies were in each other's company, and the morning passed quickly.

After luncheon an expedition to Blakesley was arranged for the women while we went riding. Mr Ferris and I had been loaned two fine hacks from Sir Timothy's stables and we duly set out on the trails through the woods that bordered Lord Firstbridge's and our host's properties. We had not gone far when we saw a young woman approaching, riding a handsome, highly strung black stallion and with a groom on a fat little grey mare trailing behind her. She wore a smart dark green riding habit and saucily perched on her brown curls was a matching and rather dashing little beaver hat, decorated with three pheasant feathers. My heart gave a leap of recognition. As they drew alongside, Sir Timothy smiled in greeting.

"Aah, Lady Firstbridge! How nice to see you out riding again. I have missed you over the summer months." And he bowed from the saddle. "You may remember Mr Ferris and Mr Mannering from last November when you kindly invited us to dine."

We bowed in turn as she nodded and smiled.

"Yes, of course I do. How pleasant to see you again. My husband is in London, but you would be most welcome to call."

She glanced at me and I felt the draw of those compelling eyes. Something about her had changed, I noticed—a new maturity to that gaze. Again I felt the stir of interest that had lingered with me for so long after my previous visit.

"My dear wife would no doubt wish to see the new heir again. She tells me he is a beautiful boy."

Her ladyship blushed with pleasure We fixed the time for late morning the next day and as her mount appeared rather restless, after a few more casual remarks, we said farewell and moved on. *She is a mother now,* I thought and felt vague regret though why, I could not fathom. I shook myself out of my reverie and joined in the laughing chatter before all three of us cantered back to Leafybrook.

The following day saw mama, Lady Badger and the two oldest Badger girls seated in the carriage and, with the men mounted on horseback, our cavalcade set off for Amberleigh. Mother admired the grounds as we approached the hall and expressed her delight when admitted to the drawing room.

"Lady Firstbridge, this is one of the most beautiful rooms I have ever seen!" she exclaimed as her ladyship drew her to the French doors to admire the lake. I could see this pleased our hostess who blushed at the praise.

"Not my design I'm afraid," she said modestly. "The first Lady Firstbridge, my predecessor, is the one most deserving of your compliments."

James then arrived with his nurse, and the ladies fussed over him. I found my eyes continually returning to our hostess. She seemed happier than I remembered and motherhood had given her an added glow. The desire to keep her in conversation and make those wonderful eyes smile engulfed me. For the first time in my life I felt an overpowering sense of protection and found myself at a loss to explain it. My mother, who is an astute woman, had noticed my attention to our hostess and I could see the worried question in her eyes. Being attracted to a married woman could only lead to disappointment, I could almost hear her saying. But what could I tell her? I didn't even understand it myself.

We spent a week at Leafybrook. Lady Firstbridge joined us for dinner one evening and I met her several times when out riding. Those lovely eyes stayed with me long after I had returned to London.

Chapter Twenty-three.
Emily.

After the months of no riding it felt marvellous to be back on Firebrand again, however, I must admit, he is *not* enjoying the side saddle at all. My nether regions also suffered due to the long break, and it was a blessed relief when Nettie applied a soothing balm—my own concoction—for the first few days. Thankfully, the pain soon faded. That first ride was doubly pleasurable when I met up with Sir Timothy and his guests. I invited them to call the next day and then persuaded them to stay for luncheon.

I *do* like that Mr Mannering, and his mother is a charming woman. He sat beside me while we ate and he talked so easily I felt I had known him forever. I saw admiration in his eyes and blush thinking about it. Am I so starved for affection? Is it wrong to enjoy compliments from a man other than one's husband? It is not flirtation, so deftly practised by Sophie and the *ton*—*that* has a hard, sly edge to it, filled with double entendres—but something much warmer and more personal. He will return to London and forget me no doubt, so I shan't feel guilty that for a short while I have felt what it is like to bask in the warmth of someone's regard. I shall treasure these last few days, and when I am low, remember again the feelings they gave me.

******

127

My lord has returned from town and is in a strange mood. At dinner last night, for no reason that I could see, he suddenly started shouting and swearing at me. He stood, knocking over his chair and as I cowered in shock in my seat, Bekkit instantly appeared, calmly held him in a vice-like grip and murmured in his ear. The footmen looked on in astonishment. At a command from the valet, one came forward and righted the chair; his lordship then sat down and proceeded to eat his dinner as if nothing unusual had happened. Bekkit glanced my way but made no comment. However he stayed watchfully in the shadows against the wall until I withdrew to the drawing room.

My husband did not join me there, for which I gave thanks, and the next morning at breakfast he continued to be his usual silent self, however something had changed. From that moment forward, whenever my husband appeared, invariably his valet would not be far away. I don't trust Bekkit. There is something odd in his manner and when he looks at me I feel most uncomfortable. Once I found him in the nursery leaning over James' crib, the nurse watching nervously. When questioned he made some weak excuse and bowed himself out. After that I stationed a footman at the door with instructions to deny Bekkit entry, for I feared for my baby. Strange isn't it that I no longer think of James as *our* son.

******

Lord Firstbridge is not well. I have been told by Bekkit that it is a heavy cold and the doctor has been called. I find Dr Caukwell an enigma. He is an associate of my husband's and frequently accompanies him to London, neglecting his other patients I fear. I gather my husband pays him a retainer and I have been instructed to occasionally include him in my dinner invitations, however I find him both pompous *and* obsequious—an unsettling combination. He often refers to his noble connections and his Edinburgh degree, but I have subtly asked him questions of a medical nature which he has been unable to answer to my satisfaction. I suspect he is a charlatan, but a clever one. I requested a footman to send Dr Caukwell to me in the drawing room after he'd seen my husband. Eventually he appeared and I rose to greet him. He bowed over my hand and held it a little too long.

"Milady, a pleasure to see you again," he murmured as if this were a social occasion.

"How is Lord Firstbridge, doctor?" I asked rather brusquely.

"I have bled him milady and given him a purge of my own devising. There is much improvement," he replied in his ponderous tones. The man is a fool! But it is no use questioning him further or I shall be subjected to a lot of nonsense disguised in medical-sounding jargon. After he'd gone I mixed up one of my soothing elixirs and sent a footman with it to milord's rooms.

A few mornings later, my husband must have recovered from his cold because he appeared at breakfast, dressed for riding, his crop in his hand and Bekkit with him. I presumed he had been out for an early morning gallop. He gave me my usual peck on the cheek and sat down to his papers and breakfast. I eyed him from under my lashes. He looked no different, and I at last began to relax and took a mouthful of toast when he surged to his feet, his face red with rage and, before Bekkit could stop him, rushed at me with the crop raised.

"You filthy whore!" he roared and I froze in horror as the whip came down across my shoulder raising a painful welt. I cried out and stumbled from my seat, my back throbbing with agony.

Then Bekkit crushed my husband to him until slowly his struggles ceased and he went limp. Gradually he returned to his senses and seemed rather confused and unaware of what had passed. The footmen looked at each other and one tentatively approached me.

"Are you alright milady? Should I call your maid?" he asked softly.

"Thank you, please," I whispered. "I shall be in my book room." And I fled.

By the time Nettie bustled in with warm water and a cloth I had gained a little composure. She gently bathed my injury and applied a soothing cream to the welt, all the while condemning milord to the bowels of hell.

"He must be mad milady. I heard about the first time he used cruel language towards you. We shall just have to make sure you keep well out of his way. And to call you that foul name when you are a little angel!" Her hands were still gentle though her face scowled with rage. Obviously the footmen had told her what had passed and I flushed with shame.

"Hush Nettie. You must not talk of the master like that."

But I knew something had changed; I was no longer ignored by my husband. He seemed to actively hate me and I could not fathom why. The problem would be when we had guests, I realised. Would these strange moods come upon him then? If he suddenly flared up in front of them I should die of embarrassment. How could I avoid him? Exhausted with worry and pain, Nettie marched me off to bed, telling me I should rest for an hour. She brought me a hot chocolate and tucked me in.

"I don't know what I would do without you Nettie," I whispered, and then looked towards my husband's bedroom and wondered if I should sleep at all, though he had not come through that door since I'd told him I was increasing, all those months ago.

Of course Nettie had anticipated my thoughts. She'd jammed chairs under the doorknobs and prepared herself a pallet so as to sleep at the foot of my bed that night. By law, my husband could beat me as much as he wished, but my dear Nettie would have something to say about *that,* she firmly informed me. She has a heart as brave as a lion.

Chapter Twenty-four.
In which Bekkit watches and plans.

Bekkit had observed the beginnings of his father's illness while they were in town. It had come on quite suddenly. He had been dressing his lordship, who appeared to be his usual taciturn self, for a gaming evening with his friends at Boodle's, though the valet had noticed a recent, rather unhealthy pallor and a difficulty in articulating the few words used to address him. The friends arrived and after they'd departed, Bekkit took a restorative glass of his lord's best brandy before settling to his evening chores.

He did not expect them back until almost dawn, so it surprised him when his father returned a few hours later, laughing and shouting and in high good humour as if he were deeply in his cups. His friend, Viscount Pellman, who accompanied him, looked a little worried, as well he should, for Lord Firstbridge *never* showed high spirits such as these, and had a reputation for holding his liquor.

For the next few days, the earl behaved normally; wining and dining at his various clubs, attending the theatre and a boxing match out of town, though Bekkit noted it had been sometime since his lordship had demanded his bodyguard services. He began to think he had imagined the odd behaviour when another attack occurred.

His lordship had invited Viscount Pellman for dinner before they attended a masquerade at the Vauxhall Gardens.

Bekkit had not been present and only heard of it when a servant came to fetch him. Apparently, as the meal was being served, Lord Firstbridge suddenly swept the dishes onto the floor and in a furious voice accused the footman of trying to poison him. Somehow his guest calmed him and sent for the valet. In the meantime, as the startled servants cleaned up the mess, his lordship carried on eating and talking as if nothing had happened. Upon Bekkit's arrival, the worried viscount signalled him over.

"I say my good man, Firstbridge is behaving a little oddly this evening. Perhaps it's better we don't attend the masquerade after all. Might overexcite him. Wouldn't want to make a scene, you know," he whispered anxiously, eyeing his friend with concern.

The fact that his lordship seemed to have forgotten his evening plans entirely, made everything easier. The valet stayed discreetly by the wall as the meal concluded and Viscount Pellman joined his host in a glass of port before making his farewells. His lordship returned to his room and Bekkit prepared him for bed in spite of the early hour. Nothing was mentioned of the Vauxhall Gardens visit.

******

He observed his father's personality changes with fascinated interest—unreasoning fury switching in an instant to placid acceptance—and experimented with carefully worded suggestions. It had not been difficult to persuade him to sign bank withdrawals, these requests greeted with almost childlike acceptance and forgotten in the next instant. Bekkit was far from being a fool; he knew he had to be careful and not raise Netherby's suspicions, but this new development held much promise.

From then on he accompanied his master everywhere, no longer just on his lordship's forays into the darker side of London society. No introductions were made and eventually Lord Firstbridge's friends accepted the valet's presence as one of his father's idiosyncrasies and largely ignored him.

To Bekkit, accompanying his parent to clubs and routs, gave him a false sense of belonging. Occasionally, he was even addressed as if he were a normal guest and this served to feed his fondest illusions. Gradually, over the months, his father's altered moods became more frequent. The situation was now becoming so unpredictable, it appeared increasingly obvious to his valet that it was no longer safe for his lordship to move in society without his delusions becoming common knowledge.

Things finally came to a head. When Bekkit felt trapped and needed an escape, he dosed his master with laudanum, locked him in his room, then donning his lordship's clothes, would visit the more notorious gaming hells, further living out his wistful fantasies. He sensibly frequented those that his father did not. There, he called himself Sir John Wolffe and if his likeness to his lordship occasioned a query, he planned to claim a distant relationship. Nobody ever had. He spent lavishly, occasionally winning, but more often losing, large sums of his lordship's money at the gaming tables and became known as a handsome tipper, thus, always welcome. Then one night he heard a rumour about his lord's unusual behaviour—only a snippet—but it put him on his guard.

He sat at the faro table, enjoying a rare winning streak, standing beside him, a beautiful woman in an extremely low-cut gown which displayed her assets to their best advantage. There came a pause in the play while the banker shuffled the cards. Opposite, sat a raddled, absurdly dressed old dandy, his eyes glued to the expanse of white flesh leaning so fetchingly over Bekkit's shoulder. Next to the dandy lounged a much younger version, but clearly on

134

the same path. The young one raised a scented handkerchief to his nose and tittered maliciously.

"Hearing odd things about Firstbridge, don't y'know. Dicked in the nob they say."

Then the play began again and Bekkit heard no more. So disturbed was he by this chance remark he did not stay to avail himself of the obvious invitation from the woman at his side, but collected his winnings and excused himself from the game.

He returned to Firstbridge House, deep in thought. He liked things the way they were but the overheard comment gave him a warning he could not ignore. His manipulation of his father depended on discretion, so, soon after that, he made the decision to return to Amberleigh, and his lordship docilely agreed. Bekkit had hoped that the country air and quieter life would slow down his lordship's illness, and make it easier to hide from the world. Unfortunately, Amberleigh made it worse.

"They're all thieves! I won't have it. Where's my pistols? I must have them with me at all times. Well, don't just stand there! Oh, you're one of them as well, no doubt! Filthy Bastards!" And so Lord Firstbridge raged and thrashed wildly in his valet's firm grip until the fit passed.

Bekkit was continually having to secretly unload the weapons—a madman with a loaded gun endangered him as well.

Lady Firstbridge also appeared to be a trigger for the violent episodes he soon discovered, as the bouts continued, increasing in frequency.

"There's the bitch! I'll make her pay for what she's done. A bullet's too good for her!" And more of the same when he happened to come across Emily in a hallway, the valet's strong arms being all that stopped him from attacking her.

The only times Bekkit could safely rest were when his father was drugged. It had become a strange household; he had never been *just* the valet. Now, as well as his father's bodyguard, he also acted as his keeper. He smiled to himself at the change in his circumstances and enjoyed the power it gave him over the man who had never acknowledged him.

He'd visited the baby once, out of curiosity, and looked down at the son who would inherit everything, all that should have been his in a fairer world. Her ladyship had suddenly appeared and questioned him.

"What are you doing here Bekkit? she'd asked sharply.

He'd turned to face her with a smirk. "Oh just passing your ladyship and thought I heard the babe cry." He'd almost said 'my brother' just to see the look on her face.

They both knew that he had no business in that part of the house. He walked away and heard later that a footman now guarded the nursery. No matter, he would make his own plans for a comfortable future. *He who laughs last, laughs longest.* Bekkit liked that proverb.

Chapter Twenty-five.
Emily.

An atmosphere of fear pervades Amberleigh. It is almost physical in nature and reflects the dismal weather outside. Mrs Peebles has been to see me. Nettie had gone to the village to do some personal shopping and I sat alone in the book room, gazing at the fire and feeling very low, when the housekeeper knocked at the door and I bade her enter. She bobbed a curtsy and stood in front of me with her hands clenched in front of her skirts and a grim look on her face.

"I'm sorry to bother you milady. I know you have much to contend with." We both knew to whom she alluded. "But I am having trouble keeping staff. That Bekkit is preying on the prettier maids," she continued stiffly. "Peebles has spoken to him but he seems to be a law unto himself these days."

I sighed. "Yes I understand the problem Mrs Peebles. Try and schedule their work well away from areas he frequents. I shall speak to him myself."

Mrs Peebles curtsied again and left, a look of relief on her face. But I'd told a lie. I knew I wouldn't mention the housekeeper's complaint. I wanted as little to do with the valet as possible. The few times that he'd requested an interview, he'd watched me and I'd felt my skin crawl at his stare. How finely he's dressed these days, a sparkle of a gem in his cravat and flashing rings on his fingers.

******

We no longer entertain and refuse all invitations. The rare caller is turned away at the door on some pretext or another. My husband has stopped travelling up to London, so Amberleigh has become almost a prison. Everybody hears the shouts and pistol shots.

"The maid who cleans the fireplaces is terrified to enter milord's bedchamber and will only do so if a footman accompanies her," Nettie told me one morning. "And apparently his lordship sleeps with a loaded pistol in his hand. Obsessed with burglars, so they say." Nettie is a mine of servant gossip. I am ashamed to say I listen to it all, as I have hardly seen my husband in months.

Christmas proved a sad affair, the only happy spot, James wonderful, drooling smile, with one shiny pearl-like tooth beading his gum. My main concern is for his safety, so his nursery has been moved to a location well away from the family part of the house with not one, but two footmen guarding the door with instructions to let no one through but Nettie, James' nurses or myself, and especially not my husband or his valet.

I spend a large part of the day with my baby, feeding and playing with him, or reading stories; he is my delight in this dark place. I have also brought in a wet nurse to attend to his night-time feeds as I am too afraid to leave my room after sunset. My other refuge is the stillroom. It relaxes me; the pleasant smells and concentration required to mix my herbal remedies helps me forget our perilous situation, and I always leave there, feeling calmer. Sadly, I no longer believe the library is safe.

Nettie and I crept into the church for the Christmas service but slipped away before friends could stop to talk with me. I have not seen Uncle Rudolf or Sophie for an age and suspect they have returned to town. I know the Badgers are worried but what can I do? I eat my meals in the nursery, the book-room or my bedroom. I have no idea if my husband even knows I am hiding from him. He still occasionally takes his dinner in the dining room but according to Nettie, is not even aware that I'm not there. And Bekkit is always with him. In fact I'm told that his valet sits at the table and speaks to the staff as if he were master. I should assert myself as mistress of the house but fear the consequences—very weak-willed and timid of me, I know.

One day, on my way back from a trip to the nursery I came upon my husband in the hallway, without Bekkit, and looking terrible. His feet were bare and his shirt hanging loose. Blood-shot eyes in a sallow, unshaven face, glared at me. His matted hair was a tangled mess and I could see bald patches with festering sores. Even from a few yards away, I could smell his stale sweat and something unpleasant I did not recognise. I noted all this in a matter of horrified seconds. He also held a pistol in his hand. I froze—there was nowhere to hide—and of course he saw me. He raised his arm and I could see it trembling as he took aim. Thoughts of my baby left motherless and unprotected flashed through my mind. A *click* sounded and I realised with relief that the pistol was unloaded.

I turned to escape but he broke into a shambling run and, lungeing forward, whipped me with its barrel, screaming invectives as blows rained down on my head. I tried to protect myself as I fell, and my cries brought a brave and burly footman, who courageously tackled his master to the floor. Suddenly, Bekkit appeared, and after dragging his lordship to his feet and disarming him, led him away with a frowning backward glance at me.

"Better you avoid him milady, seeing as you seem to bring on his attacks."

Bloodied and barely conscious, I hardly needed his advice to know *that*.

Nettie had arrived by now and looked with horror at my sorry state. She put her arms around me and together with Nathan, the footman who had come to my aid, helped pick me up from the floor and got me to my bedroom. We had considered finding a new sleeping room but after Nettie located keys to both the door into the small sitting room and the one to the hall, we decided that would do. I asked Nettie to thank my saviour as I lay prostrate, blood seeping into the bedcovers. Luckily I discovered my nose appeared to be unbroken when I gingerly prodded it, but everything ached and one arm positively throbbed with pain. Swellings marred my face and head, one eye had closed and blood matted my hair. Nettie gently probed my arm, the one I'd lifted in a vain attempt to protect myself.

"You are going to be black and blue milady and I suspect this arm is broken, not badly, fortunately," she said grimly as she gently proceeded to splint it. "Having brothers always falling out of trees helps me to recognise the signs," she added, trying to cheer me a little, I was sure. "Perhaps we should call for Dr Caukwell?" Nettie suggested this half-heartedly, knowing my distrust of the doctor.

"No!" I replied emphatically, and shuddered at the thought. No doubt he would want to bleed me and I had already lost enough blood. Nettie did not mention it again. I have been told my husband never remembers these violent interludes, which is a relief, as I should not like Nathan to be let go for having laid hands on his master when he came to my rescue.

Not long after the beating, Sir Timothy, who refused to be turned away this time, paid me a visit. Nettie did her best to hide the damage but though the swellings had gone down, my bruised face showed a riot of colour and the splint on my arm could not be hidden. I asked for him to be shown to my book room. I took a deep breath and entered. He stood warming himself at the fire, for the weather had turned bitterly cold and gloomy. He came forward to greet me when he heard the door open and in the candlelight did not immediately notice my wounds.

"Hullo my dear. Penny and I have been so worried about you, she insisted I come by and check."

As he walked towards me his face went from cheerful, to puzzled, to horrified.

"Oh Emily, what has happened to you!" In his agitation he called me by my given name but I did not mind. He always feels like an uncle to me. I had thought about what I would say to him, what lie I should tell, but I could hardly say I had walked into a door and be believed. No doubt the servants' gossip network had been busy too and he would be at least partially aware of the situation.

I cleared my throat. "Please do not worry Sir Timothy." His eyes took in my battered face and broken arm. "It is not really as bad as it looks," I finished lamely.

"My dear, it looks *every* bit as bad. Who has done this to you?" But of course he probably already knew.

"It seems my husband has taken a dislike to me, I am afraid. I mostly stay out of his way but unfortunately he came upon me unexpectedly."

As a magistrate, Sir Timothy would be well aware of the right of a husband to beat his wife, but my injuries were much more brutal.

"I shall call on Lord Firstbridge and speak about this," he replied indignantly.

With fright, I grasped his hand with my good one. "*Please* don't mention me, Sir Timothy. Don't draw me to his attention."

He stared at me for a few moments, frowning. "Very well, but I shall still call on him and assess the situation and let you know." He looked grim.

After that we had tea and talked about James and his own children until he finally and reluctantly took his leave.

Lord Firstbridge received Sir Timothy, with Bekkit in attendance, and apparently conducted himself with no appreciable sign of his madness. No doubt his valet had prepared him for the interview, hiding the ugly sores on his head and giving him something to calm his frightening moods. Of course I did not need a report from Sir Timothy to know the outcome of their conversation. Nettie heard it all from the servants, who by now knew that their own safety relied on listening at doors for knowledge of the whereabouts of the master and his valet, the mood of his lordship, and what places to avoid.

Sometimes his rages are inspired by delusions other than the one he'd created around me. He accused the staff of stealing, screaming that they were in league with burglars and pointing his pistol menacingly. There were now a few bullet holes in the wainscotting—Bekkit did not always manage to unload it—but so far no one had been shot. However, I felt it would only be a matter of time. My husband is cunning in his madness and hides cartridges from his keeper. I know, because one afternoon I'd crept into the library to get a book and found a small box of bullets with a packet of gunpowder on the bookshelf. Should I remove them? Might he remember and come looking ? I quickly picked up the packet and box, chose my book and fled.

******

"His lordship showed no unusual signs my dear; perhaps a little vague and he doesn't look well, but not enough to permit me to interfere." When Sir Timothy called to see me next, his face looked so disturbed, I tried to comfort him.

"I have taken precautions, sir, so please do not worry. And Bekkit is fairly vigilant." The fact that I had to rely on my lord's valet made me feel a little sick.

"Well, I insist, if you find yourself in the least bit of danger, you and the baby must come straight to me. Penny is very worried about you and so am I." Sir Timothy stared at me with an earnest frown. He is such a dear man and his concern for my safety almost moved me to tears. However, he would also be aware that if my husband demanded me back, he would be powerless to deny him.

"It is comforting to know I have somewhere to turn, if it gets too bad," I whispered to the empty room after Sir Timothy had gone.

Chapter Twenty-six.
In which Emily's plight is discussed.

Sir Timothy was a good man. As a loving husband and father he could not comprehend how it was necessary for a man to injure his wife in such a way. His dear Penny had never given him cause to deliver more than a gentle verbal chastisement and he could not believe that a sweet young girl like Emily deserved *any* physical punishment.

Leaving the neighbourhood, while he worried about Lady Firstbridge, bothered him, but he had urgent business in London that could not wait. January brought with it unpredictable storms so he must take advantage of any spell of reasonable weather to make the journey. When Mr Ferris received a letter advising of the pending visit, he insisted that Sir Timothy stay with him in return for the many pleasurable times he had been a guest at Leafybrook Park. And so Simon, who had also been invited to dinner, heard of the troubles of his grey-eyed lady.

They were sitting around the fire, Mrs Ferris embroidering a baby gown for her stepdaughter and the gentlemen enjoying glasses of an excellent brandy after a delicious meal, when the subject of Lord Firstbridge's violence entered the conversation.

"Poor Lady Firstbridge," sighed Sir Timothy. "She is having a terrible time with that husband of hers, but I'm powerless. I suspect he is losing his mind, however, when I spoke to him, he appeared sane so I cannot intervene," he added gloomily. And then he described the injuries Emily had received at the hands of her husband. As he spoke to a fellow magistrate, he did not consider this gossip.

Simon sat up, immediately alert and aghast. His Lady of the Grey Eyes in danger? What could he do? He knew it for foolishness; had enjoyed pleasurable fantasies about her in his dreams and no doubt she had not given him another thought. If he had been aware of the warmth with which Emily remembered him, he would have been delighted. Then an idea came to him. As each weighed the perils facing her ladyship, he spoke tentatively into the solemn silence.

"Perhaps, sir, we could put someone into the household who would help keep her safe?"

Sir Timothy looked at Simon with interest as the idea took hold. "Hmmm, that is a good suggestion young Simon. Now I think about it, Newton, my wife's lady's maid has a nephew who is one of Firstbridge's footmen. I seem to remember him being a striking young man. Lady Badger pointed him out to me in church. I shall get my wife to speak to Newton and arrange a meeting. Yes, an excellent idea." And he smiled with satisfaction.

With a sigh of relief that he had done at least some small thing to ensure Lady Firstbridge's safety, Simon relaxed, but he found himself longing to be the one protecting her from harm. The conversation moved to other matters and gradually his worried thoughts subsided, to re-emerge and invade his dreams that night.

Chapter Twenty-seven.
In which we meet a striking young man.

Nathan admired Lady Firstbridge enormously. She always remembered the servants' names and never failed, with a sweet smile, to thank any small service done for her. Her husband, on the other hand, he did not like at all—had never liked. Even before the beginnings of his lordship's odd behaviour, Nathan had summed him up as a cold and arrogant man. When you were a footman spending hours mimicking a statue, serving at table or out and about, opening carriage doors, and following behind the mistress carrying her parcels, you had plenty of time to observe and evaluate the follies and foibles of your betters.

At one and twenty, Nathan stood at six feet six inches in his stockings, with a fine, well-developed body to match his imposing height, dark blonde curls grown long enough to tie back in a queue, and leaf-green eyes.It was no wonder he had set all the maid's heart's aflutter when he came to work for Lord Firstbridge. His Aunt Flora, a friend of Mrs Peebles, had been instrumental in getting him this job at Amberleigh and his proud mother firmly believed that he would one day rise to be butler of a great house.

Nathan had other dreams, however. He yearned to become a soldier and spent his long, boring hours of standing to attention in the draughty hallways of Amberleigh, dreaming of heroic battles against the French and that monster Napoleon, with himself leading the charge and destroying all before him. The only thing that stopped him going immediately to enlist was his widowed mother who needed his financial support. Nathan sighed.

He kept his face carefully blank as Bekkit walked past. He suspected him of being as bad if not worse than the master and thought it unnatural that Lord Firstbridge's by-blow had been trained as his valet. Something dark and dangerous about the man disturbed Nathan. True, he had fine looks, almost a younger version of the father he grudgingly admitted, but he'd seen the way Bekkit stared at her ladyship; overly familiar—and gloating. The vague rumours he'd heard about his lordship's unhealthy tastes and the unvalet-like skills at which Bekkit supposedly excelled, made him uneasy.

Seeing the valet reminded him of the incident when he'd tackled the master to the floor. He could have lost his job over that but he couldn't bear to see her ladyship, or any woman for that matter, beaten so cruelly. Her screams for help had brought him running and he'd acted instinctively. Bekkit had then appeared and between them they'd subdued his lordship. Nothing had been said since, and he'd breathed easier when, after a few days had passed, it appeared that Peebles had not been ordered to let him go.

His thoughts drifted again and he wondered why his ma had told him to call on Aunt Flora at Leafybrook Park on Sunday afternoon, his half-day off. It would take him some time to walk there and he begrudged the waste of his leisure hours. He'd much rather spend them at the *Horse and Saddle* in the village supping with his friends. Still, ma had been insistent so he'd better oblige. Thinking of his aunt brought to mind a lady's maid closer to home. That Miss Perkins— Nathan admired her feisty temperament and grinned to himself as he pictured her. She protected her mistress like a lioness with her cub, and just as well, with Bekkit and the master prowling around.

Oh well, another two hours on duty then he would be relieved and get a bite to eat in the servants' hall. Perhaps more than a bite, he admitted to himself. After all he had a big body to keep fuelled, even bigger than that pesky valet, he thought with satisfaction. Luckily the cook had taken a fancy to him and slipped him extra portions, she being a good, solid English woman; not like that queer little Frenchie who used to be at Amberleigh. Long before his time of course, but he'd heard the stories.

******

When he arrived at Leafybrook Park, Nathan paused with his hands on his knees to catch his breath. He'd run all the way so as to take up as little of his free time as possible. He would get this visit with his aunt over quickly and hopefully still have time to call at the *Horse and Saddle* for a pint on his way back to Amberleigh. The barmaid had a wicked smile. He knocked at the kitchen door and the maid who opened it, told him to wait. To his surprise, Rankin, the Badger's butler, and not his aunt, soon appeared.

"Come with me young man. The master would like a word with you."

Rankin escorted Nathan, now a little disturbed, through the baize door that separated the service rooms from the family living area and then to Sir Timothy's study. What on earth was going on? He knew Sir Timothy was the local magistrate and frantically searched his memory to see if there had been any mischief he'd recently committed that necessitated his being called up before this formidable man. Had his tackling of Lord Firstbridge finally been revealed? But that'd happened a while ago. Surely something would have been said before now?

148

"Mr Nathan Fisher, sir," announced Rankin as he held the door open. The young man felt slightly sick as he walked into the study.

Sir Timothy had been sitting behind his desk when Nathan appeared but stood to greet him.

"Take a seat lad, and don't look so worried. You've nothing to be afraid of."

Nathan relaxed a little but still remained wary. He felt uncomfortable sitting in this grand room.

"No sir. I mean yes sir," he stammered.

Sir Timothy sat down again. "I asked to meet you Nathan… you don't mind if I call you Nathan?"

He had no time to even open his mouth before the magistrate went on speaking.

"I have a rather sensitive task for you and I wish for it to be kept between the two of us."

Nathan could only nod. He had no idea what task Sir Timothy referred to but thought it best to agree.

"I am concerned about the safety of Lady Firstbridge but it is a delicate matter. Hrrmph. I don't quite know how else to word this but I fear she may be in some danger." Here, he looked steadily into Nathan's eyes and hoped that he had not made an error in his judgement of this young man, whose character had been so lavishly praised by his wife's lady's maid. He felt assured when he saw comprehension dawn there.

"I understand sir. What do you wish me to do?"

Sir Timothy smiled with relief. "I want you to keep an eye on her ladyship; see that she comes to no harm. And report to me if you have any worries about her safety or that of the child." He watched as the footman thought about his request.

"I'm happy to help, sir, but there is one problem. Peebles, Lord Firstbridge's butler, is my superior and he is the one to assign me my duties. He will have to be brought into your confidence, sir, perhaps with a letter from you explaining the situation? I don't think you need fear his disapproval as I believe he is fond of her ladyship and we all know how things have been lately at Amberleigh."

"Excellent idea Nathan." Sir Timothy reached for his quill and a sheet of paper, dipped the pen in the ink pot and wrote quickly. He sanded and folded it then handed the note to the young man.

"There, my boy. Show that to your superior and if there is any problem let me know."

He rose, and Nathan knew the interview had ended. He couldn't believe it when Sir Timothy, himself, escorted him to the front door!

Nathan ran home, stopping at the *Horse and Saddle* for a quick pint. He brimmed with excitement at his special mission, too full of it to even flirt with the barmaid. It felt like being one of Wellington's spies! A pity he could only share it with old Peebles, but he knew his duty. He'd keep an eye on that slimy Bekkit as well, though he hadn't mentioned *that* to Sir Timothy.

Chapter Twenty-eight.
Simon.

I sat at my desk, trying to finish a report on a case to be brought at the Old Bailey but finding it hard to concentrate. Some months had passed since Sir Timothy's revelations but still a pair of lovely grey eyes kept distracting me. Had she recovered from her injuries? Was she even safe? I felt so powerless. At least a secret protector had now been stationed in Amberleigh, and watched over her. He would contact Sir Timothy directly if danger threatened. This comforted me a little, but I wished that I was the one guarding her.

Sighing, I shook my head as if to force the vision of those compelling eyes away and resolutely concentrated on the task in front of me. When completed, I must undertake a commission for Mr Ferris to call on a Mrs Tindall, a distant relation of my employer's late wife, whose son had been accused of stealing. At last I came to the final sentence. With a flourish, I signed and sanded it then passed it to a clerk to be noted in the records.

Straightening my coat, I put on my hat and gloves and picked up my cane. I had lately taken up fencing under the tutelage of the great Angelo and as my detective work often took me into less salubrious neighbourhoods, a sword-stick was a useful weapon. I checked my timepiece, and with a nod to the doorman, left the building and walked briskly down the street, my eyes searching for a hackney to deliver me to an address in a fashionable part of the city.

I eventually arrived outside a charming townhouse of warm red brick and after paying the jarvey, approached the front door. A bang of the knocker brought a doorman who took my hat, gloves and cane and the butler, after glancing at my card, escorted me to the drawing room. I bowed over the hand of a middle-aged woman of statuesque proportions who looked close to tears and obviously in a great deal of distress.

How may I be of service madam? Mr Ferris has only given me the barest facts; I understand some valuable jewellery has been stolen and your son is the accused."

Mrs Tindall burst into sobs and paced the room. "Yes! How could my brother believe it of his own nephew!" she wailed, a handkerchief pressed to her face.

Gradually I extracted the story from the distraught woman. Apparently, her son, Peter, a young dandy, who mixed with a rather dubious set and invariably overspent his allowance, had been blamed for the highway robbery of the jewels when his uncle and aunt, Lord and Lady Edale, were travelling to Bath to take the waters, his lordship apparently being prone to gout. Because of my work with the *ton*, I had made a point of familiarising myself with the various connections and intermarriages of the aristocracy, so already knew that Lady Arabella Edale was Lord Burncliff's sister and therefore my grey-eyed lady's aunt.

"Along with the immediate family, my Peter also knew of the secret compartment in the coach," explained Mrs Tindall. "*That* came about because of the loose talk of Andrew, the Edale heir," she added resentfully. "I know his father admonished him severely when his indiscretion became known and he swore then that he had told no one else but Peter. My brother threatened to have my son's tongue cut out if he ever breathed a word," she cried indignantly. "And now he's blaming him! As if my boy would do anything so base as to rob a coach! I have warned him about over-spending his allowance too, but you know how these fashionable young men behave and he never listens to his mother!" She fixed me with a tragic glare.

Peter's forbidden knowledge and his debts combined, explained why he was under suspicion. After bidding a tearful Mrs Tindall farewell and promising I would do my best for her son, I took a hackney to the prison. There was the inevitable bribe to the prison guard, who I then followed through the cold, dank passageways, a pomander held to my nose that did little to reduce the appalling odour of damp, human waste and despair. We passed other cells where gaunt faces peered out and begged for my help. Filthy, clawed fingers grasped the bars but let go with anguished howls as the gaoler rapped them with his truncheon. Finally, we arrived at young Mr Tindall's cell. I knew money had changed hands to make him reasonably comfortable; he had it to himself at least. The guard opened the door and indicated I should enter, then locked it behind me.

A narrow bed with a thin mattress, though it had warm coverings, sat against one wall and a shelf extended from another to hold food and drink, some books and a candle in a candle holder. A rug lay on the stone floor and a small, barred window gave a little natural light, but nothing could displace the odour of decay.

"Just shout when yer ready to leave, guvner," the gaoler grunted through the grille and disappeared back the way we had come. With all the moans and screams I could hear, I wondered how my voice could be identified in this grim place.

Looking pale and miserable, the young man, who'd been sitting on the bed with his head in his hands, rose to his feet on my entry. His clothes were in disarray and his hair wild. I wanted to leave this awful place as soon as possible, so wasted no time in stating my reason for being there.

"My name is Simon Mannering, Mr Tindall. Your mother has asked me to prove your innocence, so firstly I shall ask you a question which you must answer truthfully. Did you steal the Edale jewels?"

"No Mr Mannering! Of course I didn't! And I don't know why my uncle blames me. I would be a fool to steal from my own family, no matter how to let my pockets were, *and* when they knew I was aware of their hiding place!"

I looked at him keenly and heard the desperation and indignation in his voice. I have become a fairly good judge of character in my work and can usually detect a lie when I hear it.

"Have you ever told anyone else, perhaps when you were in your cups?" I asked, watching him closely.

"No! I am sure I have never been *that* bosky," was his bitter reply.

"Have you ever ridden *in* the Edale coach?"

No, never! If I accompanied them, I rode on horseback. Andrew told me about the secret place but I never actually saw it." Then he hesitated, pinched at his bottom lip and looked uncomfortable.

"Well, actually, a few months ago, Andrew and I and another friend *did* take the coach for a little jaunt; Lord Edale never knew of it. My uncle had just purchased a perfect matching four and the coachman was trialling them. Andrew bribed him to let him handle the ribbons and I came along as his groom. I must say he tooled the carriage smartly and kept those cattle in good order in spite of being a trifle disguised," he added admiringly. "Our friend Patrick played 'milady' and managed some very girlish-sounding shrieks." In spite of his predicament the young man smiled at the memory of the sounds coming from inside the swaying coach.

I became instantly alert. "Who is your friend Patrick?"

"Oh that's Patrick Niall, a thoroughly good fellow, always up for a lark," Peter replied.

I searched my memory—the name had rung a bell. A man quite a bit older than his friends, a rake and a frequenter of gaming hells, he had been seen in the company of some of London's more notorious fences. His name had appeared in a Bow Street Runners report that had recently crossed my desk. Could the solution be that simple? I must not jump to conclusions without checking all the facts I reminded myself.

"Thank you Mr Tindall, you have given me something to work with. Don't give up hope," I said, smiling kindly at the young man's anxious face. I banged the door and shouted for the guard.

Next, I called on Lord Edale. He was at home and the butler ushered me into the drawing room. I hoped the all-pervasive smell of the prison wasn't still clinging to my clothes. Lady Edale stood beside him and I could see a faint family resemblance to Lady Firstbridge, though I considered *my* lady far superior in looks. *My* lady? When had I started to think of her as mine?

"Good day milord, milady, I have been asked by Mrs Tindall to look into the theft of your jewels." I bowed over her ladyship's hand and wondered if she knew of her niece's unhappy circumstances. Should I inform her of my acquaintance with Lady Firstbridge? No. As this would be a professional call and not a social one, I kept silent.

Lady Edale looked thoughtful then exclaimed. "Of course, you are making quite a name for yourself young man. Viscount Bothrell had only praise when you solved his rather delicate little problem."

I winced. I had been paid very handsomely for that. I have now come to believe there are no secrets in the *ton*.

"Oh don't worry my boy, Lord Edale and I were told in the strictest confidence. Now what's this about our stolen jewels? I thought we had caught the thief, young Peter, but he hasn't led us to our property yet," complained her ladyship with a frown.

Lord Edale then rumbled. "Yes Mr Mannering, Peter will stay in Newgate until he confesses, in spite of his mother's pleas. Though I did make sure the boy was not in too much discomfort," he added looking a little discomforted himself. He produced an ornate snuffbox and offered it to me. Having never acquired the habit, I politely refused.

"Would you please give me the name of your coach builder, milord. I wish to clarify a few points." I had wondered how many of his employees knew of the secret compartment included in the design.

"My coach was especially commissioned from William Felton and I am extremely pleased with it—well sprung, beautifully finished." Lord Edale was a big man and I imagined it would have to be very sturdy.

"Also, if you could give me a list and description of the jewels stolen, that would be most helpful."

"Lady Edale has made out a list," he informed me. "We have already given a copy to the Runners." He summoned the butler to fetch it from his desk.

"And, by the way, I think it's highly unlikely your nephew is the culprit," I added. I could not see Peter Tindall as a highwayman, no matter how hard I tried. To me he had seemed a rather a timid fellow.

Both husband and wife stared at me. Lord Edale spoke first. "Well, as to that, we shall have to see. There were two of them you know. One had the voice of a gentleman even though he tried to disguise it, but the other sounded common and definitely a bad 'un. Might bring that young rascal, Peter, to his senses, cooling his heels in prison. Been mixing with a rum lot."

I had the feeling his lordship felt very uncomfortable accusing his nephew of theft.

"I should like to speak to your son as well. Where might I find him at this time?"

Her ladyship sighed rather wistfully. "Our son will be dining at his club, White's, Mr Mannering. We see little of him these days. Young men lead their own lives. With our oldest daughter now wed and Lucy, our youngest, gone to pay her a visit, the house feels quite empty."

The butler returned with the list, I bowed myself out and took a hackney to St James's Street. feeling rather hungry by now, after a busy day, and it now being late afternoon, I decided to dine there. On the way I tasked my brain with remembering Lord Edale's family name. Brookton? Brookington? Yes that sounded right. But young Andrew used the courtesy title of Viscount Livington I recalled. I enquired of the doorman and had him pointed out to me in the coffee room. As I walked towards him I observed a substantial young man, built very much like his father—sans his expanded girth—with a pleasant face and a quietly elegant taste in clothes. He sat reading a newspaper, the steam rising from a hot drink at his elbow.

"Lord Livington?" I bowed politely and the other man looked up enquiringly.

"Yes, how may I help you?"

I introduced myself. "I am investigating the theft of your mother's jewels and I wonder if you could verify something for me?"

At first Livington appeared startled and looked me up and down appraisingly, but nodded in assent. "You don't look like a Bow Street Runner, Mr Mannering."

"No, I'm a private individual, milord, with an interest in puzzle solving," I answered, and then repeated what Peter Tindall had told me about the coach ride.

He broke into a broad grin. "Yes, an amusing lark," he confirmed, then sobered. "Poor Peter, I don't think he is a thief but who else could it be?"

"That is what I am going to find out," I replied.

Invited to join Lord Livington and his friend, who had just arrived, we moved to the dining room and I spent the next two hours enjoying their company over a delicious meal of pease soup, followed by fish with wine and mushrooms, and a roasted fillet of pork. It ended with a variety of cheeses and preserved fruits. After a final glass of port, I made my farewells, bundled myself into a hackney, and arrived back at my lodgings, a little the worse for wear but more convinced than ever that Peter was not the culprit.

Chapter Twenty-nine.
Simon.

The following morning I talked with the coach builder and it was very illuminating. Mr Felton appeared to be a most amiable fellow who, after assuring himself that I was not a spy for his opposition, took me through the building of a carriage—in minute detail.

"May I enquire about the designs of your secret compartments sir?" I asked when the flow of information had slowed a little.

He put a finger to the side of his nose and looked knowing. "Well, as to that young man, they wouldn't stay a secret for long if I told all and sundry, now would they? I keeps *that* information to meself, y'see." He tapped his head. "This is where it's stored. Then there are no drawings of me cunning designs to be stolen," he finished proudly.

After thanking Mr Felton for his time, and reasonably sure that the coach builder's apprentices and journeymen had not been involved in the theft, I returned home to ponder over what I had learned.

That afternoon I returned to the Edale's townhouse and asked for permission to sit in the coach. A footman took me to the stables and introduced me to the coachman. I duly admired the four beautiful matching bays, then I was walked the few yards to the coach house and proudly shown the new carriage. When I brought up the escapade with the young men, he looked most uncomfortable and begged me not to mention it to his lordship.

I had to admit Mr Felton had outdone himself. It shone glossy black with wheels and trimmings outlined in gold and the Edale coat of arms emblazoned on the doors. The steps were lowered, I climbed in and looked around. The interior exuded luxury and I could understand the carriage builder's pride in his workmanship. A young groom called the coachman away so I took the opportunity to poke and prod at the rose velvet and silk padded seats and walls and the inlaid wooden floor. I found cleverly concealed cupboards for storing heating bricks, pistols, travelling rugs, food and drink and even a chamber pot, but nothing resembling a hiding space for valuables.

Then my eyes moved upwards. I stared thoughtfully at the ceiling, curved and moulded, with an elaborate raised medallion decorated with painted leaves and flowers. On an inspiration, I reached up with both hands and twisted. The decoration turned smoothly and came loose. To one side, in the shallow cavity exposed, I saw a small door. Locked now, I knew that it had been forced open during the robbery and had since been repaired. Behind it would be a black velvet-lined compartment. Nodding to myself, I replaced the medallion. I made no mention of this discovery but it confirmed in my mind that if I could find it, then so could Patrick Niall who, from all reports, appeared a sharp and cunning man. Somehow he had discovered the secret compartment on the day of the drunken ride.

Had he staggered and grasped at something to stop falling and opened it accidentally? He would have known immediately what it was. Or had he deliberately searched for it? Then he would have patiently waited until the Bath trip. It took little effort to impersonate a highwaymen, just a mask, a horse and a pistol. I knew there were two of them—one to cover the coach's occupants and another for the coachman and groom. In fact the more daring of the young town rakes thought taking to the High Toby a capital amusement.

I had arranged for some of my small 'soldiers' to observe Mr Niall's movements, and if he had an accomplice it would eventually be known. Over the months, through my work for my step-father, I had also built up my own network of informers. To them I had given a description of the lost jewels and soon discovered that, as yet, they had not surfaced in the hands of the more notorious fences. This suggested to me that the thieves were still to make their move. I needed to catch one or the other in the act of disposing of the gems. The trap had been set; the only thing required now was patience.

In the course of my enquiries I learned that Peter Tindall had been released from Newgate. His mother's pleas and my assurance of his innocence had finally convinced Lord Edale. A very shaken young man had contacted Mr Ferris and found out where I lived so that he could express his thanks in person. As the landlady's doorman ushered him into my small parlour I noted a change, no doubt caused by his sojourn in Newgate. It was obvious that Mr Tindall normally dressed as an extremely fashionable young man, but now, even his attire seemed to have lost its exuberance. Enduring the prison's horrors would have a profound effect on any man.

"I'm eternally grateful to you for getting me out of that hell hole, Mr Mannering." He shuddered as he dropped into the chair I'd indicated, and accepted a glass of brandy. "I realise what a fool I have been and regret causing my mother so much anguish. I suppose Uncle Richard had good reason to be suspicious of me. I receive a generous allowance but my gaming debts have been…" Here, he paused uncomfortably and took a gulp of his drink. "So I can understand why. But dammit! How could he imagine I would rob my own family!" His voice filled with anguish as he reiterated the words he had used in prison.

It made me feel quite old listening to him. At Peter's age - he must be all of nineteen - I had not been in a position to squander money on the throw of a dice. I knew Mrs Tindall was a widow, so I took pity on him.

"At the risk of sounding like a father figure, perhaps this episode will lead you to re-think the direction in which you have been going. Take it as a warning that it is time for you to shoulder your responsibilities and give purpose to your life. You have much to be grateful for after all. Things will be coming to a head soon. I can't say more at present, but there will be other scandals to overshadow your fall from grace and it will soon be forgotten." *God! I sound pompous,* I thought ruefully, but my words were having an effect. Tindall nodded, finished his brandy and rose to go.

After fervently shaking my hand, he left with assurances that he would immediately take himself off to the country to stay with friends. Consequently, he had already left town when the shocking news splashed across all the papers that Mr Patrick Niall—deeply in debt—and an unsavoury character known as One-eyed Jack, had been arrested by the Bow Street Runners for highway robbery, and the Edale jewels returned to their rightful owner.

I heard that Lady Edale wasted no time in calling on her favourite gem cutter and very soon was the possessor of a stunning collection of paste replicas.

Chapter Thirty.
In which Bekkit makes more plans.

Bekkit remembered his lordship before the madness had consumed him. To have an unassailable belief that one's exalted birth and wealth made one superior to all others came naturally to his father. He'd always done exactly as he pleased without expecting retribution. The law was different for the aristocracy Bekkit knew. They were judged before their peers in the House of Lords which would hardly condemn one of its own if at all possible, he thought bitterly.

Having now experienced both states himself—power and powerlessness—Bekkit appreciated the difference. As he laid out his master's morning toilet in the dressing room, he thought of the madman next door who would be wanting his coffee soon—that's if he woke up lucid. Bekkit never knew in what condition he would find him.

It amused him to play the dutiful valet during the increasingly brief moments of his master's sanity and he took great satisfaction in being rather too violent when subduing him during his insane episodes. Added to that, Lord Firstbridge's addiction to opium had become obvious. He had to be dosed at closer intervals now to keep him under control. With his shaking limbs, slurred speech, and profuse sweating, he made a sorry figure. Bekkit freely admitted to himself that he enjoyed taking out his own frustrations on his father for all those years when he'd meant nothing to him. Now, his lordship couldn't live without him.

To his surprise, her ladyship, whom he had judged as rather timid, had shown surprising courage, bolstered by that virago of a lady's maid. She, he would like to break. It would be an exciting challenge. He thought of his future. When his lordship died, and it couldn't be long now, should he comfort the desolate widow? His smile was without humour.

Then again, should he move on? He had enough put aside to live well as a gentleman. He could go to America and start afresh, or perhaps India. Another scheme now occurred to him; it would have to be accomplished soon before his father descended completely into madness and would require a little persuasion, but it would be a fitting retribution...what a delightful idea! He must think on it further—and his smile grew even broader, but no less calculating.

Chapter Thirty-one.
Emily.

Spring is here! My arm has healed and only a slight bump remains to remind me of that terrible day. Sir Timothy insists on calling at least once a week to assure himself I am well. I have also arranged to meet with my husband's steward.

"Come in and sit down, Mr Netherby," I called, when Nathan opened the door to my book room and ushered him in. After much thought, and knowing the state of my husband's health, I had decided to question him about his lordship's financial affairs. For my son's sake, I needed to understand the sources of the earldom's great wealth and exercising my brain might lift me out of the long depression and utter helplessness I had felt for months. I asked him to be seated and smiled my most beguiling smile.

"The reason I have invited you here, Mr Netherby, is to learn from you. You appear to me to be an excellent man of business and I do not question your decisions or wish to interfere in any way, but I would like to familiarise myself with the Firstbridge investments." I paused and watched his face warily. Would he think that as a woman I should not be poking my nose into things that should not concern me? I had been told by Nettie that he had witnessed one of my husband's mad attacks and had been badly shaken, so hoped this would encourage him to confide in me.

"Milady, I hardly think finance is something with which a lady should be involved," he replied stiffly and rather patronisingly. I had expected this predictable answer and as I knew Netherby didn't like Bekkit—no one did—I tried a different tack.

"It is just that I am concerned with the hold his lordship's valet has over his master, Mr Netherby. Since my husband's ah… sickness, Bekkit seems to have become particularly affluent, flaunting jewellery way beyond the wages of a servant. I would like to know how he is achieving this."

I had hit upon the perfect way to open the floodgate. In his outpouring of words I could hear the steward's frustration.

"Large sums of money requested by his lordship disappear into Bekkit's pocket milady—and there is nothing I can do about it," he fumed. "I have been desperately trying to find a way of stopping this drain but as long as his lordship signs the withdrawals, I can do nothing." He looked grim and beaten.

"Well, I suggest we put our heads together, Mr Netherby. Perhaps between us we can find a solution to the problem." I had no idea how, but at least the man would not be fighting Bekkit alone. After that he became much more amenable to explaining my husbands investments. I even managed some intelligent questions and when he had explained a few points I started to enjoy myself. We have now formed a comfortable working relationship and I am beginning to understand the true extent of the Firstbridge wealth and it astonishes me; graphite, coal, gold and silver mines, sugar cane farms in the West Indies, shipping, and estates all over England and even Wales, Scotland and Ireland. I shuddered to learn that my husband even owns slaves!

Now all Mr Netherby and I have to do is find a way to foil Bekkit.

******

My one delight is my fast-growing boy. James is now over six month's old and sitting on his own. Thankfully I think my husband has forgotten his very existence, his baby noise safely hidden by distance. I believe his lordship no longer even remembers that he has a wife. Sometimes the howls coming from his rooms are quite anguished and there are occasions when Bekkit needs the help of our burliest footmen to control him. Between the Peebles, Mr Netherby and Nettie, I am kept informed of the situation but it's as if we are all holding our breaths, waiting for the next disaster to come crashing down upon us. How will this living nightmare end? There are times when Nettie holds me as I cry myself to sleep. What should I do? My greatest fear is for my son. I must protect him at all costs.

Occasionally, Bekkit requests an audience to report on my lord's progress, though of course I am already well aware of things, and I make sure Nettie remains in the room with me. His tone is overly familiar and his eyes rove over my body as he speaks.

"Lord Firstbridge has moments of lucidity milady but they are fewer and fewer. The disease that grips his brain is overwhelming him I fear."

Bekkit is so finely dressed these days one would take him to be master of the house. Mr Netherby and I are at a loss as to how to deal with him; his control over my husband is total. He is too cunning to overstep when withdrawing money from my husband's bank account and the steward seethes with impotent fury.

I dismissed the valet and paced the floor. How, at seventeen, have I found myself in this desperate situation? I thought of Dr Caukwell, but abandoned that idea immediately. Perhaps I should consult a London doctor? However, I do not entirely trust the medical profession, having studied some of the treatments for madness with my father; they filled me with horror. I have no tender feelings for my husband but I would not submit him to the supposed cure fashionable at present—water therapy they call it. The description appeared in one of papa's journals. Inhumane.

And the hospitals for the insane are…bestial. I would not consider them even for my worst enemy! One hears stories of women forced into them by fathers simply because they would not marry their parent's choice, or husbands who wished to remove their unwanted wives. There are even visits paid by the *ton* to ogle the poor, chained creatures as if they were a side show.

Somehow I must endure.

******

Nettie's mother is dying. She'd received a letter from her father and was in tears.

"You must go home Nettie, dear," I said as I hugged her close.

"How c-can I leave you, Miss Emily, when you are in s-such danger," she sobbed, torn between me and her family. But I insisted.

"Nonsense Nettie, we have managed for months, and a few weeks without you will not make a lot of difference. You pack your bag and I shall arrange to have the coach readied. Send me word when you wish to return."

I finally persuaded her, and as I waved her goodbye and the coach rumbled down the driveway, I realised with a chill feeling that I was now truly alone. Aunt Arabella has written to me a few times so I am not entirely forgotten by my family, but she is unaware of my situation, and how can I even begin to explain to her the awful state of my marriage. I remember Uncle Richard's promise to go to him if I ever needed help but he is so far away and I hardly know him. Only Sir Timothy and Lady Badger understand and worry for me.

Some time after Nettie left, Bekkit accosted me in the hallway outside my bedroom. He glanced around as if to make sure we were alone.

"I would like to discuss his lordship, milady."

He came so close, looming over me, I could smell brandy on his breath, see the pores on his face and the glow of his predatory eyes. Fear nibbled at me, however I put steel into my voice and spoke as haughtily as I could.

"Pray make an appointment in the usual way, Bekkit."

But he ignored me and suddenly trapped me against the door, pressing his body against mine so that I could feel his engorged manhood. It terrified me. He knew it and laughed in my face, then savagely kissed me, forcing his tongue into my mouth and groping at my breast. On the edge of my vision I saw a hand reach for the bedroom door knob. He knew of my vulnerability now Nettie had gone. Somehow I freed my mouth and managed a yelp before he crushed my lips again. That is what saved me. I heard running feet then a voice say respectfully.

"Excuse me, milady, but Mrs Peebles asked me to remind you of your appointment with her this afternoon."

With an oath Bekkit released me and glared at the footman whose face remained politely attentive. The valet started to say something to him, then, changing his mind, turned back to me and muttered under his breath so that only I could hear.

"We have not finished, milady." He leered at me and my blood ran cold, then he stalked away. I thanked heaven that Nathan had come to my rescue. I remembered that he had also been my saviour when my husband had so viciously attacked me many months before.

"Thank you Nathan. I am so glad you were nearby. You have rescued me again." I felt sick and still trembled with shock.

"I'm watching over you milady so don't fear," he replied earnestly. "I won't let that excuse for a man hurt you." His voice sounded quite savage.

I knew there had been no appointment with the housekeeper; that had just been an excuse to save me from Bekkit. Repeating my thanks, I locked myself in the bedroom, and paced the floor. My husband's valet has become dangerously powerful; with so much control over his lordship, their roles were now reversed, but what could I do? At least I had a guardian angel in Nathan, but as a footman, he could not be with me all the time. I knew Nettie had her own problems but selfishly longed for her return.

******

Bekkit cannot be alert for twenty-four hours in the day. My husband, when he escapes from his gaoler, has now taken to wandering through the halls at night; occasionally I hear shouting and even shots. One night my door knob rattled and there were animal-like grunts accompanied by swearing. I lay stiff with fear but nothing further happened. Then I heard Bekkit's voice coaxing my husband away and breathed again. Perhaps I should move closer to the hidden nursery. Sleepless nights are wearing me to a shadow and I am full of indecision. Nettie, come back soon. I need you!

170

Chapter Thirty-two.
In which a footman guards and a valet schemes.

Looking back, Nathan had not been surprised at how well old Peebles had taken Sir Timothy's letter. He'd read it with a slight frown then looked hard at the footman. "Well young man. I'm pleased to see that someone out there has a care for our mistress. I shall arrange your duties to coincide with her waking hours and make sure you are stationed nearby." Peebles hesitated before he added gruffly.

"Beware of his lordship's valet as well. He has a lofty opinion of himself these days."

For Peebles to criticise Bekkit to a mere footman, showed Nathan how troubled the butler was about the situation.

"Yes, sir, I won't let harm come to the mistress," Nathan had replied confidently. Though Bekkit topped six feet, he towered over him.

At the outset, he had given a lot of thought to his mission. Of course, no obvious weapon could be carried; in fact, being a village boy, growing up, fists and feet were the only things he'd ever used and usually his size scared the troublemakers off anyway. So what could he keep on his person that would not excite comment? He racked his brain but nothing came to mind. Then he recalled a childhood fight with the village bully who had thrown a hand full of dirt into his face and proceeded to pummel him while he lay blinded. *Yes!* At the first opportunity, he'd gone to the wood stack and, after checking that no one had noticed him, filled a pocket he seldom used with sawdust. He'd grinned to himself and felt quite pleased at his inventiveness. Now he was armed!

******

Nathan took his guard duty very seriously and when he'd heard his ladyships muffled cry, he'd not been far away and had an excuse already on his lips as he turned the hallway corner to see his mistress struggling in Bekkit's arms. He longed to smash his fist into that leering face but he'd kept his true feelings hidden as he told his lie. Lady Firstbridge's eyes had been wide with fright, but she'd lifted her chin and nodded her acknowledgement. Bekkit muttered something which Nathan couldn't hear and had then walked away.

In spite of her obvious distress, her ladyship had thanked him sweetly, gone into her bedroom and shut the door. Nathan dared not leave his post but how he would've loved to have gone after the valet and beaten him to a pulp for the way he had mishandled the mistress.

Bekkit scowled. It would take a fool not to notice that damned footman, who seemed to be always hovering near whenever he approached her ladyship. At first he'd thought he only imagined it—though Nathan's size made him hard to miss—but then it became more than just coincidence. The man never made it obvious, but Bekkit wondered. Had her ladyship requested him as her bodyguard? Or might it be Peebles' doing? He knew the butler disliked him and feared his now almost total control over the master. No matter, the

172

footman may be formidable but Bekkit knew he could deal with him.

Perhaps a small scare would be enough to frighten him off. Yes, a little knife work would keep his hand in. There had not been much call for it of late. He wouldn't kill him—that would ruin his plans for the future, should he be caught. No, just slice him up a mite so he would learn to keep out of his way. Bekkit nodded to himself as he measured out his lordship's next dose of laudanum.

Chapter Thirty-three.
In which a footman is in danger.

Nathan yawned and rubbed his eyes; this guarding business was exhausting—trying to be always on the alert, and forever checking where his nemesis would most likely appear next. If Bekkit stayed in his master's rooms it would be so much easier, but once his lordship had been drugged, the valet roamed freely. Everyone in the house now knew that Bekkit managed his lordship with opium. At least that meant Nathan didn't have to watch quite so much for the madman. He even felt a little sorry for the living wreck Lord Firstbridge had become. No matter how cold and unpleasant he had been before the sickness gripped him, no man deserved to end like that. Then he remembered the way his lordship had treated the mistress, and changed his mind.

When would Miss Perkins return? He'd not heard. At least then there would be two of them to guard her. Dreaming of the lady's maid filled the long, boring hours for Nathan. But dreams were all it could ever be. A lady's maid would not be interested in a lowly footman, no matter how handsome and well put together. He thought her full of pluck and had to admit her dimples and upturned, freckled little nose were attractive. Nathan came back to the present with a jolt. He must keep his thoughts focussed and not go drifting off, he reminded himself.

At present her ladyship worked alone in her still room, the door closed, and he stood not far away in the rather cool, poorly lit passageway that lead to it. This part felt isolated, separated as it was from the rest of the kitchen complex by a series of larders that blocked any noise from the bustle and traffic of the scullery and main area. Through the wall he could hear his mistress quietly singing as she worked and this helped alleviate the unnerving silence and gloom of his post, but for some reason he was feeling decidedly uneasy. His granny had the second sight and sometimes he wondered if he had a touch of it too.

To combat the long hours of standing still, Nathan had developed a series of muscle tensing exercises and he'd moved to the scrunching up of his buttocks, when from the corner of his eye he saw a flicker of something in the shadows, and the hairs on the back of his neck stood to attention.

"Hullo Nathan, what are you doing down here? Keeping an eye on her ladyship, eh?" Bekkit, with a slight smirk on his handsome face, walked towards him. A speculative look in the valet's eyes and the way he moved put the footman on his guard.

"I might say the same of you, sir," he replied warily. Nathan sensed trouble. What reason could Bekkit possibly have for being in this part of the house?

The valet stepped closer. "I don't like people poking their noses into my affairs," he hissed, and dropped swiftly into a fighter's crouch. Simultaneously, a ratcheting sound whispered and the dim light caught the glint of a lethal looking knife that suddenly appeared in Bekkit's hand. Nathan had heard of the hooded snakes of India that mesmerised their victims, and stared with a sense of unreality, his eyes tracking the blade weaving to and fro in front of him. Like lightning the valet struck. The footman stepped back, but not fast enough. He felt a thump on his

175

forearm followed a split second later by a sharp pain. Glancing down, he saw blood welling through a slash in his sleeve.

Nathan swore and backed a few steps, watching that deadly knife. Yelling for help would bring no one. The only person near enough to hear would be her ladyship and he must protect her, not put her in danger. Had she even locked the door? His longer reach would not get past that knife and to get closer would expose vital parts of his body. He couldn't run because the passageway ended at the stillroom and *that* door he must guard at all costs. Bekkit blocked the only exit.

Then his survival instincts kicked in. He'd almost forgotten his secret weapon! With a shout he jumped forward which, for a moment, confused the valet. Almost within range now of the blade, he simultaneously thrust his hand into his pocket and threw sawdust into his assailant's face. This he instantly followed with a hard kick between Bekkit's legs. The valet gave an agonised scream and crumpled to the floor clutching himself, the knife dropping with a clatter.

Nathan stood trembling, blood flowing in a steady stream down his arm. *Now* he believed the vague rumours he'd heard about Bekkit's un-valet-like skills and with a sinking feeling knew that he could never best the valet in a fight, no matter how superior his size and strength. Only the sawdust and good luck had saved him. Why had Bekkit attacked him? He must have guessed that he guarded Lady Firstbridge. Shock and loss of blood made Nathan feel a little faint, his stunned mind trying to take in what had just happened.

The stillroom door open behind him and light shone into the passageway. He turned to see her ladyship's surprised face.

"What on earth is going on Nathan? I heard a shout." Then her eyes took in the figure of Bekkit curled up on the

176

floor, making mewling noises, and the blood dripping from the footman's arm. With a startled gasp, she beckoned to him.

"Quickly. Come in here and let me see to you. You can tell me what happened while I stem the bleeding."

Pressing his other hand to the injury, Nathan silently followed her into the room and his mistress guided him to a chair. He watched as her ladyship slipped a key from her apron pocket and locked the door. With deft fingers she pushed up his sleeve exposing a nasty gash. She then pressed a folded wad of cloth against the wound and gradually the bleeding slowed, then stopped, while Nathan haltingly told his tale.

"What a clever idea to think of such a simple everyday thing as sawdust to use as a weapon, Nathan."

He coloured with pleasure, then tried not to wince as Lady Firstbridge dowsed his wound with alcohol, stitched it closed and smeared it with honey, one of her favourite remedies she'd told him cheerily. But he knew from her pale face, that fear lurked not far below the calm exterior.

"How has Bekkit become so bold as to feel he can do such a thing with impunity?" she wondered out loud as she wound the bandage around his arm.

"He's guessed I'm watching out for you and obviously doesn't like it, milady." Already the throbbing pain in his arm felt less. "I probably shouldn't tell you but Sir Timothy has set me the task of keeping you safe. He thought the master would be the danger but I fear that Bekkit is even worse. Thought to frighten me off, he did, but I'll not desert you milady." Nathan set his jaw with determination. "I don't know the why of it, but he *won't* succeed."

He had a fair idea what Bekkit had in mind however, after witnessing the scene outside her ladyship's bedroom, but he did not intend making his mistress even more afraid. For her part, Emily felt a little better knowing Sir Timothy had done what he could to help. She tied the bandage off and sat down at her work bench with a weary sigh.

"How I wish Nettie could return soon, Nathan. It's very selfish of me when she has her own family woes to deal with, but I'm lost without her." Emily knew it to be highly irregular for her to be discussing her problems with a footman, but at the moment she lived in a constant state of worry and Nathan's was a friendly ear.

He smiled. "Yes, Miss Perkins is clever." Then he blushed again and hoped her ladyship hadn't noticed. To cover his embarrassment, Emily quickly spoke.

"Do you think Bekkit is still out there? We can't stay in here forever." She glanced fearfully at the locked door.

"Given what I did to him, I don't think he'll be in any shape to harm us. I'll take the key if I may, milady, and have a look."

Emily passed him the key and though he was no knife fighter, he picked up a blade he'd noticed lying on the work bench, just in case, and slowly and carefully unlocked and opened the door. They were both greatly relieved to find the valet gone. Only dribbles of congealing blood and sawdust remained, dark patches trailing across the floor. Nathan escorted his mistress safely to her bedroom, but he feared what Bekkit's next move would be.

******

Two days later, Nathan stood on guard as his mistress interviewed Bekkit in her book room. He made sure the door remained open so he could watch carefully. He wondered how long it had taken the valet to recover from his kick in the ballocks and smiled grimly to himself. As the valet had passed, he'd noticed with satisfaction that his eyes were still a little bloodshot. Nathan watched as Bekkit handed her ladyship a paper which she read with a look of horror. They

178

talked for a while longer then the valet left the room appearing very self-satisfied. He'd smirked at Nathan and glanced at his arm as he strode confidently by. What was that shit-sack up to now?

Lady Firstbridge almost ran to her bedroom and Nathan followed in her wake. She looked ill and close to tears but said nothing. He felt helpless and wished for Miss Perkins' speedy return. Her mistress needed her now more than ever, with both her husband *and* Bekkit to deal with. He sighed glumly. Everything seemed to be getting even more complicated.

Chapter Thirty-four.
Emily.

No one else seems to be aware of Bekkit's attack on Nathan so we both decided to say nothing. Who could I turn to? Certainly not my husband. It had become increasingly obvious that I must stop dithering and seek outside help, but still I hesitated. A few days after the knife incident, the loathsome valet requested another interview. Surely he would not try to repeat his attempt at forcing his unwanted attentions on me with the footman nearby? I presumed there would be a further dreary report on my husband's condition. How wrong—terribly wrong—I was.

Nathan, who has become my shadow, accompanied me to the book room and opened the door to admit Bekkit; he did not need me to tell him to leave it ajar. He could see into the room but could not overhear our conversation. With Nettie away I felt uneasy, however it gave me a little confidence to know my guardian was near. Bekkit strode in with no sign in his posture of the injury inflicted by my protector. He looked like a cat with a bowl of cream and started speaking immediately.

"Milady, I have come to advise you that I have been named by Lord Firstbridge as your son's guardian in the event of his death." And he waved a legal-looking document at me.

With horror I took it and read. Part of my shocked brain registered that Bekkit's first name was John. Such an inconsequential thing to catch my attention. He had always been just...Bekkit. The letterhead looked official, some solicitor in Blakesley, not my husband's. The signature appeared to be his though, written with a trembling hand and affixed with the Firstbridge seal. It had been witnessed by strangers, people Bekkit must have brought in, for I did not recognise their names.

"How can this be?" I choked out, for when James had been born, Sir Timothy had told me in confidence that he would be my baby's guardian if anything should happen to my husband, a thought that had greatly cheered me.

"Your husband has finally recognised me as his son and therefore considers me a suitable protector for my brother," he replied in a gloating voice. Then he took the document from my unresisting hands and with a bow, left me.

Nathan, standing watching in the hallway, could see my distress but words were beyond me. I flew to my room and threw myself onto the bed. A new horror had been visited upon me. Bekkit knew how much I loved my son and that I would do *anything* to keep him safe. It took little imagination to see how he would control me. I sobbed into my pillow and longed for Nettie's comfort.

My storm of weeping finally ceased and I lay there, drained and hopeless. Things had at last come to a head. I had finally reached *point non plus* and would have to write to Sir Timothy and ask for his advice. Surely he would be able to tell me if that horrible document could be overturned. It might not even be legal. Filled with a new determination, I washed my face and went to visit my son. James always makes me feel better. Whatever the outcome, his safety is *everything* to me. My dithering must end. I would write that letter tomorrow.

As it happened, circumstances took charge and altered everything.

Chapter Thirty-five.
In which Nettie is with her family.

Life was so unfair. When her ladyship needed her more than ever, pa had written to say ma had been cruelly struck down. Nettie's heart felt torn in two, but her dear Miss Emily, such a sweet and generous person, had insisted she go to her parents. More than Lord Firstbridge, she feared that horrible Bekkit. Who would think that such a pleasant-looking young man could harbour such an evil nature. She knew he no longer dined in the servant's hall but sat at his lordship's table every night, bold as brass, whether his master dined there or not, and these days he seldom did. The valet put on airs and graces and behaved in a very familiar manner with her ladyship when they met for him to make his reports about his lordship's state of health. Nettie always remained in the room and watched him carefully.

The last time, when he'd stood too close to Miss Emily and looked at her so insolently, she'd seemed almost overwhelmed by him, however Nettie felt that *her* presence gave her ladyship the courage to face him down. She'd noticed how her mistress's shoulders straightened and her chin tilted up when she dismissed the valet. He obviously enjoyed the effect he had on her, so Nettie gave him her best glare. Bekkit had looked challengingly back, an amused and knowing smile on his face as he'd left the room—curse him! Now she couldn't be there to protect her mistress, Nettie hoped a guardian angel watched over Miss Emily to keep her safe. True, Sir Timothy lived nearby but not *in* the house to see what that valet got up to each day and how bad things were getting.

******

When Nettie returned to her family, she found everyone in a state of despair. Pa had temporarily hired a man to run the inn while he sat with ma. Her two older brothers who cared for the horses and acted as postillions were managing on their own but it needed a firm hand to organise the maids and maintain the inn's high standards. She could see how much pa needed her; his tear-stained face had greeted her when she'd stepped out of the Firstbridge carriage.

"Fancy, my little girl riding around in a lord's coach."

He'd tried to sound jolly as he gave her a welcoming hug but she heard the grief in his voice. Her mother looked terrible, the once pretty face gaunt and grey. Nettie's parents held hands as if her father could pour himself into ma, trying with the strength of his love to make her better. The doctor called and looked grave as he took Nettie aside and explained that the end could not be far. She returned to sit at her mother's side and clasped the frail little hand in her own; it felt just skin and bone. She forced a smile onto her face.

"Now ma, you are not to worry about a thing. I'll soon get everything running smoothly. You know how I love to ring a peal over a nodcock." She could see her ma relax and try to smile and knew how worried she'd been.

The cure for a breaking heart is hard work, so Nettie became a whirlwind. The hired man, cook and maids found themselves chivvied into giving of their best, and soon she had everything running smoothly. She would dearly love to have spent more time with her mother, but knew that what she did would give her ma peace of mind.

In spite of the doctor's prediction, her darling mother lived another two weeks. She clung to life for her family's sake, Nettie believed, but in the end, the disease that ate away at her insides overcame her precarious hold on life. Her father, who had always been so strong and cheerful, collapsed like a falling tree and Nettie could not bear to leave him.

Her ma's funeral included everyone in the village. Even the local gentry, who had enjoyed her mother's wonderful hospitality, made an appearance at the church. After, at the funeral repast in the inn's common room, the roar of many voices echoed off the walls. When the door finally closed on the last mourner, her father sat in the bedroom, holding one of his wife's night rails to his face, breathing in her scent and quietly weeping.

Nettie kept her own grief to herself and supported her family. Her two younger brothers were bereft having lost their mother while still only boys so they needed her to hold them while they cried out their sorrow. She wondered about their futures. Her two older brothers were being trained to take over the running of the inn but the younger boys had no desire to stay, so she decided to discuss this with her ladyship when she returned to Amberleigh.

******

She remained with her family until her father could cope again, employing a competent woman to oversee the inside staff, and fearing every moment for her Miss Emily's safety. The day she sent for the Firstbridge carriage lifted a great weight from her shoulders. Nettie arrived back to hear startling news.

Chapter Thirty-six.
Simon.

Dear Simon,

I have need of your special puzzle-solving skills. A rather self-important fellow, cousin and once heir to Lord Firstbridge, has raised concerns about the recent death in a fire of his friend, a Dr Caukwell. You may have met the good doctor on one of your visits here. An autopsy has been performed on what was left of the badly burned body showing that the neck had been broken. This may have been caused by a fallen beam. The corpse, what was left of it, lay before the fireplace in the study where the blaze originated and the question needing an answer is what had he been doing there in the early hours of the morning? My supposition and that of the surgeon who conducted the autopsy, is simply that he smelled smoke and came downstairs to investigate and became trapped. Perhaps the study fire had not been banked properly and a smouldering log fell out onto the carpet. The fire burned fiercely, so it is hard to tell. However, to put all suspicion to rest, I should like you to stay for a week and use your unusual skills to unravel the sequence of events, at your convenience of course. Please let me know what dates would suit.

Kind regards,

Your humble servant,

Timothy Badger, Bart.

I placed the letter on my desk and stared thoughtfully out of the window. I would have to ask permission of course, but I had every intention of returning to Northamptonshire as soon as possible. My heart beat a little faster at the thought of being close to Milady Grey-eyes again, for I would most definitely call on her and convince myself of her safety, in spite of Sir Timothy's assurances.

I showed my stepfather the letter.

"By all means, Simon. Finish up those few reports we've been working on and you are free to go. And don't forget to give my regards to Sir Timothy and Lady Badger."

I sent a quick note to Sir Timothy advising him I would be there in three days. Rather than take the mail coach, I hired a post chaise and spent the journey drifting between thoughts of my coming assignment and delightful daydreams of Lady Firstbridge. Well after dusk we drew up at the entrance to Leafybrook where Sir Timothy and his cheerful wife waited in the lamp light to greet me.

"Simon, my boy, it's been a while since you visited us. I knew my little mystery would entice you here."

I retrieved my valise and dismissed the post chaise, whose postillion and groom would spend the night at a local inn, at my expense, before returning to London in the morning. Sir Timothy patted my weary shoulders as I accompanied my host and hostess into the hall. A chill still hung in the evening air even though we were now moving from spring to summer. They led me to the drawing room fire and a glass of brandy was thrust into my hands. With a murmured thanks I sipped it gratefully.

"I'm not going to bother you tonight, Simon, but further events have occurred since I wrote you. We'll discuss them tomorrow. Lady Badger has arranged for a tray to be sent to your room—we have already dined—so you may relax and not worry about changing for dinner. I know you don't have a valet, but if you need his services, my man will be happy to oblige."

I am accustomed to managing for myself, so smilingly declined. When the housekeeper escorted me to my room, she told me a bath was being prepared. I found my bag unpacked and a tray piled high with a tasty selection of meats, relishes, cheeses, bread, fruit and cakes. The footmen brought in the tub, filled it with hot water, and soon I soaked in bliss, a glass of claret in one hand and a filling sandwich in the other. I drowsily wondered what new development had occurred but tiredness affected me too much to care. Tomorrow would be soon enough to find out. I struggled from the bath, dried myself and, donned my nightshirt. The footmen removed the tub and I crawled wearily into bed. The maid had run a warming pan between the sheets and in this soothing comfort I closed my eyes. As I drifted into slumber, my last thoughts were of Lady Firstbridge.

******

Over breakfast the next morning, Sir Timothy broke the startling news.

"There has been murder done at Amberleigh," he announced grimly.

I went cold and my shock must have shown on my face.

"No, no, it's not little Emily," he hastily assured me, "Nathan, the footman I set to guarding her, has been doing his job, but that madman, her husband, appears to have murdered his valet and then dropped dead himself."

"When did this occur Sir Timothy?"

"Not long after I posted you the letter about the doctor's death. Lady Firstbridge sent for me and from my observations and the autopsies, it appears to be straightforward, however, I would like you to write a report

188

for me after you have interviewed the Amberleigh staff and her ladyship. So now you have three deaths to investigate."

"Certainly sir. I'll get on to it straight after breakfast." My fear at the thought of harm coming to Lady Firstbridge eased. "I would like to see the autopsy reports for all three deaths but firstly perhaps you could show me the house where the doctor died. I'll start with that."

Sir Timothy had his curricle brought to the front entrance and soon we were bowling along at a brisk pace. I admired my host's handling of his mettlesome pair and his dexterity with the whip.

"Yes, I am a founding member of the B.D.C. you know," he remarked proudly.

Every young gentleman knew and longed to belong to the Bensington Driving Club, or its rival, the newly established Four Horse Club, and I was no exception. When Sir Timothy offered to give me some pointers, I almost forgot the purpose of my visit, I was so delighted. The short drive passed in most pleasant instruction.

Dr Caukwell's house, or what remained of it, sat on the edge of the village a few miles from Leafybrook Park. Parts of it were still standing but the rest remained as a blackened skeleton and several village boys, with the promise of a sixpence a day, had been charged by Sir Timothy with protecting the ruin from thieves until I had done my inspection. So far, no family member had come forward to claim Dr Caukwell's belongings. After paying off the young guards, we climbed gingerly through the ash and charred timbers and Sir Timothy showed me the exact spot in front of the study fireplace where the body had been found, lying under a fallen beam. The scorched bricks of the chimney remained as a gaunt finger pointing to the sky.

The only live-in servant, the cook-housekeeper, who had survived and now resided with her daughter in the village, had slept at the back, a good distance from the seat of the fire. Both her bedroom and the doctor's had remained remarkably unscathed, the wind having blown the flames away from that side of the house. The staircase being deemed unsafe, we borrowed a ladder from a neighbour some distance away and I climbed gingerly into the second storey and walked carefully around the doctor's bedroom.

One wall had been a touch scorched but otherwise there appeared to be no damage. The furnishings were rather austere with a bed, a clothespress, a chest of drawers and a chamberpot and washstand tucked away discreetly in a corner cupboard. A rug, rucked up, lay on the floor. Ash had drifted in with a wind change and coated everything.

I looked inside the drawers and the clothespress. It surprised me to see the doctor's clothing still present and I could tell at a glance it was of good quality. The bed covers were greatly rumpled as if someone had left it in a hurry and the pillow still had the indentation of the doctor's head. I absentmindedly straightened the rug with the toe of my boot and as I did so a glint caught my eye. I stooped to pick up a metal button with a small piece of dark fabric attached that had perhaps come from a coat and fallen into the folds. I returned to the clothespress and soon discovered that no button appeared missing from any of the garments, so I put it in my pocket and having satisfied myself there remained nothing else to see, climbed back down to the ground floor. I did not mention the find to my host.

After returning the ladder, we went to the daughter's house to interview the doctor's housekeeper, a small, weepy woman I suspected of being a little deaf, but she had nothing of real importance to add. She had been woken on the night in question, most likely by the crash of a beam falling, smelled smoke, seen the flames and been too terrified to check on the doctor before running to her daughter. No, she'd heard no voices nor seen anyone. The village fire brigade had arrived but the house was well alight by then and there was little they could do to save it.

We drove back to the hall, and following luncheon, sat in Sir Timothy's study while I read through the three autopsy reports. The one for Lord Firstbridge filled me with horror. Milady Grey-eyes was in danger! I looked fearfully at my host.

"Sir, h-has Lady Firstbridge been…"

He hastened to reassure me. "No, my boy, I thought of the same thing, but the surgeon assured me there is a period in the disease when the infection is dormant. It can last for many years, even decades, before it finally flares up to destroy its host. I spoke to her ladyship immediately and advised her to visit a doctor in Kettering; he is rather an expert in that field. She has done so, and advised me that all is well with her and baby James."

I heaved an enormous sigh of relief. I believe Sir Timothy and Lady Badger were well aware of my feelings for the mistress of Amberleigh. And now she had been made a widow, I'm ashamed to say, I felt only gladness.

I sent a note to Lady Firstbridge asking if it would be convenient for me to call the following morning to interview the staff. A reply rapidly returned saying she would expect me at eleven. I went for a walk and thought about that button and scrap of cloth in my pocket and the irony that if the doctor had stayed in his bedroom he would most likely have survived the fire. Lady Badger served a very nice dinner; William was away at university but the two oldest daughters played and sang for us and the evening concluded with an exciting game of whist.

Lying in bed, with hands behind my head, I thought about my appointment with the mistress of Amberleigh. Would I still feel the same when I looked into those amazing eyes again? I must not let her distract me from my investigation but it would be hard. She would be in mourning of course but surely that would be just a social formality. Who could mourn the monster that her husband had become? I thought of tomorrow's meeting with elation.

Chapter Thirty-seven.
Simon.

I had come alone, riding one of Sir Timothy's horses. He deemed it wiser to allow me free rein to question how I saw fit, without another's influence. The butler ushered me into Lady Firstbridge's book room, where she sat waiting with her lady's maid. I had already been informed that Miss Perkins had only recently returned to Amberleigh from a family bereavement. Her ladyship was sewing what looked like a child's garment.

I realised she'd had barely more than a year and a half before being plunged back into mourning again. After laying her work aside, she rose and came towards me, a smile of happy recognition on her face and her hands extended in welcome. I took them in mine and lost myself in those lovely grey eyes. I had the almost irresistible urge to sweep her into my arms and cover her with kisses but I forced myself to concentrate.

"Milady, I am sorry to intrude at this time, but Sir Timothy has asked me to write a report on the disturbing events of last week." As I bowed over her hands it broke the almost mesmerising eye contact. When I looked up again they were sad and her face drawn.

"Yes, I understand Mr Mannering. You will know, if you have spoken to Sir Timothy, that the past months have been…very difficult," she murmured. I released her and she then asked me where I would like to begin.

"I shall be as quick as possible milady. Firstly I would like to speak to your staff, if I may. Where would be convenient?"

She showed me to her late husband's study where the desk had been cleared and paper, ink and pens prepared for me. A very tall young man in footman's livery accompanied us.

"This is Nathan. He will be at your disposal and see to anything you may require Mr Mannering." Then with a shy smile she left us.

I spoke to Nathan first, observing him carefully, and feeling satisfied with what I saw. "I know of Sir Timothy's arrangement and I thank you for your protection of her ladyship," I began quietly.

The footman looked grim. "This house has been full of danger for a long time, sir. Her ladyship lived in fear of both her husband and that *valet*, but Peebles made sure I always stayed near her once he received the note from Sir Timothy." He spat the word 'valet' with venom. "No one is sorry they are both gone," he added with satisfaction.

Shame filled me that I should be so jealous of this young man who had been Milady Grey-eyes' guardian when I could not. "What can you tell me about the morning of the deaths?" I then asked.

"Well, sir, I accompanied Polly, that's the maid who cleans the grates. She wouldn't go into his room without a footmen, scared of the pistol you see. We went up at seven thirty as usual and the first thing we saw was the valet, lying on the floor near the bed in a pool of blood and coffee, the tray with broken china lying beside him. Polly screamed and I had to catch her when she fainted. I left her lying on the floor and checked if Bekkit still breathed—he didn't. I could see he'd been shot through the heart—his chest a right mess.

194

Then I checked Lord Firstbridge. He lay on his back in the bed with the pistol in his hand. Dead too, but I could see no obvious injury." He looked solemn at the memory. "After that I ran to get Peebles."

"Did you hear a pistol shot that morning?" I asked.

"No sir. Before I came up with Polly we were in the servants hall having breakfast. After seeing Polly into his lordship's bedroom, I would normally station myself outside her ladyship's room. We did tend to ignore odd noises like that anyway, his lordship being rather fond of firing at imagined burglars. You probably know of his mad fits through Sir Timothy. It was common knowledge hereabouts. I can show you some of the bullet holes in the walls if you like," he added.

I thanked him and asked to speak to Polly next. She came in timidly and in a gentle voice I told her to sit and asked for her name. She was shaking with fright as she perched on the edge of the chair.

"P-Polly sir."

"Now Polly, I want you to tell me exactly what you saw when you went into Lord Firstbridge's bedroom to light the fire on the day he died."

Polly immediately burst into tears. "Oh sir, it were terrible! Blood everywhere and Nathan, that's the footman, had to catch me when I fainted," she sobbed.

It became hard to get the girl to speak coherently. Recalling it all again reduced her almost to hysterics but I had Nathan's clear report so didn't detain her further.

One by one I interviewed the rest of the staff and heard about the atmosphere of fear his lordship's insanity had created, the gradual change in the status of Bekkit, his lordship's obsession with burglars, and his sleeping with a gun in an always candlelit room. One question I asked repeatedly—had no one heard the shot that killed the valet? I knew the time of his death because his lordship's coffee always came at seven. And Firstbridge must have died soon after as Polly cleaned the grates at seven thirty. Some had heard a pistol's report but the answer never varied. No one thought it unusual to hear shots, screams and shouting. Best to ignore it and stay out of danger was the often repeated refrain. And poor Lady Firstbridge and young Master James were most at risk. They had all seen their mistress bruised and bloodied on several occasions.

On hearing this I seethed with impotent fury. Curse the man to hell! If he had not already been dead I would have been tempted to finish him myself. Now I truly understood Sir Timothy's concerns. Slowly and patiently I formed a picture in my mind of the scene.

At one thirty, Lady Firstbridge invited me to luncheon and I spent the next little while trying to make her smile. In the afternoon, at my request, Nathan took me to Lord Firstbridge's bedroom; he showed me exactly where the bodies had lain. I then dismissed my guide and stood still, absorbing my surroundings. The room spoke of great wealth, sumptuously decorated with an un-curtained four-poster bed, carved of exotic woods and covered with a beautifully embroidered silk coverlet and plump pillows. The walls were wood-panelled to waist height and above the panelling, a gold-embossed maroon wallpaper reflected the light from the large windows. These were framed by dark gold, velvet curtains, held back with elaborate ties. There were many candle holders, though at the moment the candles were unlit. Priceless paintings hung everywhere. I am no art connoisseur but I recognised a Giotto, several by Gainsborough and a Titian, to name but a few. The bloodied rug had been replaced but in spite of its rich appointments and warm colours, the room felt dark and somehow depressing. I berated myself for these fanciful notions and walked through to the dressing room. Decorated in a similar fashion, it had two walls of beautifully finished cabinets plus a long mirror, a sofa, a comfortable chair, a writing desk and chair, and a dresser. In one corner, behind an ornately carved wooden screen, stood a spacious copper bath tub. Both rooms had fireplaces, now empty.

Standing in front of the desk, I eyed it thoughtfully. I considered myself an expert at ferreting out hidden drawers, one of the quirks of my puzzle-solving mind and my instincts told me that this desk would surely have one. After only a few minutes and a bit of fiddling I discovered its secret; within, I found a series of rather disgusting etchings. These I put into my pocket, not wishing Lady Firstbridge to see them. The drawer also contained gambling vowels from prominent gentlemen of the *ton,* stuffed in untidy bundles. I whistled when I saw the amounts. These were worth a fortune and some were dated back more than a year. Amongst them was a sizeable collection tied together and signed by Dr Caukwell.

The doctor's vowels went into my pocket and I proceeded to the valet's room. The maids had stripped it bare; the top mattress sat rolled up on the unmade bed, the set of drawers and the clothespress empty. However, I had already been told of the discovered paperwork showing a very substantial bank account in the valet's name, the jewellery, expensive clothes and the bundle of hidden valuables. I stood in the centre of that cold and impersonal space and frowned. Something felt not quite right; then I realised what had puzzled me—the almost undetectable smell of smoke in a room with no fireplace.

My eyes swept across the few pieces of furniture and stopped at the bed. Though the upper mattress had been rolled up, the thin under mattress still lay over the rope base. Slowly I pulled it back. Underneath, pressed flat, lay rough, dark workingman's trousers and also a coat. I picked it up and sniffed. *Yes!* I had found the source of that faint smoke smell. I could see a button and a small patch of cloth

197

missing. I felt in my pocket for the one I had found in the doctor's bedroom. It matched those on the jacket and the fabric appeared to be the same!

Now, I believed I understood what had happened. I took one last look around, passed back through the dressing room and into Lord Firstbridge's bedroom. I crossed to the other door which opened into a small sitting room. I had been told that beyond would be her ladyship's room, another dressing room and then the one for the lady's maid. As Miss Perkins had been sent home for a family bereavement and had been away on the morning of the murder she would have nothing to add. Satisfied that I had all the information I needed, I poked my head into the hallway to find Nathan patiently waiting for me.

Returning to the book room, I came upon her ladyship playing with her son. Miss Perkins, with a look of contentment on her face, sat watching. The baby crawled towards his mother and hauled himself up at her knee. She looked at him with such naked love, I turned away feeling that I intruded on so private a moment, but she swept him into her arms and welcomed me with a smile. I knew, before I took my leave, that I had one last question. I felt uncomfortable but I must ask it.

"Forgive me milady, but did you hear the pistol shot that killed the valet? I noticed that only one room separates you from Lord Firstbridge's bedroom."

She sighed and looked incredibly sad. "Yes I did Mr Mannering, but in this house gun shots were largely ignored as they were a frequent occurrence. Better to stay ignorant—and safe." She said no more.

As it had now begun to rain, Lady Firstbridge offered me the use of the carriage to return to Leafybrook Park so I tied my horse to the back and said goodbye, with promises to advise her of my findings as soon as I had finished my report. She came to the door with me and my last view of her, as the coach carried me away, was of a little black-clad figure, partially obscured by the rain and looking lost against the magnificent facade of the hall. I must put her out of my mind and focus on my report I firmly reminded myself. But it would not be easy.

I found Sir Timothy in his study and we sat together with glasses of brandy. I handed him the etchings.

"I removed these from the secret drawer in Lord Firstbridge's desk," I said, keeping my voice level. "They were with scores of vowels—a small fortune's worth."

With a grimace, he glanced at them, then without a word screwed them up and threw them into the grate.

I talked about the link I had found between the fire and Amberleigh. "I believe, sir, that the doctor owed Lord Firstbridge a great deal of money." I produced the bundle of vowels I had pocketed and placed them in front of my host. "Perhaps he attempted blackmailing his lordship into forgetting the debts. The autopsy indicated quite clearly that his lordship's syphilis had progressed to a life-threatening stage and the doctor would be aware of that. However, as I found no blackmail letter, it is only a supposition but still a reasonable one I believe. If there *had* been a letter, no doubt he burned it. Firstbridge would not want his affliction made public knowledge. It would create a very unwelcome scandal. Insane, Lord Firstbridge may have been, but he still seemed to have times of lucidity according to the staff. Whatever the reason, he sent his valet to kill the doctor, and I am very sure of my ground here." I pulled out the button and explained how it matched the smoke-scented clothing hidden in the valet's room.

"I gather from your description, the doctor was not a big man, and I believe his neck was broken in the bedroom, and during the struggle he tore the button from his assailant's coat. Bekkit then carried the body down to the study and started the fire, making sure all the doctor's records were destroyed in the process. No doubt he noticed the missing button when he returned to Amberleigh but no one would be able to trace it back to him once he'd destroyed the evidence. His own demise soon after prevented him from doing so." I paused in my report and Sir Timothy nodded in agreement.

"The housekeeper's room is well away from the doctor's and as she is apparently a sound sleeper and I believe a little deaf, she told me she heard nothing until the crash of falling timbers woke her," I added.

"I think your summary is fairly conclusive Simon." And he looked pleased with me.

I continued talking. "Now as to the other deaths, both you and Nathan informed me of the position of the bodies. From the trajectory of the bullet and combined with the fact that the murder weapon was in his lordship's hand, I believe his lordship shot his valet. I'm afraid the reason for the killing will never truly be known. Perhaps Lord Firstbridge, in one of his sane moments, realised his valet had been stealing from him and they had an argument, but more likely he shot him during a fit of madness, for the staff say he slept with a pistol and had an obsessive fear of burglars. I understand his valet usually made sure it was kept unloaded but this time his luck ran out. However it happened, his lordship killed a man who had already committed murder so it makes an odd sort of justice. As for Lord Firstbridge, the surgeon has already concluded his horrifying disease caused his death. I read the autopsy report, remember," I added grimly, a look of distaste on my face.

"Write it up my boy and I shall sign it. Congratulations on a job well done." And Sir Timothy lifted his glass in a toast.

A week's leave had been given to me so, after writing out my conclusions the following morning, and satisfied with the result, the time had come to enjoy myself. The thing that would please me most would be to see Milady Grey-eyes. Using the excuse of presenting my report, I rode over the following afternoon. Lady Firsbridge greeted me with most gratifying warmth and after I had explained my understanding of the gruesome events, we forgot about the horrors of the past and just enjoyed each other's company. Sir Timothy, Lady Badger and I were invited to dine the following evening and I returned to Leafybrook, lighthearted and hopeful.

Mr Netherby, the steward had also been invited. He is a pleasant faced, middle-aged gentleman, well-spoken and refined. I noticed, with twinges of jealousy, how he doted on his mistress. In the drawing room, where we had gathered before dinner, James came to meet the guests and bid his mother good night. He has already developed a small vocabulary and amused us all with his happy baby talk. When the nurse finally carried him away to bed he objected loudly.

What a happy household it felt now, I mused, looking at the animated faces around the dinner table in the soft candlelight. And then my eyes turned to my hostess. She is the centre of this small universe; has survived a time of terror and despair to come through it all as a stronger woman, though I knew her to be only seventeen. My heart swelled with love and at that moment I finally admitted to myself how much she meant to me. She had been scarred by her horrific marriage so I would be patient and quietly court her, but I determined that Milady Grey-eyes would eventually be mine. Her mourning would last for a year, so I had plenty of time.

Chapter Thirty-eight.
Emily.

It is wonderful having dearest Nettie back. She has been away for so long seeing to her mother's funeral and helping her distraught father settle their family's affairs. When she stepped down from the coach I gave her a big hug.

"Oh Nettie, I missed you very much. I hope your papa isn't too lost without you and your mother. Terrible things happened here while you were gone. I did not like to write and burden you as you already had enough to deal with. First the doctor died in a fire, then Bekkit was shot and Lord Firstbridge died." It gave me such relief to let it all flood out. Poor Nettie. She'd come back to hear more woes.

"Don't you stress yourself Miss Emily. Pa's managing, and I found a good woman to help him. I know I shouldn't say this, but I'm glad his lordship and that valet have both departed. They made your life a hell, and that's most likely where they are now." Her face looked grim. Then she smiled. "Now don't you think about it anymore. I'll just put my things in my room and join you for a nice cup of tea and a chat about all the things James has learned while I've been away. I missed him terribly."

Nettie is such a comfort, I felt better already. I fetched James and we settled in the book room. He crowed with delight at seeing her—she has always spoiled him terribly—and managed a few wobbly steps towards her open arms. With James sitting happily in Nettie's lap, we talked.

"I wanted to ask you about my younger brothers Miss Emily. They don't want to work at the inn— pa's got the two older ones for that. Robbie is very good with horses and Davie wants to be an engineer—he's mad about mechanical things. I don't know the first thing about how to arrange an apprenticeship and wondered if Mr Netherby would be able to help." While she talked Nettie bounced my chortling son on her knee.

"That's a good idea. I'm sure he'll know how to go about it, and as for Robbie, he can come here. We can always use a good lad in the stables" I sent for Mr Netherby and soon matters were settled, much to Nettie's relief.

I gather the funeral services of Lord Firstbridge and Bekkit were very discreet and felt only relief that I did not have to attend. In my more fanciful moments I wondered if they *were* keeping each other company in hell as Nettie had suggested.

Sir Timothy has managed to mute the scandal. Bekkit already being dead, meant he could suppress the facts of the doctor's murder, and I am sure that something else will soon excite the interest of the gossipmongers. Nettie and I are both in black and I feel I have been in mourning forever, though I can't wait for my current one to end. I think of the contrast in my feelings this time— grieving for my father had been true and meaningful. This farce I enact for my late husband is just that—a performance for society. I feel nothing but a great release and joy that my son is now safe.

At the funeral repast after my husband's interment, Mr Jeremiah Wolffe, his distant cousin whom I had never met, was introduced to me. He appeared to be a rather pompous young man, plump and soberly dressed, not at all how I had imagined him after overhearing some of milord's disparaging remarks. He has asked to meet the new Lord

Firstbridge at some future date; he is still the heir until my son reaches adulthood and has children of his own. I cannot see any objection, so he is to call at Amberleigh soon.

******

Upon his arrival, I asked Peebles to show Mr Wolffe to the library. It seemed a more fitting setting than the drawing room, or my informal book room, for such a serious fellow. When I joined him he stood, hands clasped behind his back, gazing through the open french doors into the garden. He turned and came towards me with a polite smile on his face and bowed over my hand.

"How pleasing it is to see you again, Lady Firstbridge. You shine in the eyes of the Lord."

This address startled me a little. "Why, thank you Mr Wolffe," I replied, as I bade him be seated. I presumed he meant it as a compliment.

"I am aware of my late cousin's iniquities and thankfully you have not been blighted by them. *Be aware and of sober mind. Your enemy, the devil, prowls around like a roaring lion looking for someone to devour. Peter Chapter 5 Verse 8,*" he intoned as he solemnly stared into my eyes.

I could not think of a single adequate reply and into the awkward silence blurted. "Would you like to meet James now, before his afternoon sleep?"

"Most assuredly. *Children are a gift from the Lord; they are a reward from him. Psalm Chapter 127, Verse 3,*" he replied, still pinning me with his eyes.

I could see conversation was going to be difficult. Sir Timothy had told me that Jeremiah Wolffe and Dr Caukwell had been friends when the doctor lived in Oxford and owing to the wide age gap, I wondered how they had found a common ground, they seemed such different people. Perhaps it had been a friendship of expediency, the doctor discovering that Mr Wolffe was an earl's heir. It is my cynicism showing again.

A footman was summoned to have James brought to the library and send the maid with tea and cakes.

While we waited, I made small talk. "I believe you were a friend of the late Dr Caukwell." I framed this question as a statement. The doctor's funeral had taken place during the deaths at Amberleigh, and I wondered if Jeremiah had attended.

"The Lord giveth and the Lord taketh away. Job Chapter 1 Verse 21," he quoted piously.

I persevered. "How did you meet?" I knew my blunt questioning to be rude, but talking to the man was not easy.

"Robert assisted the local apothecary. My mother is an invalid and I frequently called on his services."

"I'm sorry to hear that, but I'm afraid I know little of my late husband's extended family," I interjected apologetically.

"Then he left Oxford," he continued. "and we lost touch. The next time we met, some while later, he had become a physician. Mother found him a comfort and he served her devotedly. She went into a decline when he moved his practice here. We did keep in touch though, and when I had not heard from him in a while I made enquiries and discovered he'd died." He looked suitably sad.

This advancement from apothecary's assistant to physician all sounded rather suspicious to me and hardened my belief that Dr Caukwell had been a fraud. I changed the subject. "And what are you intending to do with your own life?"

"I am planning on taking holy orders and hope to obtain a living upon completing my degree. I understand the earl has several in his gift," he said hopefully.

"I believe they are all taken but I will have to consult with Mr Netherby, the steward, to be sure," I replied, relieved to hear him speaking sentences without a biblical quotation dangling from the end.

Thankfully, James arrived with his nurse. She put him down and he staggered towards me with arms outstretched.

"Mama, mama!" I picked him up and cuddled him, smelling his lovely little boy smell.

"James, this is your father's cousin. Say hullo, darling."

He looked at this strange man from the safety of my arms. "Huwo," he said then turned to me with a shy smile and put his arms around my neck. My heart melted.

"Start children off on the way they should go, and even when they are old they will not turn from it. Proverbs Chapter 22, Verse 6," Jeremiah said solemnly.

With an effort I did not roll my eyes, however his next comment redeemed him a little.

"He is a fine, healthy looking little boy, Cousin Emily. You must be very proud of him."

Hmmmm. I had become 'Cousin Emily' now. And then it occurred to me that perhaps he had been hoping for a sickly child? I mentally chastised myself for my uncharitable thoughts.

His nurse had brought James' blocks down so I sat him on the floor and after he'd decided the stranger could be safely ignored, happily played with them while we talked. Afternoon tea arrived and I waited to hear a relevant quote, but instead Jeremiah eyed the cakes and biscuits and filled his plate. We discussed his studies and his dreams for the future. I find with young men, it is best to ask questions about their own doings, for then I can sit back, keeping an interested look on my face—with the occasional nod thrown in—and never say another word. So it came as a surprise, when shortly he leaned forward and fixed me with his intense gaze again.

"Your beauty should not come from outward adornment, such as elaborate hairstyles and the wearing of gold jewellery or fine clothes. Rather, it should be that of your inner self, the unfading beauty of a gentle and quiet spirit, which is of great worth in God's sight. Peter, Chapter 3, Verses 3 to 6."

I'd had enough biblical quotations for one day, and the direction they were taking seemed to be getting personal. I feared he would be spouting the *Song of Solomon* next and that, I would not allow.

"It is so nice of you to call Mr Wolffe, but it is time for James' nap and I always like to put him down myself. I shall check with the steward about the livings and let you know." I rose to my feet, which forced my guest to do likewise, a cloud of cake crumbs scattering to the floor. After clutching my hand and offering profuse thanks, I finally managed to get rid of him.

"Oh Miss Emily, I think he's taken a fancy to you and intends to come courting," Nettie teased when I later recounted the conversation.

I paled at the thought. "I hardly think it likely; I would be much too scientific for him, I'm sure. His conversation is definitely suited to a career in the church," I added firmly.

******

Since the funerals and Mr Mannering's questions, Nettie has never again mentioned the deaths in my presence, for which I am thankful. I never want to speak or think of my late husband or his valet ever again.

******

James is one today! I can hardly believe it. I am so looking forward to teaching him to ride when he is a little older. Dear old Bluebell will be perfect for him. I invited his cousin Charles and the younger Badger children for a birthday luncheon. Sophie, who has returned from town to escape the heat, is increasing again and looking rather drawn. Now of course I understand how she feels. Poor Sophie. She had been so radiant with her first, too.

The birthday party proved a great success. I look at my darling boy who is now Lord Firstbridge. Such a big title for so small a fellow. I insist the staff refer to him as *Master* James. I cannot bear the thought of him carrying that weighty load when he is so young. The nurse finally came to take my ice-cream-covered boy for his afternoon sleep. Sophie sent Charles home and the Badger children amused themselves with games, while we ladies settled down to tea and conversation. What a happy day it has been.

When my husband's will had been read, as I'd already known, Sir Timothy became my son's executor and his guardian. If his lordship could not bring himself to name me, then who better? That would be the only time he had pleased me—then I remembered he'd allowed our son to be named after my papa, *and* Mrs Crombie for my lying-in, so apart from giving me my beautiful baby, that made three good things in that horrible marriage.

My dowry is returned to me as my widow's portion but Mr Netherby has invested wisely so it has increased in value. I shall definitely reward him for his efforts. The bulk of the rest, which is enormous—apart from a few smaller requests—goes to James on his twenty-fifth birthday. In the meantime it will be administered by Mr Netherby and Sir Timothy.

I destroyed the vowels that Mr Mannering found in the secret drawer, wanting nothing to do with them. After Bekkit's death, I had searched for and found the document he had persuaded my husband to sign, and burned it. Only I and the solicitor who composed it were even aware of its existence and as the valet is now dead it no longer matters.

Tomorrow, James, Nettie and I will receive Dr Jenner's cowpox vaccine. I am a little worried but Dr Stanhope, the young physician who moved into the neighbourhood after Dr Caukwell's demise, assures me the procedure is safe, much safer that the smallpox inoculation favoured by the royal family. We will be a little sick and feverish he tells me but will be protected from the ravages of that dreadful disease. I have also encouraged the staff to be vaccinated at my expense and even convinced Sir Timothy of its efficacy. He in turn has persuaded Mr Mannering and the Ferris's to have the vaccine. Dr Stanhope, who trained in Edinburgh, has many progressive ideas and is a follower of Dr Alexander Gordon so I like him immensely.

I have so much hope for the future. Though, to all intents and purposes, I am still in mourning—and I feel rather hypocritical about that—I have decided to visit the city in a few months to make some decisions with regard to the town house. Mr Netherby says that as it is hardly used, now that my husband has gone, it would make good financial sense to rent it out. Sir Timothy trusts my judgement and is happy to endorse my decisions. I intend taking James with me, as by then the dangerous, hot months would have passed. I have never been to town during summer but apparently the heat is most unpleasant I have been told, and the smell from the Thames is appalling. While I am there I shall be ordering a whole new wardrobe, not in blacks and greys and purples, but all of the most fashionable colours. When next summer arrives I shall be re-born.

And then there is Mr Mannering. We have become such good friends. Sir Timothy invites him to stay often and when he is there I see him every day, either out riding, calling on me, or when I dine at Leafybrook. I know he is fond of me, his eyes are so full of tenderness, but he always behaves with perfect propriety. As we have become good friends, he has asked if we may speak on first name terms and I have agreed. "Simon." I say it out aloud when I am alone, the name so dear to my ears. Have we become like brother and sister? But I don't want him as a brother, I tell myself. I am so confused.

When he is in town, he writes to me regularly and I await his letters with warm anticipation. They are full of his detecting adventures and scandals of the *ton*, written in such a way as to make me laugh. I am not sure how I would react if he kissed me. The attention I received in my marriage from both my husband and that vile Bekkit seems to have created in me an aversion to any physical contact, except of course with Nettie and my baby. I am torn!

Then I think of Sir Timothy and Lady Badger; it is obvious to everyone how much they love each other. Lady Badger is increasing again I hear. And I remember the affection of my own parents too. When my year of mourning is up, perhaps Simon will become more than just my friend. I feel my heart give a little flutter. After all, I never loved my husband nor he me. Surely it is different between a man and a woman if there is love? The Badgers and my parents are good examples. I have just finished a reply to Simon's latest letter and on a sudden impulse I kissed the paper next to my signature before I sealed it. I wonder if he does the same when he writes to me? I blush at my thoughts.

Chapter Thirty-nine.
Simon.

Milady Grey-eyes has moved to town! She is still in mourning so cannot attend balls and routs but I have called on her and invited her to dinner at my mother's request, or rather *my* request channelled through my mother. Lady Edale has discreetly introduced the widowed Lady Firstbridge into society and already the *ton* are knocking at her door. She is young, beautiful, wealthy, and well-connected. Fortunately she has not been touched by the scandal of her husband's demise which is as it should be. I will have to keep a careful eye on my rivals, I realise.

I know Lady Edale looks on me with favour but would she still do so if she knew I wished to court her niece? I have no independent means; everything I have has been earned by my own hand—or rather head. Is what I do classed as trade? I know the *ton* are very much against anything that smacks of it, which is quite hypocritical, as many of them have shares in all sorts of business enterprises. There is a duke in my antecedents so I could make sure I brought that up in conversation. Then I feel ashamed of myself. Emily puts more value on qualities other than wealth and titles. My time with her has shown me a warm, generous heart and an ever curious mind.

The dinner party went very well. The 'special' guest looked ravishing in a pale silvery-grey silk that matched her eyes. My mother watched me and I knew she could see what

I felt. I'm sure I positively glow when I am near my darling, who returns my attention with delightful smiles; this gives me hope. Dare I believe it is love? Mother has heard a little of that terrible first marriage and I know she feels lucky herself, to have been wed to two such kind and considerate gentlemen. Though she has not said anything to me as yet, remembering the time before my two sisters were born, I suspect that she is increasing.

******

It is St Nicholas's Day and I arrived in Grosvenor Square in a flurry of snow, with an enormous bunch of hothouse flowers for Emily, a posy for Nettie—I am allowed to call her that, now we have become friends—and a book of children's stories for James. Laughter and music greeted me as I entered the drawing room. A huge tree—decorated with candles in tiny brass holders, oranges and paper flowers—takes pride of place. Flames leap in the fireplace, its mantle decorated with greenery and the scents of fir needles and mulled wine sweeten the air. Emily—in my heart I still call her Milady Grey-eyes—face flushed with laughter, drew me forward.

"Oh Simon, thank you for the wonderful flowers. We have been playing such fun games. Do please join us."

I looked around the room and saw Andrew, Viscount Livington and Lucy Brookington—Emily's cousins, William Badger and the oldest two Badger girls, who had been invited to stay with Emily, and several other young ladies and gentlemen I didn't recognise. I noticed Nettie, now more Emily's companion than lady's maid, sitting knitting by the fire. At the moment a game of charades was underway causing much hilarity. I felt rather old in this youthful gathering, though I am but four and twenty, however I joined in the fun, glad to see my hostess so happy. At times I forget how young she still is and how she has missed out on so much.

Chapter Forty.
Emily.

I must admit, I've had to change my rather childish and dismissive opinion of the city. Though I shall always prefer the country, these past few months in town have opened my eyes. Oh I still believe the *ton* are parasites on society, their vapid, self-indulgent lives shallow and empty, for the most part ignorant and uncaring of the terrible poverty perhaps only a street away, but the city itself is a marvel. Dirty, smelly, dangerous, are true descriptions, but also exciting, vibrant, and full of a brash energy.

This day, Simon was escorting Nettie and me to the Tower of London to see the menagerie of wild animals. I had never visited with my father as he'd disapproved of the conditions in which they are kept but I wanted to see for myself. I longed for the time when James would be old enough to join us on these outings. We stopped the carriage well short of the west gate and sent it home, as I wished to approach on foot. A hackney would be hired for the return journey. As we walked I had the feeling of eyes watching me. Turning to look back I saw a small street urchin trailing us. When he saw I'd spied him, he grinned and skipped up to Simon.

"'Lo guvner. 'Oo be the pretty ladies wiv ya?"

Simon stopped, looked down and smiled. He fondly tousled the boy's hair and received a glare in return. "Spiff, let me introduce you to Lady Firstbridge and Miss Perkins. This is my friend and business associate, ladies."

Spiff solemnly bowed, then a cheeky grin lit his face again. And so I learned more of Simon's other life as he told me of Mannering's Militia, with his small 'soldier' looking on and nodding in agreement.

"Would you like to join us Spiff? We are on our way to see the wild animals," Simon asked with a smile.

"No fanks guv. Seen 'em plenty o' times. Easy sneakin' by vem beefeaters," he boasted. With that he saluted us and melted back into the crowd.

We continued on our way, and Simon looked down at me. "You know Emily, if that little rascal had not wanted to be seen, you would never have spotted him. It is clear he desired to meet you."

I wondered why, but as we approached the Tower of London, I forgot Spiff in the excitement of the adventure ahead. We spent some hours exploring that amazing fortress, and though I enjoyed other aspects of my visit, the crown jewels being the highlight, I agreed with my father and felt very sorry for the animals trapped in their small dark enclosures. The smell could only be described as nauseating.

I did not realise it at the time, and neither did Simon, but from then on, whenever I left my house, I had a secret, miniature guard. There came a time when this made me very thankful.

On my behalf, Simon, with the help of one of his friends, well-versed in horseflesh, had bought for me from Tattersall's, a sweet-natured, well mannered dapple grey mare called Moonbeam, very similar in looks to my Bluebell, but taller, and broken to side saddle. I had been furious when I discovered I was not expected to attend the male-dominated Tattersall's sales, though I learned later that some women braved them, those involved in the industry as buyers and sellers, but these were few and far between.

When it comes to horses, I am quite knowledgeable—I am my father's daughter after all. Nettie watched as I paced up and down the drawing room in a temper.

"It is ridiculous that I cannot choose and purchase my own horse!" I fumed. But like so many places in London, women were not welcome, though in this case not completely forbidden, however I had reluctantly accepted the fact that a man would have to buy it for me and naturally I called on Simon, who was happy to oblige. He'd left with a long list of my preferences and a rather bemused look on his face.

During the fashionable hour I rode Moonbeam in Hyde Park with Simon and other friends I had made in town. I'd had a groom bring Firebrand down to London as I couldn't bear to be parted from him but though I had occasionally ridden him in the side saddle at Amberleigh, he had not taken to it happily, much to my disappointment. In temperament he is full of mischief but not mean with it, however, I must admit he is prone to fits of disobedience, and needs to be handled firmly, which is no doubt how he got his name. So, early in the mornings when the ton slept, I would take him out for exercise, riding astride and with a groom for company.

I had been doing this for some weeks, as long as the weather remained settled, when I received a dreadful fright. On this particular gloomy morning, well wrapped up against the cold, with no wind or rain threatening, I rode Firebrand through the park. A mist shrouded everything and I could barely make out the trail. As usual, I walked the stallion until he accepted that I was in charge, then I allowed him to trot, followed shortly by a canter. No one else rode in the park at this early hour—the *ton* are largely night creatures—so I indulged in a gallop which I knew Firebrand had been anticipating. We pulled up where the trail passed through a

216

small copse, the trees ghostly shadows, with my beautiful black fellow full of himself, snorting and prancing.

The groom, mounted on Moonbeam, had dropped quite a long way back. I heard her whinny but they had disappeared into the mist. Soothing Firebrand with words and neck stroking, I waited for them to catch up. Suddenly, from amongst the trees stepped two men clad in a mishmash of tattered uniforms. Firebrand snorted and side-stepped but they were on to me before I could flee. I screamed and fought as one dragged me from the saddle and further into the trees. The other tried to hold my horse, but Firebrand gave a shrill whinny and reared, pulling away from the grasping hands and cantering off. I heard the thunder of Moonbeam's hooves and the grooms shout. "Milady!" But by now my mouth had been covered with something filthy and the man dragged me further into the underbrush. Then we stopped and the one holding me growled in my ear.

"Stay still 'n' shut up 'n' we won't kill yer." His breath smelled rancid and the sour odour of his unwashed body was overwhelming.

"Oo's first?" said the other and frightening memories overwhelmed me.

I felt hands tearing at my riding habit. The layered clothing and divided skirt made it hard for my molester as I fought and scratched in a frenzy, my panic giving me added strength. Suddenly, through my terror, I heard the sounds of something hard hitting flesh and my attacker shuddered and lay still. Small hands rolled him off me. Trembling in shock, I turned my head to watch the other rogue being beaten to the ground by four little figures, like pixies dancing around in the mist. A group of scruffy young boys surrounded me, all armed with cudgels—and one I recognised. It was Spiff.

"Spiff at yer service m'lady," he said as he bowed.

The other children watched and with wide grins, copied their leader. I sat up and pulled my clothes together.

Still shaking and fighting for composure, I at last found my voice.

"Well Spiff, it is very nice to see you again and I thank you for saving me. I'll tell Simon and you will no doubt get a reward, however, in the meantime, I should like you all to join me for breakfast." I struggled to my feet and looked down at the unconscious assailants. "We should tie them up and I expect you know what to do with them better than I."

At that moment my groom, white-faced, pushed his way through the bushes, dragging the two horses behind him.

"Milady, are you alright?" He eyed the boys and the two men.

"Yes thank you, Taylor, all due to my knights in shining armour. They will be joining me for breakfast."

The groom looked at me oddly but said no more and helped with the restraining of the villains. We tore strips from their tattered clothes to bind them and left them where they lay. As the early morning mist slowly dissipated, our strange cavalcade left the park.

When we arrived back at Firstbridge House, I sent the groom to the mews with the horses, then took my band of heroes around the side to the kitchen door. The butler did not need a shock at this early hour of the morning. I sent a footman to fetch the Watch and explained about the men in the park. The cook seemed a little upset to hear I intended eating in the kitchen with my guests but when I related how they had saved me, she nodded with approval. After clucking her tongue at her mistress's foolishness, riding alone except for a groom at that hour, she bustled around preparing an impromptu feast. Of course, Nettie came flying into the kitchen with Nathan—who had come to London with us— close on her heels. It had not taken long for news of my escapade to spread upstairs.

"I *knew* I should have stopped you going on those early morning rides with just a groom for company, and you mounted in that unladylike fashion!" She'd repeated cook's scold almost word for word, her face pale with fright.

I patted her arm. "I'm sorry I upset you but these brave lads came to my rescue and knocked out the two rogues that attacked me. I suspect they were returned soldiers from the military rags they wore."

Nettie turned to the boys with a beaming smile. "How marvellous that you were there. Lady Firstbridge is very special to me, I would hate to see her harmed. You are such brave lads to tackle two grown men." Her compliments were so effusive I thought the boys would burst with pride.

She joined us, and Nathan went with a note to Simon. We were in the middle of our jolly breakfast when he arrived. Nathan brought him to the kitchen and he grasped my hands, such a look of fear on his face.

"Emily, I have been sick with worry all the way here. You are all right my…?"

Had he been going to say, 'my love', but stopped himself in time?

"Yes I owe my deliverance to Mannering's Militia," I assured him with a warm smile.

The boys had been looking on with great interest—had even paused in their eating to watch this revealing scene.

"Please join us. My champions can tell you all about it." I included Nathan in my invitation so two more chairs were pulled up to the kitchen table and the other boys deferred to Spiff, who gave Simon a very professional report of my adventures. After praising them for the rescue, he turned to me and spoke in a voice that brooked no argument.

"If you intend continuing to ride at that hour Emily, either Nathan or I shall accompany you."

Simon looked very determined and I didn't disagree with him for it had given me a bad fright. My experience had shown me the darker side of this complex city.

When the boys could no longer squeeze in another mouthful, Simon rewarded them lavishly, and after I gave each a kiss on the cheek, which caused a great deal of teasing and blushing, they disappeared down the road shouting and laughing. Nathan and Nettie returned to their duties and Simon came upstairs with me to the drawing room. I would have to bathe and change before the usual stream of callers—I knew I smelt of horse and something unpleasant—but he seemed not to want to let me out of his sight, which was most satisfying.

"Emily, when I imagine what might have happened to you—it does not bear thinking about!" He took my hands again and looked at me with anguished eyes.

"I have learned my lesson, Simon. I shall be careful in the future and now I know I have little guardian angels, I shall be a lot happier. I must bathe; I have to wash away the smell of those men." I pulled a face and shuddered.

After promises that he would return in the evening to dine with me, Simon reluctantly left. I soaked in my bath and tried not to think of the attack. Instead I thought of Simon's dear, stricken face and his very revealing agitation.

Chapter Forty-one.
Simon.

Spring is coming to an end. I have been assiduous in my attention over the previous months, accompanying my dearest to the theatre, the Tower of London, the museum, lectures at the Royal Society—anything that I thought would appeal to her. We have even attended a few balls, now her mourning is almost over; separately of course. I am building up my own connections in the ton so am receiving a satisfying number of invitations. I know how Emily loves to dance and watch jealously as her card fills quickly, though I always make sure we have the supper dance together—and a waltz. Other than her scare in the park, which my boys foiled, I think she has enjoyed herself. I had no idea they had been keeping an eye on my love. They have adopted me, and that Spiff is a worldly-wise child, so they are no doubt aware of my feelings for Emily and have included her in their protective shield.

I knew that Mr Netherby had arranged for tenants to move into Firstbridge House on the last day of June and Emily would then be returning to the country. With the end of her official mourning now at hand, I am still not sure how to go about telling her how much I love her, though she surely must realise it by now.

When I turned fifteen, not long before the death of my father, he and I had talked, man to man, about the hazards of consorting with prostitutes and it had left a lasting impression on me, so much so that years later when my drunken friends had suggested we pay a visit to a famous Cambridge brothel, much frequented by students, I begged off, using my pockets to let as an excuse. Other than hasty pecks on my mother's and sisters' cheeks, my only experience with females amounted to a nervous fumble with a maid at my student lodgings. In fact, though I enjoy looking at pretty girls as much as any man, until I met Emily I had never been stirred by a Grand Passion. Now at five and twenty, I had become an acknowledged expert in crime but still a veritable virgin in love! And to make it worse, my heart's desire has been emotionally as well as physically abused and so made wary of any expressions of intimacy. I could not afford to be clumsy in my lovemaking. I needed help.

I had kept in touch with one of my Cambridge associates, Jeremy Stanford, Viscount Bendon, a young man of the world, so feeling rather uncomfortable, I arranged to meet him at White's, with the intention of asking his advice. Ben, as he is known to his friends, shook my hand vigorously and clapped me on the back.

"Great to see you again, Mannering. Been hearing good things about you around town. Making quite a name for yourself. How is that nice grey mare going? The one I helped you buy for your lady friend? "

Ben is a Corinthian; a pugilist of note, a first rate shot, an acknowledged whip, and races his own yacht. If that wasn't enough, the ladies consider him exceedingly handsome, with blonde, curly hair, cut in the latest fashion and laughing, blue eyes. I remembered how I had admired and looked up to the older man during our sojourn at Cambridge, and felt flattered that he had deigned to befriend a penniless young man of no particular consequence. It was he who had accompanied me to Tattersall's to purchase Emily's mare.

We sat in an alcove where a private conversation would not be overheard. Occasionally other members would nod in greeting as they passed but mostly we were left alone with our brandies. I talked of generalities, as I tried to think of a way to bring up the subject closest to my heart.

Finally Ben leaned back in his chair and looked at me with a wry smile. "Something is on your mind Mannering. Now out with it."

I could not put it off any longer. I felt my face flush as I blurted out. "I'm in a bit of a quandary, Ben. Ummm, how do I approach a lady to make my intentions known? I've never even really kissed a girl," I confessed miserably.

To do him credit, Ben managed to keep a straight face at my declaration, though I could read the mirth in his eyes. "I say, that is a bit of a problem."

Ben, I knew, remained unmarried, though over the years I'd known him, had maintained discreet liaisons with a number of actresses and opera singers.

"I suppose one day I'll have to get leg-shackled and produce an heir, but in the meantime, I'm practising," he'd told me once with a wicked grin.

Apart from his official townhouse, he owned a charming place in an area of London frequented by the demimonde and there he kept his current ladybird.

I, sick with nerves, had barely sipped my first glass but he had been drinking steadily, refilling from the bottle standing on the table between us. I think this increased his sense of bonhomie and perhaps inspired him to make his startling offer.

"I'll tell you what, Mannering, How about I give you a night with Maria? She could teach you a trick or two," he offered generously, and smiled benignly at me.

To say he had stunned me, was an understatement. I had never for a moment considered anything like that. Obviously my face must have shown my thoughts for he roared with laughter. A few heads turned our way, but thankfully no one approached.

"She's a good sort, my Maria, and a lot of fun. I assure you my boy, you will come away with all the tools you'll need to win your lady."

And that's how I found myself, the following evening, climbing the steps to a bright, blue-painted front door with a polished brass knocker and neatly tamed potted shrubs each side. I held a bunch of flowers in my sweaty, gloved hand and a dainty and expensive, gold bracelet in my pocket for…after.

A saucy maid opened the door, dressed to match it, with a crisp white apron and a cap perched on a riot of red curls.

"Ah, you must be Mr Mannering. The mistress be expecting you," she twinkled, her Irish brogue strong.

She took my hat and gloves then led me to a charmingly decorated parlour, where the current lady of the establishment greeted me. Beautiful in a dramatic sort of way, with masses of black curls bound with a scarlet ribbon, Maria wore a matching dress of a silky fabric that clung to her abundant curves. A ruby necklace rose and fell on a delightful bosom. Warm brown eyes that tilted up at the corners studied me with interest; a pretty little nose and full red lips completed the picture of seductive beauty.

"How nice to meet a friend of my Ben. Colleen would you please put these lovely flowers in a vase for me," she said, and a dimple came and went. I'd thrust them forward as if to create a barrier between us. I have to admit it —she terrified me.

I wondered how she felt at Ben's casual offering of her charms, but whatever her thoughts, she smiled kindly

224

and patted the sofa for me to sit beside her. Her perfume subtly hinted at roses. Before long she had skilfully overridden my shyness and I found myself talking freely about my detection adventures while we sipped glasses of wine. It could have been any drawing room in the *ton*, except we were alone, and the air almost throbbed with a sexual tension.

More in control now, I had started to enjoy myself, when suddenly Maria leaned closer, put her hand on my knee, and looking at me from under her long lashes, gently began to stroke along my thigh. Devil a bit! I broke out in a sweat and my eyes widened in panic. Have I mentioned that her voice sounded as smooth as honey? Golden and sweet.

"Come, Mr Mannering, may I call you Simon, I have something I want to show you."

I choked on a mouthful of wine. After coughing and spluttering into my handkerchief, I got my breath back and like a marionette, she drew me to my feet and led me up the stairs and along a hallway. I knew where we were going—to her bedroom! I'm embarrassed to say that by now it would be hard to miss the very obvious bulge in my trousers. I defy any man to be affected otherwise in the presence of this intoxicating woman.

And so began my education in lust—not love; the difference to me appeared obvious, but it was certainly enjoyable. In exquisite detail she showed me how to please a woman and in return drove me to mind-blowing madness. When we experienced together what Maria called 'the glorious explosion' I thought I would leave my body behind with the intensity of it. As I lay exhausted, my arm splayed across her breasts, Maria turned to look at me, an odd little smile on her face.

"Who is Emily, Simon? You called out her name."
I didn't reply. I couldn't. Milady Grey-eyes was no part of this. Instead, I ran my hand down Maria's body and

225

marvelled at the softness of her skin, my mind anticipating bringing all this pleasure to my darling, for I doubted there had been any tenderness or magic in her marriage.

I left Maria just before dawn. I thanked her for all she had taught me, both in the giving and the receiving, pressed the gold bracelet into her hand and gave her a chaste, farewell kiss on the cheek. It seemed strangely formal after the torrid ones we had shared but that interlude had now ended. Even at this late hour, there were still hackneys to be hired. It took me home to my lodgings, and feeling detached from reality, l stripped and fell exhausted into bed. The other lodgers, clattering noisily down the stairs, woke me at midday.

For some minutes I lay thinking about the things I had learned. It felt like a vivid dream. Then I climbed out of bed and surveyed my clothes lying where I'd dropped them. With a resigned shrug I started tidying them away. I don't employ a valet but was seriously considering it after spending two hours trying to remove the scent of Maria's perfume. It being Sunday, I asked Mrs Brendon if I might have a bath. Her odd-job man hauled it up the stairs to my room and filled it with much huffing and grunting.

I lay and soaked until the water had cooled, re-living again my extraordinary night and reminding myself that I must take Ben out for dinner to thank him. Now I would have to put all that knowledge into practice. My plan must be both subtle and sensitive if I wished to win my heart's desire, but I could hardly wait.

Chapter Forty-two.
Simon.

I decided I would call the following morning and seal my fate. I had sent a personal note to Nettie as I needed her help to get my love on her own without her continual stream of visitors. Lady Firstbridge had become a magnet for the penniless lesser sons of the ton. I knew, after discreet whispers from Nettie, that she had already refused several hopeful offers. I hadn't forgotten the more eligible heirs either; I worried about them the most, though I had long since realised that titles did not overly impressed my darling.

Nettie looked on me with favour so I knew she would make sure we were left undisturbed. I had planned to arrive a little earlier than is fashionable so that when shown into the drawing room, my love would be without her usual cluster of admirers. And so it proved. She rose and came towards me, smiling her enchanting smile, looking so beautiful in a dress of softest pink, her hair in a tumble of shining curls, it took my breath away. Nettie sat by the fire—though it is early summer, the weather is still quite cool in the mornings—with her inevitable knitting.

She bobbed her head and said innocently, "Oh, I have almost finished this ball Miss Emily, I shall have to fetch another skein." And with a wink of encouragement to me, slipped from the room.

The moment had come. Taking both her hands in mine, but leaving a small distance between us, I took a deep breath and began. "I have something to confess to you Emily. You have been Milady Grey-eyes from almost the first time I met you, and though I didn't realise it at the time, you had also claimed my heart." Here, I paused anxiously.

"Oh Simon, love is a wonderful thing," she answered shyly, looking down at our clasped hands then raising those glorious eyes to mine.

Still holding her, I gazed into that dear face and murmured, my voice husky with emotion. "Let me show you what a kiss is like when one loves someone as much as I love you, my darling."

Emily's eyes were wide and a little wary as I gently lowered my mouth to hers, the kiss soft and sweet. She did not pull away as I had half feared. The wariness seemed gone as she looked up at me wonderingly and then standing on tip toes, kissed me back, the lightest flutter of butterfly wings. I groaned inwardly, the effort of keeping myself under control was torture but I must not make a mistake.

My tender, gentle kisses moved from her mouth to her jaw line and down her neck beneath her ear, my breath warm against her smooth, delicately-scented skin. I felt her small shudder of pleasure. With infinite care I drew her to me so that we melted into each other and allowed my kisses to deepen. She tasted so wonderful that my heart swelled and my whole body burned for her as I felt her fingers twine in my hair. Suddenly she pulled away and for a moment I thought I had pushed too hard, but her face was flushed and her eyes starry.

"Oh Simon, this must be what Mrs Radcliffe is always talking about."

I looked a little nonplussed until she explained and then I burst into laughter.

"Oh Emily, my sweet goose, I didn't think it possible to love you more." And holding her close again, I demonstrated that real life is far better than the written word.

Chapter Forty-three.
In which Nettie is satisfied.

Nettie had discreetly left the lovers for a decent interval, and now she peeped into the room to see her dear girl wrapped in Mr Mannering's arms. She had already told the footman at the front door to turn away any callers for the next hour. Nettie smiled delightedly, and gave a little cough of warning before entering. She had quite forgotten the skein of wool.

As the lovers hastily stepped apart, Emily, her face glowing with joy, exclaimed "Oh Nettie, Simon and I are to be wed. I wanted you to be the first to know."

Perfect!

Chapter Forty-four.
Emily.

My Simon wasted no time. With the help of Mr Ferris, he applied for a special licence and we were married at St George's in Hanover Square within the week. My wedding day couldn't have been more perfect. For once London had a clear blue sky and the morning promised to be mild and still. Nettie is a marvel. In very short order she'd arranged for the church to be filled with flowers, planned the wedding feast, bought a glorious cake from Gunters and bullied my favourite modiste—I suspect another faux French woman—into creating a masterpiece for me to wear. Silver gauze embroidered with pearls over a shimmering pale blue silk. Nettie twined pearls and white rosebuds into my hair and I carried a spray of white roses. She even arranged an honour guard of Mannering's Militia, much to Simon's delight. Somehow, she miraculously got them bathed and outfitted in smart new clothes in time. For me, the week before the wedding passed in a trance-like state of happiness.

Simon looked so handsome and proud, with eyes only for me, as I walked down the aisle on Sir Timothy's arm. As he'd been like an uncle to me and was my son's guardian, I'd asked him to give me away. The heady scent of massed flowers will always remind me of that moment when I became the wife of my dear friend and one true love. Most of the ceremony remains a blur in my memory but as the ring was slipped onto my finger I experienced one of those incredible moments in life—a nexus, when all the events in my past felt inevitably connected to that point.

The wedding breakfast was held at Firstbridge house. The Badger family had rented a nearby townhouse for the Season as their two oldest daughters were coming out together, so they attended along with Uncle Rudolf, who came without Sophie, as she had miscarried and remained unwell. I'd spared a thought for my poor aunt in my happiness and had written a long letter of condolence. The Ferris and Edale families were there, my cousin Sarah happily increasing. Aunt Arabella had not been sure if she approved of what she considered my socially, rather uneven match, even though she likes Simon.

"Of course he *is* related to the Duke of Letchford, so I suppose that counts for something," she grudgingly conceded when I'd informed her I intended marrying him.

Fortunately, as a widow, I needed no one's permission. She admitted then that Uncle Richard had told her of a few disquieting rumours about Lord Firstbridge, but she'd scoffed at the time. Now, she understood better.

"I think, seeing you so happy Emily, perhaps for this second marriage, it is more important than status." So she reluctantly gave her approval.

Uncle Richard, on the other hand, appeared delighted. He put his arms around me and it felt like being hugged by a bear.

He rumbled in my ear. "My dear niece, you deserve this after all you have been through. I only wish I had been closer at hand to protect you. Such a lot for a young gel to cope with. I have been doing my utmost in the House to give women more protection in the law, but it's an uphill struggle."

I gave him a kiss on the cheek and praised him for his efforts.

Simon and I were sitting holding hands when Ben, who had been best man, came over to speak to us.

"I'm almost tempted to get caught in the parson's mousetrap myself, the two of you look so disgustingly happy," he laughed.

I'd noticed him eyeing Rebekah, my new sister-in-law, with interest and wondered if she would be the one to finally lure him from his bachelor ways. She *is* very beautiful and I found her both charming and witty.

The war has finally ended and we had thought of visiting Paris for our honeymoon, but with the move from Firstbridge House looming, we decided to leave it for the present. The city is bursting with excitement following Napoleon's defeat and banishment to Elba and when we had tried to book a suite at the Pulteney for our wedding night, we discovered it to be packed with foreign dignitaries, as with every other good hotel in London. So we spent our honeymoon at home. To be honest, neither of us cared where we were, as long as we were together.

How can I describe to you the joy of our wedding night. Simon overwhelmed me with tenderness as he educated me in the pleasures of the marriage bed. I never realised that such ecstasy existed. It was a revelation. A few days later, he confessed to his night with Ben's mistress. We were lying in each others arms, sated and feeling delighted with each other, when he told me.

"My darling, I used to be a callow young man, who knew nothing of how to please a woman. I needed desperately to bring you pleasure, I loved you so much, and I wanted it to be wonderful for you, so I went to Ben."

He stroked me as he talked but then stopped and I could tell something made him uncomfortable. I turned and pressed myself against him, our legs entwined, and waited. Finally, with his arms wrapped around me and looking into my face in the dim candlelight, the words haltingly came.

"Ben offered me a night with his mistress. All the physical things that bring us both pleasure, she taught me. It was not love, but what I learned has given ours an even deeper meaning."

I could see both his relief at finally admitting it, and his tension as he waited for my reaction. In the pleasant afterglow of our lovemaking, I examined this revelation with as much dispassion as I could muster. Being a well brought up young lady, who had been taught nothing of man's baser desires, should I be horrified? No, I decided. True horror had been my experience in my first marriage. It would be ridiculous to deny the delights that an unknown woman had gifted me. I kissed my husband deeply and he relaxed. We made leisurely, sensuous love again, and afterwards we talked. I even saw its funny side. Now, whenever I see Ben, I have a quiet giggle and I see him looking questioningly at me. I can never tell him the reason.

******

When we aren't in the bedroom, we ride in the park or go for long walks, even attend lectures at the Royal Society, lost in our private world of happiness, while the house is preparing to be evacuated around us. Nettie organises it all. She is amazing; she not only acts as my lady's maid, but is overseeing our removal from London, which is just as well, as I am of little use. Penny Badger is a treasured friend and I have made quite a few others while I have been in London, but Nettie will always be my nearest and dearest.

"I am officially making you my companion, and no longer my maid, Nettie," I tell her gaily as she pins up my curls one morning, a few days before our move. "Though I hope you will still do my hair, you are so good at it. *Tu m'es tres cher.* You are very dear to me."

"Merci, Madame Mannering. *Vous etes tres gentil,"* she replied with a grin.

Nettie's French is coming along famously. I must contact M'sieur Duprés when we return to my old home to arrange lessons for her. I wonder how much my young friend, Raoul, has grown and look forward to seeing him again. He has been writing to me regularly, in French of course, to make sure I would not forget, so I know he and his great uncle are well. His letters had been a bright spot in my life during the time at Mornington and then through the nightmare of my marriage.

Because of all its unhappy memories we have made the decision to let Amberleigh. It is to be tenanted by an extremely rich nabob from India, until James comes of age. Our home in the future is to be Sweetwater. A whole new wing will be added to make room for an expanding family—Simon and I are doing our part to make this happen—and for frequent visits from the Badgers, as they will no longer be our near neighbours and Simon and I both value their friendship. Mr Netherby is moving his office there as well and will live in the dower house.

Over the months of Simon's courtship, James accepted the new male in my life with his usual happy exuberance and the day he called him 'papa' brought joyful tears to my eyes.

Penny called while our menfolk attended a boxing match and brought her new baby to visit. Letitia is the prettiest little thing, and only eighteen months younger than James so hopefully they will grow up to be friends. The children were eventually taken to the nursery while we sat together in the drawing room, and discussed marriage in general, over tea and biscuits.

"Yours is such a happy one, Penny. Obviously Sir Timothy adores you. It is wonderful with Simon and I can't imagine a time when we won't love each other as passionately, but how do you keep everything so fresh after decades?" I knew they had been married for twenty years and hoped she wouldn't mind my frankness. I would never have dreamed of having this conversation during my first marriage, but I know her well now and she is a generous-hearted and wise woman.

Penny patted my knee. "I came out at seventeen and had many hearts laid at my feet but I only gave mine to one. He was not a baronet then but I knew he was for me when he came visiting my older brother." She smiled softly as a faraway look in her eyes relived the memory.

"We were married not long after, and many of my friends made matches too. I soon noticed that those who had wed for money and title, though they led glittering lives, were eventually discontented and unhappy. And in that unhappiness they searched for love elsewhere but never seemed to find contentment. I reasoned that somehow I must keep that first passion alive within my marriage, and then I stumbled upon the answer." An impish grin lit her face. I was all attention.

"The secret, my dear, is to be inventive. Never let complacency into your lovemaking. That is a sure way to have them wandering. And it goes without saying you must have trust in each other. However, you need have no fears for many years, Emily. By the look in your Simon's eyes, I'm surprised he could tear himself away long enough to attend that match."

I blushed when I recalled what we had been doing that morning.

******

Occasionally, I notice Nathan mysteriously disappearing. When I questioned Simon he gave me a wicked grin and a kiss.

"Oh, I've been rather distracted of late, love, can't imagine why. Nathan has been doing a few small jobs for me. I have to say he is taking to investigating with enthusiasm."

I nodded in understanding. "Yes I can believe it. He came up with that very original weapon—the sawdust. To me, that shows ingenuity." I had long since told Simon about the attack.

"Yes, he's wasted as a footman. I had thought of making him my valet, though I've managed for years without one and I do think the detection work will suit him better. He says I'm the brains and he's the brawn, but he underestimates himself. Perhaps I should make him my partner." Simon chuckled as he hugged me close. I thought that an admirable reward for my brave protector.

Mr Netherby has come to London in the last few days to facilitate the smooth handover to the new tenants of Firstbridge House—a merchant family from Birmingham. All sorts of exciting plans are in the making. At my request, he has already made arrangements to free and re-employ the slaves on our West Indies properties and has discussed with Simon our idea of setting up a trust to fund orphanages in the city. We have already purchased a house for Mannering's Militia and set up a schoolroom and an apprenticeship programme. I have talked to Spiff a few times now; he is a bright and engaging, worldly-wise child, and is eager to learn. I'm sure he will go far.

Sadly, with our move to Sweetwater, Simon's time as an assistant to his step-father is coming to an end. And if the *ton* wish for his help with their problems, they will have to be patient. He is keeping his rooms in London for the moment and, with Nathan, will most probably visit every few weeks to check on Mannering's Militia and attend to any business. Mrs Brendon will no doubt write if the mail is piling up.

The day has finally arrived. Sweetwater with all its happy memories, touched with a little sadness, is waiting for me.

Life is wonderful.

Epilogue.
1882. In which Emily's great grandson, Simon, receives a bequest.

Simon looked at the long, beautifully carved mahogany box. It lay on the desk in his bedroom and as his hand ran over its surface he remembered his great grandmother, Emily, with love and sadness, now that she was gone. It seemed almost impossible to imagine life without her, she had been such a large part of his—her wonderful enquiring mind, the charities that she passionately supported, the all-embracing love with which she surrounded her family, and those brilliant, intelligent grey eyes that seemed to see into the soul —eyes that he had inherited. When he was troubled, he could not count the number of times he had gone to her for advice, and it had always been thoughtful and wise. She'd lived through the reigns of three kings and now a queen— long enough to see the law changed so that married women could buy, own and sell property and keep their own earnings, in spite of Her Majesty's disapproval.

A tear trickled unheeded into his carefully cultivated side whiskers. At nineteen, he'd been told he looked very much like his grandfather, James, at the same age, though he had his grandmother Letitia's dimples. He knew the history of the box, had been shown its contents as a child and been fascinated by the stories of the Amazon jungle. He kept reminding himself that great grandmama had been very old when she'd died and had led a full and happy life. The death ten years before of her beloved second husband, his step-great grandfather after whom he'd been named, had dimmed her joy but she'd told him then, through her tears, that when one had a love as great as theirs, it became one's duty to live the rest of one's life to the full, for both of them. As a nine-year old boy he'd not understood—but now, as a young man, he was slowly coming to appreciate what she'd meant.

Removing the key from his pocket he inserted it into the lock. He opened the box, expecting to see the blowpipe, a few darts and a tiny pot containing the dried remains of a poison now known as curare. A surprise awaited him. It also contained what appeared to be a small bundle of letters tied together with a pink ribbon. On the outside sheet he saw his name written in his grandmother's neat handwriting. He picked it up and removed the ribbon. No, not a collection of letters, just one. Intrigued, he crossed to the wing chair by the cheerful fire, sat down and started to read.

My dearest Simon,

If you are reading this then I am no more and it is my conscience speaking. Other than my parents, we have been a lucky family, each generation healthy and long-lived. You were named after my second husband, a man your father and grandfather loved and admired. You were still a boy when my Simon died so would not have known him well, but you may remember his cleverness at solving puzzles.

On the other hand, my first husband, your true great grandfather, Lord Miles Firstbridge, is seldom mentioned, as your grandfather, being so young when he died, has no memory of him. You may however have heard rumours of a family scandal, carefully hushed up at the time, as are so many amongst the wealthy and powerful. Here then, my

240

dearest boy, is the true story of what happened all those years ago.

The family doctor, who lived in the village near Amberleigh, burned to death in his home. Suspicions about the cause of death were brought to the attention of the local magistrate and coroner, Sir Timothy Badger, your other great grandfather. He asked my Simon, who already had a reputation as a solver of crimes, to come up from London and investigate. He wasn't 'my Simon' then of course, but I knew him through Sir Timothy. Before his arrival, two more deaths occurred. My first husband shot and killed his valet and then died himself. The three deaths were linked and it appeared that your great grandfather had ordered Bekkit, his valet and natural son, to kill the doctor because he was being blackmailed. Apparently Dr. Caukwell had been treating him for a terrible disease and had threatened disclosure if the huge gambling debt he owed my husband was not forgiven. Exposure would have meant social disaster. Simon surmised that following the first murder, my husband quarrelled with his valet, or perhaps he mistook the valet for a burglar, your great grandfather having by then descended into bouts of madness due to his illness. For whatever reason, he shot Bekkit and his own death followed soon after. The autopsy showed that his lordship's organs were riddled with infection. That is supposedly what killed him.

You, your father and grandfather are gentlemen to be proud of, partly I am sure because you have all been influenced by a good and compassionate man, my Simon. On the other hand, I hate to hurt you my darling but my first husband, your ancestor, had been utterly selfish and corrupt. He most likely began as a spoilt, undisciplined child with too much wealth at too early an age. Ignored by his parents and brought up by servants, he became accustomed to always doing exactly as he pleased and ignoring any consequences.

241

Or perhaps I am making excuses for his behaviour and evil came naturally to him.

Later, his hatred of his heir—a cousin—proved quite venomous. As I learned the full horror of what he had done to me, I tried to find a little pity for his desperate actions, however, the fact that he had turned Bekkit, his own flesh and blood, into a monster to serve his obsessions, is unforgivable. I am not making excuses for my own actions dearest, and you may think me a coward for waiting until after my death to confess, but here is the true story of what happened before and after Dr Caukwell died. You will surely destroy this letter but I hope that at least you will have an understanding of what drove me.

My first husband had always been cold towards me and after our son, James, was born, his sickness gradually took hold and until his death our marriage seemed as close to a living hell as one could get. As his madness worsened, the whole household lived in fear. My husband's valet had complete control of his master's life by now and Bekkit accompanied him everywhere, even at the dinner table. He dressed in his master's clothes, wore his jewels and commanded the staff in his name.

I feared for my baby's life as your great grandfather roamed the house with a loaded pistol. On the rare occasion when I came across him, and I took great pains to avoid this happening, he would beat me for no reason—other than some twisted idea in his mind—until his valet could draw him off. So you can imagine the atmosphere we all lived in. And then the fateful letter arrived.

I had been feeling very distressed that day. Bekkit had just shown me a document purportedly signed by my husband and making him my son's guardian upon his lordship's death. That loathsome valet would control me through James. It filled me with despair and I had decided, at last, to ask Sir Timothy for help when the blackmail letter arrived. My Simon was right in assuming that there had been one but it had been addressed to me, not my husband. I recognised the doctor's handwriting immediately. I have a good memory and every word of that terrible letter is burned into my brain.

Lady Firstbridge,

I regret it has come to this. I am in serious debt to both your husband and others and I see no other way to overcome my problem. I have therefore decided to disclose to you the unpalatable truth. Lord Firstbridge has been impotent for many years. I have been treating him for this condition to no avail. He is also in the last stage of syphilis which has lain dormant for a long period. His erratic behaviour has come to my attention and this is a clear indication that that is no longer the case.

You will understand the implications with regard to your son. I am persuaded a certain cousin would greatly appreciate this knowledge and no doubt would spread the scandal wide; perhaps even convince the court to put aside your son because of your husband's impotence. If you could see your way clear to supply me with the means to honour my debts—the sum of two thousand pounds should cover them—I shall be much obliged and assure you that milord's cousin will not be made privy to this information.

Your servant,
Robert Caukwell MD
Fellow of the Edinburgh College of Medicine

I read those awful words, feeling myself go hot and cold. I had always thought the doctor an imposter and a blackguard; this letter confirmed it. How could I find such a large sum? Other than the household allowance and my generous quarterly pin money, I had nothing. Then the implication of my husband's impotence hit me. If he could not have fathered James, then who had? With a flash of understanding and feeling ill, I now realised the significance of the black silk hood my husband had insisted I wear when he came to my bedroom. He told me it was to protect my sensibilities and in my innocence, I'd believed him.

My son was definitely a Wolffe—his likeness to my husband was obvious. With horror, the truth slowly dawned on me and the meaning of the leering and knowing looks I had received from Bekkit became clear. My husband had arranged for his natural son to rape me! Had he in his twisted mind reasoned that his by-blow carried his blood and therefore made a suitable candidate? My beautiful baby would be known as base-born, and even though he was still legally the heir, my husband's impotence made that an impossibility. Would anybody believe me innocent in this mad scheme? My character would be in tatters. And what if the courts decided as the doctor suggested? His hatred of his cousin must have led my husband to concoct this cold and cruel plot.

Once Bekkit realised I had become aware of the subterfuge, would he force himself back into my bed and without a hood this time? The only happy thing that had come from that frightening letter was that other than an occasional kiss on the cheek, my husband had never actually touched me, so I had no fear of having contracted his terrible disease, which also meant that my baby was safe.

What could I do? The valet had absolute power over the household. He had already coerced my husband into making him my son's guardian after his lordship's death. Bekkit must have bitterly resented his own illegitimacy and been jealous of James who, whilst also being baseborn, would inherit everything. If I told Sir Timothy of the blackmail, the dark and evil story would become known and your grandfather would have been branded a bastard. We would be at the centre of a terrible scandal.

A woman had even less power over her own life then, my dear. My husband owned me and could abuse me if he chose, and I had no recourse in the law. As long as his lordship lived, Bekkit could do with me as he wished. And after his death, my son and all his wealth would be in the valet's power. I didn't care for myself, but I would die to protect my baby. I had two choices. The first, to go to Sir Timothy and tell him everything—all would be exposed, with the added risk that James might be disinherited; the second, to give the letter to Bekkit and see if he had a solution. Perhaps he could frighten the doctor into silence. By now, with the fear and worry of it all, I felt desperate and could hardly think straight, but a decision had to be made.

I took the doctor's letter to my husband's dressing room where Bekkit lounged on the sofa drinking brandy. His lordship had been heavily sedated so the valet could relax his vigil. As I mutely handed it to him, he smiled knowingly and his eyes travelled over my body; I felt only revulsion. I watched him read it and, of course, he immediately understood the implications. Society would learn of his master's disease, the cause of his madness, and also of his impotence. Once the full story was known, and with the chance that James might be disinherited, Bekkit could lose everything. The guardianship document he had shown me would then be next to useless, and his power over me would be gone. With a frown, he read through the letter a second time, then tossed it on the fire.

Leave this with me my dear lady. I shall deal with it, never fear," he smiled and my skin crawled at his overly familiar address. Within twenty four hours the doctor's house burned down and he died with it. I guessed who had been responsible; it seemed too much of a coincidence. At least my Simon had been correct there. I felt guilt at my part in the doctor's death but then I reminded myself he had been a blackmailer. As I'd expected, once he realised I knew of the disgusting deception, Bekkit informed me that I need never sleep alone again and we could continue our charade. I realised I had exchanged one trap for another and still had the valet to deal with before James would be safe. Telling him I had my courses, which meant he would leave me in peace for the moment, and feeling detached from reality, I made my plan. Two mornings later, sick with apprehension, I put that plan into action.

Bekkit brought his master's coffee at seven each morning and drew back the window curtains. My husband's bed had none because of his dislike of the dark. A candle remained alight at all times and he slept with a pistol, one of his paranoias being a fear of burglars. Twenty minutes before seven I quietly opened his bedroom door and stepped into the room carrying the blow-pipe box. In the dimness I could see him lying on his back, snoring, the pistol in his hand.

As I told you when you were a little boy, I had learned how to use a blow pipe from one of my father's explorer friends. I quietly removed the pipe, somehow stopping my hands from trembling long enough to load the already poisoned dart and raised it to my lips. My husband slept on as I carefully aimed for his unshaven jowl. A hard puff and it was done. There could be no turning back now; my fate was sealed. The lethal dose I had given would paralyse him and shortly he would stop breathing. I replaced the blowpipe in the box, tucked it under my arm and waited a few moments for the curare to invade his system, then I crept across the room and leaned over the bed.

"I'm so sorry you have driven me to this milord," I whispered shakily as I carefully removed the dart, wiped the small drop of blood with my handkerchief, and put them both back with the blowpipe. When they examined his body, *hopefully the tiny puncture wound would be lost in his whiskers. I pushed the box under the bed out of sight.*

With my heart thudding, I removed the pistol from my husband's unresisting hand. It was unloaded, but I had prepared myself beforehand, just in case. It almost felt as if papa sat beside me giving me instructions; I could hear his dear voice in my head. "Now Em, you must pour the correct amount of powder down the muzzle, then the wad and ball and carefully tamp them home. Yes, fill the pan with the primer next and lock it down. Never cock it my dear, until you are ready to pull the trigger and never point it at anyone unless you intend to fire."

In spite of my nervousness, loading took only a matter of seconds. Overcoming a feeling of revulsion, I slipped under the top bedcover beside my husband, pulling it up to my eyes and being careful to keep a distance between us. I then waited, the pistol clutched in my hand.

The time seemed an eternity before a knock came at the door and Bekkit appeared from the direction of the dressing room to receive the coffee from the footman. I watched fearfully as he placed it on a wall table, then went to draw back the window curtains. He picked up the tray again and walked across the room towards the bed. Suddenly he hesitated—perhaps he sensed my eyes watching him—but then he sniffed the air. He must have smelt the gunpowder! In a panic I raised the pistol, cocked and pressed the trigger. Instantly, there followed a bang and a momentary flash. I saw Bekkit's eyes staring at me in astonishment before he crumpled to the floor, blood spraying everywhere and scalding coffee mingling with it. I knew I did not need to check that I'd killed him—I am a crack shot and at that range I could not miss.

With a feeling of revulsion, I put the pistol into my husband's hand, taking care to rub some of the gun powder residue over it and wrapping his finger around the trigger.

Then, keeping my eyes averted from the body on the floor, I scrambled off the bed, dragged the wooden box from under it and staggered back to my room.

Nettie, my maid and dear friend, had been sent home to see her family—her mother was dying—so if my crime became known, she would not be involved. I hastily checked in the mirror in the early morning light to make sure there were no blood splatters and washed my hands to remove the smell of gun powder, then threw the water out the window. The handkerchief, I dropped into the banked embers of the fireplace, where it flared up and disintegrated into ash. I returned the mahogany box to its temporary hiding place in the dressing room—it was usually stored in the stillroom—and at last crawled into my own bed. It had been only ten minutes since the shot.

My hot chocolate would be delivered at seven-thirty and I knew the maid who saw to the grates would not be here before then. I had gambled that the household had become so accustomed to unusual noises, they would not investigate the sharp report of the pistol. And so it proved. I lay awake feeling nauseous and shivering with shock, barely believing what I had done. Slowly the minutes ticked by and when I heard a faint scratch at my door—one of the upstairs maids bringing my morning drink—I climbed out of bed and unlocked it. As I took the tray from her hands, there came a shrill scream from the direction of my husband's bedroom.

Later, when Simon spoke to me, he had already interviewed the staff and knew that everyone lived in terror of my husband with his intermittent rages, his pistol and his malevolent valet. I listened with relief the next day as he laid out what he believed had happened and that the autopsy had shown Lord Firstbridge had died from the advanced stage of that terrible disease, his organs finally collapsing. He sounded so convincing, I almost believed it myself.

248

So there is the true story my darling. I killed both your true and false great grandfathers—one of them a murderer himself and the other diseased and already near to death—and have had few regrets. To me, you, your father and grandfather have more than vindicated my decision all those years ago. I tremble to think what might have happened if I had been too afraid to take the law into my own hands. For my sins I have been rewarded with a long life of joy and love so I must assume my crime has been forgiven.

Live yours to the fullest my dear boy and please remember me not too severely. I shall be with my darling Simon soon, but you are his living namesake and I am so proud of you.

Eternally yours,
Great Grandmama Emily

Simon sat staring into the fire, the final page of the letter grasped in his hands. The great grandmother he had adored and admired all his life had made him rethink what he believed he knew about her. He remembered always feeling safe and loved when with her. Everyone knew of her generosity to those in need and he could not think of one moment when she did not display a goodness of spirit. He tried to imagine what her situation must have felt like—a young, bright, orphaned girl, abused by her husband and his valet, alone and forced to face a terrible situation in a time when little, if any, safety in the law existed for women. Exposure would have brought with it a future of complete and utter ruin, none of it of her own devising. In her place, would he have made the same decisions? But he was a man; how could he even comprehend the terrible feeling of powerlessness she must have endured? His mind spun in a turmoil.

He had always idealistically believed that to take another's life could never be vindicated, but in war was not that standard set aside—for expediency's sake? Had not his great grandmother been in her own personal battle for the safety of herself and her son, and lived a blameless life thereafter?

He would eventually inherit an earldom after his father, though his grandfather, James, remained hale and hearty. Both of them were honourable men using their wealth and influence for the betterment of all. If things had gone differently, and his great grandmother had not acted as she had, then that might not have been the case. It really came down to the old adage of whether the end ever justified the means. Simon hesitated no longer. He picked up the discarded pages of the letter and standing, walked closer to the fire. He kissed the bundle in his hand.

"Good bye my darling great grandmama. I'll always love you," he whispered, then tossed it into the flames and watched until all the pages were totally consumed. He folded the pink ribbon, returned it to the box and closed it. With firm steps he walked from the room.